RIVER ROAD

JAYNE ANN KRENTZ

LARGE
PRINT

First published in Great Britain 2014
by
Piatkus
An imprint of Little, Brown Book Group

First Isis Edition
published 2015
by arrangement with
Little, Brown Book Group
An Hachette UK Company

A catalogue record for this book is available
from the British Library.

ISBN 978–1–78541–066–6 (hb)
ISBN 978–1–78541–071–0 (pb)

Published by
F. A. Thorpe (Publishing)
Anstey, Leicestershire

Set by Words & Graphics Ltd.
Anstey, Leicestershire
Printed and bound in Great Britain by
T. J. International Ltd., Padstow, Cornwall

This book is printed on acid-free paper

This one is for my fabulous sister-in-law, Wendy Born, with thanks for the background info. I will never look at a Gravenstein apple the same way again.

CHAPTER
ONE

"Who appointed you my guardian angel?" Lucy Sheridan asked. She was pissed — really, really pissed. But she was also thrilled. She was alone with Mason Fletcher, driving down a narrow, moonlit road. It should have been the most romantic night of her life — the stuff teen dreams were made of. But Mason had ruined everything by treating her like a kid who didn't know enough to come in out of the rain.

She slouched deep into the passenger side of the truck, one sneaker-clad foot braced against the dashboard, arms folded tightly around her middle.

"I'm not anyone's guardian angel," Mason said. He did not take his attention off the road. "I'm doing you a favor tonight."

"Whether I like it or not. I'm supposed to be grateful?"

"Brinker's little party is not going to end well. There's booze and drugs and a lot of underage kids. You don't want to be there when the cops break it up."

Mason's calm, ice-cold certainty was infuriating. You'd never know that he was nineteen, just three years older than her, she thought. The realities of teenage life made that an unbridgeable gap, of course. To him, she was what Aunt Sara would call jailbait.

But it was worse than that. Mason was not just nineteen — he was nineteen going on thirty. Aunt Sara said that he had the eyes of an old soul.

True, Sara often described people in weird ways. She and her business partner, Mary, were heavily into the whole meditation, enlightenment, be-in-the-moment thing. But Lucy had to admit there was something to what Sara said about Mason. He was already a man in ways she doubted any of the boys at the party tonight would ever be. He made them all look like they were still in middle school.

She was starting to think that Mason was more of a grown-up than any of the actual adults she knew, including her parents. When they had split up three years earlier everyone congratulated them on a civilized divorce. But none of their acquaintances had been in her shoes, she thought. None of them had been a thirteen-year-old kid hiding out in her room while two so-called adults fought using verbal grenades filled with accusations and the kind of sarcasm that sliced to the bone. If the divorce that followed was supposed to be an example of civilized behavior, the word *civilized* needed a new definition.

Mason, on the other hand, always seemed like a real adult — to a fault, maybe. He and his uncle and younger brother had moved to Summer River two years ago. Mason was working full-time at the local hardware store and fixing up an old house on the side. This summer he was single-handedly raising his younger

2

brother because his uncle was off fighting a war somewhere. One thing was blazingly clear: Mason took life Very Seriously. Lucy wondered what, if anything, he did for fun, assuming he actually got the concept.

He even *drove* like a grown-up, she thought morosely, or at least like a grown-up was supposed to drive. The way he handled his uncle's aging pickup truck said it all. He shifted gears with a smooth, competent hand. There were no bursts of acceleration on the straightaways, no heading into the curves a little too fast and definitely no speeding. It should have been boring. But it wasn't. It just made her feel like she was in good, steady hands.

"I didn't need you to rescue me," she said. "I can take care of myself."

Great. Now she really sounded like a kid.

"You were out of your league tonight," he said.

"Give me a break. I was okay. Even if the cops do show up out there at the old Harper Ranch, we both know that no one's going to get arrested. Chief Hobbs isn't about to throw kids like Tristan Brinker and Quinn Colfax in jail. I heard Aunt Sara say that the chief wouldn't dare do anything that might get their fathers mad."

"Yeah, my uncle says Brinker and Colfax have the chief and the whole damn city council in their pockets. But that doesn't mean Hobbs won't snag a few of the other kids tonight just to show that he's doing his job."

"So what? He'll give them a warning, that's all. The worst-case scenario is that Hobbs would have called my aunt to come get me and take me home."

"You really think that's the worst-case scenario?"

"Sure." She wanted to grind her teeth.

"You're going to have to trust me on this, Lucy," he said. "You did not belong at Brinker's party tonight."

"You do realize that by tomorrow morning everyone who is at the ranch tonight will be laughing at me behind my back."

Mason did not respond. She glanced at him. In the glow of the dashboard lights his jaw looked like it was carved in stone. For the first time a tingle of curiosity whispered through her.

"There's something you're not telling me, isn't there?" she said.

"Let it go," Mason said.

"Like I can do that now. How did you know that I was at Brinker's party tonight?"

"Does it matter?"

"Yes," she said. "It matters."

"I heard rumors that you might be there. I called your aunt. She wasn't home."

"She and Mary are in San Francisco. They're on a buying trip at an antiques fair. I left a message in my aunt's voice mail, not that it's any of your business."

Mason ignored that. "When I found out your aunt was gone I decided I'd swing by the park and see if you were there. Figured you would be in over your head."

"Because I'm not one of the A-list kids?"

"You're too young to be hanging around Brinker and Colfax."

"Jillian Benson is only a year older than me. And please, whatever you do, don't give me the lecture

4

about jumping off a cliff just because all of my friends do it."

"Jillian is not your friend."

"It just so happens she's the one who invited me."

"Is that right?" Mason sounded thoughtful. "Well, now, isn't that interesting."

"She called earlier this evening and said she was going to Brinker's party, and did I want to come along? It's not like there's a lot of other stuff to do in this town."

"So you jumped at the chance."

"Not exactly. At first I said no. I'm just here for the summer. I only know a few of the local kids. She said it would be a good way to meet people. I told her I didn't have a car. She offered to pick me up at my aunt's house."

"Real nice of her, wasn't it?" Mason said.

"What are you getting at?"

"Did you have anything to drink before I got there?"

"Just some bottled water that I brought with me. And I don't owe you any explanations, by the way."

"You didn't have any of whatever was in those unlabeled bottles that were in the ice chest?"

"It was some kind of energy drink, Jillian said. She told me that Brinker makes sure it's at all of the ranch parties. She said there's something special in it."

"But you didn't have any?"

"I didn't feel like getting drunk or high, okay?"

She had no intention of admitting that the idea of consuming the oddly colored beverage had scared the living daylights out of her. The sad truth was that she had realized long before Mason had arrived that the night was destined to be a failure. She was just not cut out to live on the edge or push the envelope or take a walk on the wild side. Everyone said she was levelheaded and responsible — not the sort to get into trouble. But those were just other ways of saying that she was boring and way too cautious. She was starting to think that she was doomed to remain on the outside of an invisible glass house forever, looking in at people who dared to take a few risks and really live their lives.

"Why go to one of Brinker's parties if you didn't want to get drunk or high?" Mason asked.

She scrunched lower into the seat. "I just wanted to dance. Have some fun. So sue me."

"But you weren't dancing when I got there."

She sighed. "Because no one asked me to dance. I finally got invited to one of Brinker's parties and it turned out no one wanted to be with me. You were right, I was out of my depth, hanging with the wrong crowd, blah, blah, blah, and it sure was lucky you came along when you did. There. Satisfied?"

Mason did not answer the question, possibly because he was turning the truck into the long, narrow lane that cut through the old apple orchard to Sara's cozy house. The lights were on inside the little bungalow. An aging van emblazoned with *Summer River Antiques* was parked in its usual place in the drive.

"Looks like your aunt is home," Mason said. He brought the truck to a halt.

"She's early." Lucy unfastened her seat belt and popped open the door. "She and Mary usually don't get back from their buying trips until after midnight."

Mason studied the front door. "That's good."

Lucy paused halfway out of the front seat. "What's good?"

"You won't be here alone tonight."

"Geez, Mason. I don't need a babysitter. As a matter of fact, I babysit other people's kids. I'm very popular as a babysitter because I'm so *levelheaded* and *responsible* and all."

"I know," he said. "Sorry."

"Oh, stop apologizing. It's not your thing."

She jumped out of the truck and made to close the door.

"Sorry about tonight, too," he added, voice roughening. "I didn't mean to embarrass you."

"Uh-huh." She looked back at him through the open cab door. "You know what? A few years from now when I'm all grown up you can remind me to thank you for your totally unnecessary rescue tonight. Maybe when I'm thirty or forty I'll be able to appreciate your noble intentions. Or not. You know what they say, no good deed goes unpunished."

"Yeah, I've heard that."

What the hell. She might as well tell him the rest.

"For what it's worth, you wasted your time tonight," she said. "When you arrived, I was getting ready to walk home."

"Not a good plan. It's a long walk."

"I would have been okay. I had my cell phone. Besides, this is Summer River, not the big city. My aunt says there hasn't been a murder here in forever."

7

"Bad things happen in small towns just like they do everywhere else," Mason said.

"Crap. Now I'm going to get a lecture on walking home alone after dark?"

She held her breath because the expression on Mason's face indicated that was exactly what was going to happen. She smiled.

"You just can't help yourself, can you?" she said. "Born to protect and serve. Maybe you should consider a career in law enforcement."

"I hear there's more money to be made in real estate," he said without missing a beat.

"I'm serious."

He ignored that. "Why were you going to walk home?"

"Because Jillian was getting drunk, if you want to know the truth. I knew she didn't want to leave. She thinks Brinker is hot. All the girls do, and some of the guys, too. Anyway, I was afraid to let her drive me home. There you have it, the whole story of my wild night out. You were right. I shouldn't have gone to the ranch, even though half the kids in town are there. You did your good deed. Get over it."

The front door of the house opened. Sara appeared. The porch light glowed on her graying brown hair. Like the other women in the Sheridan family line she was no Amazon, but her five-foot-three-and-three-quarters stature and petite frame were deceptive. Decades of yoga and hauling wood for the massive fireplace in the old house had endowed her with very straight shoulders and a strong, compact body.

8

She moved to the railing and waved.

"Hi, Mason," she said. "Thanks for bringing Lucy home. I was about to call her cell to see if she needed a ride."

"No problem, ma'am," Mason said. "It was on my way."

Lucy sniffed. "On your way, my ass." She started to close the truck door, but something made her hesitate. "About this guardian-angel thing you've got going."

"I told you, I'm no guardian angel."

For the first time there was a hint of emotion in his tone. He sounded irritated.

"Aunt Sara is big on the karma stuff," Lucy said. "You know, what goes around comes around."

"I know what karma is," Mason said. His voice was a little too even.

She realized that she had managed to insult him by implying that he didn't know the meaning of the word. In spite of how he had embarrassed her by dragging her out of the party, she felt bad. Everyone knew that Mason had been working since leaving high school. It wasn't like he'd had a lot of educational opportunities. Aunt Sara said that it was his brother, Aaron, who was destined for college. She said that Aaron had just been accepted into a very prestigious, very expensive university. She also said that Mason and his uncle were doing everything in their power to make sure Aaron didn't graduate with a load of debt.

"Let's say for the sake of argument my aunt is right about karma," Lucy said. "If it's true, then sooner or later the day will arrive when you might need saving."

"So?"

"Ever wonder who rescues a professional guardian angel when he gets into trouble?"

She slammed the door of the truck before he could answer and went quickly toward the front porch, where Sara waited. So much for the most romantic night of her life.

CHAPTER
TWO

Mason watched Lucy greet her aunt and enter the old house. He waited until the door closed behind the pair before he put the truck in gear and drove back along the orchard lane.

Ever wonder who rescues a professional guardian angel when he gets into trouble?

Lucy was wrong. He was no guardian angel. He was just doing what had to be done when he yanked her out of Brinker's party tonight. With her aunt out of town, she hadn't had anyone to look out for her. She was too naive and too innocent to know the devil when he was in disguise. If the rumors were true, Brinker was definitely straight from hell.

Mason made a note to talk to Sara Sheridan in the morning. She needed to know what had almost happened tonight.

It would have been good if Uncle Deke were in town. Deke could have explained things to Sara. She would have listened to him. People always listened to Deke. But Deke had deployed again and was not due back for several months. That meant that Mason would have to have the conversation with Sara. Together they would protect Clueless Lucy.

When he reached the main road he drove back to the scene of the party. The old Harper Ranch had been abandoned years ago. The pastures where cattle had once grazed had reverted to nature. No one had lived in the dilapidated house in decades. Tristan Brinker had commandeered the barn for his parties this past summer. The local kids were drawn to him like moths to a flame. And always there at his side was Quinn Colfax. Together they reigned over the teenagers of Summer River.

The party was still in progress, but Brinker's high-end sports car was not among the vehicles arrayed around the barn. Neither was Quinn Colfax's brand-new SUV. They were both too smart to leave their easily identifiable cars in full view of anyone who happened to drive past the ranch. It was true that their rich fathers would bail them out of jail if they got picked up. But Warner Colfax and Jeffrey Brinker would both be annoyed if their sons were dumb enough to get caught.

Tristan and Quinn were new in town, but they qualified as full-on rock stars. Their fathers were partners in a hedge fund. The headquarters of the business was located in Silicon Valley, but, like a number of other successful entrepreneurs in the Bay Area, they liked to spend their weekends in the wine country. Savvy businessmen that they were, they had figured out fast that Summer River would see the next big vineyard boom.

The relentless wave of the wine business had been rolling across Northern California for more than a hundred years. It had picked up speed in recent decades, washing away the old pear and apple orchards and the ranchlands and dairy farms in its path. Now it was Summer River's turn. The first vineyards had been planted in the foothills outside of town. It would not be long before there would be wineries springing up all across the valley.

In a few years the sleepy little town of Summer River would probably be transformed into an upmarket boutique village, just as Healdsburg, Sebastopol, Napa and the other old farm towns in the region had been changed. Property values were already starting to climb. Mason had been counting on that fact when he had talked Deke into financing the fixer-upper that was intended to help pay the steep tuition at Aaron's fancy college. When he was finished with the remodel, it would be worth nearly double what they had paid for it.

Mason continued on past the turnoff that led to the barn. He took the unmarked, unpaved side road that followed the river.

It didn't take long to find the two vehicles. They were parked in the trees. It might be a while before Brinker and Colfax returned, but Mason was prepared to wait as long as was necessary.

He parked the truck behind the sports car and the SUV, blocking the path back to the road. He got out and walked down to the water's edge. From where he stood he could not see the barn, but he could hear the muffled sound of the blaring music.

For a time he watched the full moon dancing on the river. The surface of the water appeared to move in slow motion, but the languid-looking ripples were deceptive. Summer River was deep in some places, and the currents were strong. Every year brought reports of people who went wading and got swept away. A few months back there had been another report of a car accident on River Road. The vehicle had gone off the cliff at Lookout Point and landed in the swift-running water. The driver had not survived.

Maybe you should consider a career in law enforcement.

Mason thought about that. The truth was he had never spent much time pondering his own future. Since the death of his parents he had been too busy putting one foot in front of the other, obeying his father's deathbed instructions. *Take care of your brother. You two stick together.*

But soon Aaron would be in college and headed off into his own bright future. And then there would be no one left to take care of, Mason thought. Maybe it was time to think about what the hell he actually wanted to do with his life.

But first he had to take care of Lucy.

The early indication that Brinker's party was over came when the music was abruptly cut off. Someone had probably driven past the old ranch and complained to the police. Chief Hobbs would have been forced to send a couple of officers out to shut things down. Lucy was right, it was unlikely that anyone would be arrested. The kids would scatter. A couple of the slow movers might get written up, but that would be the end of it.

The sound of pounding footsteps interrupted Mason's thoughts. He turned and saw two bobbing flashlights. A moment later Tristan Brinker and Quinn Colfax burst out of the trees and into the clearing.

They ran for their vehicles, breathing hard and trying to muffle their laughter. They each had a grip on the handles of a big foam ice chest.

"Did you see the look on the cop's face when that dumb blonde offered him a bottle of the good stuff?" Brinker laughed. "He looked like he was gonna explode."

"Think he saw us?" Quinn asked uneasily.

"Who gives a shit? He knows we were there, but he can't prove there were any drugs." Brinker slowed to a walk and fished his keys out of his pocket. "He's not going to try, either. He's done his job. He closed down the party. Wonder who complained this time?"

"Probably just some farmer who happened to drive by," Quinn said.

"What I'd really like to know is how the hell Fletcher found out that Lucy Sheridan was at the party tonight," Brinker said.

"Does it matter?" Quinn asked.

"Yeah," Brinker said. "It matters. I don't like the idea of that bastard interfering in my business."

"Let it go," Quinn said. "You don't want to mess with Mason Fletcher."

"Why not? He's just a guy who works in a hardware store."

"Look, the party's over. Let's go home and forget about Fletcher."

Mason put on his sunglasses and moved out of the shadows. He lounged against the front fender of the sleek sports car.

"First we talk about Lucy," he said.

Quinn slammed to a halt. "Fletcher? What are you doing here?"

Brinker stopped short, pinning Mason with the flashlight. The sunglasses did the job they were designed to do. They controlled the glare.

"Get away from my car," Brinker snarled. "That paint job is custom. You're going to scratch it."

Mason ignored him. "Target Lucy Sheridan again and you won't be going back to college for the fall semester."

"I don't know what you're talking about," Brinker said. "Now, get away from my car."

Quinn was clearly nervous. "Are you threatening us?"

"Something like that," Mason said.

"Who talked?" Brinker said. His voice was hoarse with anger.

"That's not important," Mason said. "All you need to know is that I know what you were planning."

Quinn was starting to look bewildered. "What's going on here?"

"*Who talked?*" Brinker shouted. He made a visible effort to get himself under control. "Never mind. I'll find out, and when I do —"

"Yeah?" Mason said. "What, exactly, do you think you'll do?"

"Get out of my way," Brinker said, his voice tight with fury. "You're going to be sorry you ever showed up tonight. Got that?"

"I hear you," Mason said quietly. "Now it's your turn to listen to me. Do not go near Lucy Sheridan again. If anything happens to her, I will assume you are responsible. Do you understand me, Brinker?"

Brinker suddenly snapped into full-blown rage. He dropped his end of the ice chest, picked up the nearest blunt object — a rock — lowered his head and charged.

"Hey," Quinn yelped. "Don't. Tristan, are you crazy?"

Mason did not move until the last instant, and then he moved very quickly, slipping out of the way. Brinker slammed into the car. There was a sharp, metallic screech as the rock scored a jagged strip of custom paint off the vehicle. Jolted, Tristan staggered back a couple of steps.

Mason walked past him, turned and looked back.

"Stay away from Lucy Sheridan," he said.

He kept walking, giving Brinker and Quinn his back. Unfortunately, neither of them took the bait.

When he reached the truck, he opened the door, got inside, cranked the engine and drove home to the old cabin near the river.

He found Aaron asleep on the sofa. The pricey new computer that Mason and Deke had given him for his birthday was still glowing. The screen showed several lines of arcane computer code.

Mason locked the front door and checked the windows. It was a nightly ritual, one he had followed faithfully since the night a police detective had told him that his parents had been in a car accident.

He tossed a blanket over Aaron and climbed the stairs to his room. He powered up his own computer, the used one that he had picked up on an online auction site.

He went through the other nightly ritual, checking to make sure that the family bank account was not overdrawn and that there were no new bills to be paid. Satisfied that the electricity and the phones were safe for another month, he wrote an email to his uncle, giving a short summary of the night's events. He told Deke that he thought the situation was under control.

He stripped down to his briefs, put his cell on the night table, turned off the lights and got into bed. With his arms folded behind his head, he contemplated the moonlit night through the window.

He had told Deke that he could handle the situation, but the truth was he had not yet come up with a plan. And it had become clear tonight that he would need one. Tristan Brinker was not just a spoiled, rich jerk. He was a full-blown psycho. Sooner or later he was going to explode. Mason didn't know much about psychology, but he had no trouble recognizing a human predator when he met one. He also understood in some intuitive manner that it had been important to distract Brinker from his initial target. He was pretty sure he had succeeded, temporarily, at least, but that did not mean that Lucy and the other girls of Summer River were safe.

First thing in the morning he would talk to Lucy's aunt and explain just how dangerous the situation was. His gut told him that it was important to get Lucy out of town — and out of Brinker's reach — as soon as possible.

Then he would have to figure out how to get rid of Brinker. He was very sure now that the bastard would not stop.

The following morning, Brinker was spotted leaving town in the shiny new sports car his father had given him. He was never seen again. Within days rumors circulated that he had been the victim of a drug deal gone bad.

Brinker's body was never recovered.

CHAPTER
THREE

Thirteen years later,
Vantage Harbor, California

Lucy was about to take the first sip of a badly needed glass of white wine when she saw the Grieving Widow bearing down on the booth.

Alicia Gatley sliced effortlessly through the noisy throng of office workers crowding the popular bar at happy hour. She was the kind of woman who turned heads — male and female — when she entered a room. From the snug designer suit and sky-high heels to her manicured nails and sleek chignon, she was a classic Alfred Hitchcock blonde. The expensive boob job didn't hurt, either, Lucy thought. But tonight the barracuda beneath the glowing façade was on full display.

"Oh, my goodness," Hannah Carter whispered. "This isn't going to be good."

"Just what we needed to finish off an otherwise perfectly lousy day," Ella Merrick added.

"She's here for you, Lucy," Hannah warned. "She blames you for what happened in court."

"No kidding," Lucy said.

Ella gave her a sympathetic look. "You were just the messenger."

"We all know what happens to messengers." Lucy took a quick swallow of the wine to fortify herself. "I told the boss that she was going to be trouble."

"Looks like you were right," Hannah said.

"I admit I hoped I would be safely out of town before she figured out that I was the one responsible for her financial disaster," Lucy said.

She was not looking forward to going back to Summer River in the morning, but at that moment — given the option — she would have preferred to be there rather than where she was, trapped in the booth with nowhere to run. At least she was not alone, she thought. Hannah and Ella were her best friends. They would not abandon her.

Hannah studied Alicia with a considering expression. "I wonder how she found out that you were the researcher who discovered that the dear departed had a second family in Canada?"

"Who knows?" Lucy said. "I suppose someone at the office let it slip. It's not like what we do at Brookhouse is top secret."

"The GW probably batted those false eyelashes at one of the male investigators on the staff who immediately fell all over himself telling her everything she wanted to know," Ella said.

"A distinct possibility," Lucy agreed.

She was the one who had nicknamed the second Mrs. Gatley the Grieving Widow. It had been a tribute to Alicia's obvious acting talents. The name had stuck.

Now everyone in the forensic genealogy department of Brookhouse referred to Alicia as the GW.

Alicia was closing in rapidly. Her carefully made-up face was splotchy with rage. The rapid-fire snap-snap-snap of her towering heels on the wood floor was so sharp Lucy was amazed there were no sparks.

"Brace yourselves," she said. "Remember, we are professionals."

"Does that mean we can't take her down when she starts calling you names and flinging wine in your face?" Hannah asked. "Just curious."

"Yes, that's exactly what it means," Lucy said. "We represent Brookhouse Research. Our behavior reflects on the firm."

"Sure, take all the fun out of the evening," Ella said.

"It won't be that bad," Lucy said. "She's pissed, so she may call me a few names, but she won't fling wine in my face. It would ruin that cool Grace Kelly thing she's got going on."

"Got news for you," Ella said. She did not take her eyes off the GW. "She's no longer channeling Grace Kelly. Looks more like the Creature from the Black Lagoon. Before she gets here, I'd like to place a small side bet. I've got five bucks says she's so mad she's going to try to bitch-slap Lucy."

"I say she'll go for the wine toss," Hannah said. "It's got more drama."

"You're on," Ella said.

"Stop it, both of you," Lucy said. "She's not going to make a fool of herself in front of all these people."

Alicia arrived at the booth and pinned Lucy with a demonic glare.

"It's your fault that everything went wrong," she raged. "You had no right to interfere with my life, you damn bitch. Who do you think you are?"

"I was just doing my job, Mrs. Gatley," Lucy said. "As I'm sure you're aware, Brookhouse Research was hired by the attorneys handling your husband's estate. The trust provided for his children."

"Bernie never told me about any children. I'm positive he didn't have any. You tracked down some deadbeats up in Canada and bribed them to pretend they were Bernie's long-lost offspring. Admit it."

"I'm sorry, Mrs. Gatley. Bernard Gatley had three children, two daughters and a son, by another woman. They are the primary heirs to the estate."

"If those so-called heirs do exist, which I doubt very much, they are illegitimate."

"The law makes no distinction," Lucy said patiently. "A man's children are his offspring regardless of whether or not he was married to their mother. But in this case that is not even an issue, because Mr. Gatley was actually married to the mother of his three heirs, who are now adults with children of their own."

"You can't prove it," Alicia said, her voice very tight.

"That's just it, Mrs. Gatley, Brookhouse Research did provide extensive proof that your husband's offspring have every right to a portion of their father's estate."

"A portion?" Alicia's voice went up a notch, hitting the shrill threshold. "They're getting the best properties and all of the stocks and bonds."

"You heard the estate lawyers and the judge. Mr. Gatley's other family has every right to their share of the estate."

Ella smiled benignly. "It's not as if you didn't get a very nice chunk of change yourself."

Alicia turned on her. "I'm only getting a fraction of what I was supposed to receive. Bernie promised me that everything would come to me. Why in hell do you think I married him?"

There was a short, fraught pause. Lucy became aware of the hushed silence that had settled in the bar.

"I really don't think you want to discuss such personal matters in here," she said very softly.

"Don't you dare tell me to shut up, bitch," Alicia screeched. "If Bernie really did have kids, why didn't they show up at the funeral?"

"The three people I found in Canada were small children when their parents split up," Lucy explained. "They lost track of their father years ago. The reality is that he walked away from the family at some point and never looked back. They believed that he was dead."

"Which he is now," Ella pointed out cheerfully.

"I sacrificed two years of my life by marrying that old geezer. And what do I get? A measly few thousand dollars. *And it's all your fault.*"

Evidently having noticed that Lucy, Ella and Hannah all had tight, secure grips on the stems of their wineglasses, Alicia spun around. She swept up a full beer glass from a nearby table and hurled the contents straight at Lucy's face.

24

Before anyone could react, Alicia stormed back through the herd of fascinated happy-hour patrons, slammed open the glass doors and disappeared out into the late-afternoon sunshine.

Lucy sighed and picked up one of the three small cocktail napkins on the table. She used it to wipe some of the beer off her face. Ella and Hannah offered their own napkins.

The man whose beer glass had been commandeered for the drama gave Lucy an apologetic look.

"Sorry about that," he said. "I didn't realize what she intended to do until it was all over."

"Not your fault," Lucy assured him.

"Disgruntled client?" he asked. "By the way, my name is Carl."

"She wasn't the client," Ella said.

"Just a sore loser," Hannah explained.

"Mind if I ask what it is exactly that you three do for a living?" Carl said.

"We work for a private investigation firm," Lucy explained. "Brookhouse Research."

"Cool. Lady private eyes?" Carl was definitely interested now. "Do you carry guns?"

"No," Lucy said firmly. "Mr. and Mrs. Brookhouse are the licensed investigators in the firm. The three of us work in the forensic genealogy department."

Carl was clearly disappointed, but he made an effort not to let it show. "So what kind of research involves forensic genealogy?"

"Generally speaking, we get most of our work from attorneys representing estates," Hannah said. "We locate missing or unknown heirs and inform them of their inheritances."

"And sometimes vice versa," Ella added. "People who believe themselves to be heirs to an estate come to us to ask us to find proof."

"Got it." The man snapped his fingers. "You're heir hunters."

"The job description covers a lot of territory," Lucy said.

She kept her tone cool and professional, wary of Carl's reaction. Many people were not even aware that searching for lost heirs was a business. Those who did know about it often considered the work to be a rather unsavory side of the private investigation business.

There was no denying that there were some shady operators in the field. They worked the margins of the trade, hoping to score big by tracking down the rare heir to a multimillion-dollar estate who was unaware of his or her good fortune. The heir hunter's goal was to convince the heir to sign a contract granting the investigator a percentage of the inheritance in exchange for revealing the source of the fortune. But Brookhouse Research prided itself on sticking to the respectable side of the business.

"Looks like I win the bet," Hannah said.

"How do you figure that?" Ella asked. "The GW assaulted Lucy, just as I predicted."

"Yes, but she didn't slap her," Hannah said.

"Didn't toss wine in her face, either," Ella said. "She used beer from a neighboring table."

"That's a mere technicality," Hannah declared.

Ella smiled, triumphant. "As those of us in the forensic genealogy trade are aware, mere technicalities often make all the difference." She held out her hand, palm up. "I believe you owe me five bucks."

"Excuse me," Lucy said. "While you two argue about the bet, I am going to go home and finish packing."

The waiter bustled over with a clean bar towel.

"The manager says that there won't be any charge for the three wines," he said.

"Thanks." Lucy took the towel and blotted beer from the jacket of her business suit. "I think I'll put the dry-cleaning bill down on my expense sheet."

"You should definitely do that," Ella said.

Hannah nodded. "Absolutely."

The waiter hovered closer and lowered his voice. "Mind if I ask what you did to make that woman so mad?"

"I'm afraid that's confidential," Lucy said.

The waiter nodded knowingly. "She thinks you're seeing her guy, huh?"

Shocked, Lucy paused in the act of dabbing at the sleeve of her jacket. "That's ridiculous. Why would two intelligent women get into a fight over a man?"

"That's so last century," Hannah said.

"What happened a few minutes ago was a much more serious matter," Ella explained.

"Right." The waiter brightened. "It was all about money."

"A *lot* of money," Lucy said.

Carl laughed. "Let me take a wild guess here. You three aren't exactly the romantic types, are you?"

"Our profession tends to make a person somewhat jaded," Lucy said. "After a while you realize that everyone has an agenda. At the top of most people's lists there is, however, usually one of two possible priorities."

"Yeah?" Carl looked expectant. "What are they?"

"Money or revenge," Lucy said. "It's amazing how often the two tend to go together."

"Wow." Carl was awed by the insight. "That's heavy, real heavy."

"No," Lucy said. "It's human nature." She slipped out from behind the table. "Now, if you will all excuse me, I'm going home."

"Found any other lost heirs lately?" Carl called after her.

"As a matter of fact, yes," Lucy said. She hitched the strap of her purse over her shoulder and started toward the door. "Me."

CHAPTER
FOUR

Mason Fletcher lounged against the sales counter, a gleaming wrench gripped loosely in one hand. He regarded Lucy with a lot of interest infused with a dash of cool disapproval. She found the combination both annoying and unnerving.

But the real problem was that Mason looked even better now than he had thirteen years ago when he had figured so powerfully in her fevered teenage imagination. Her first reaction upon walking through the door of Fletcher Hardware had been primal and flat-out breathtaking. *I've been looking for you.*

The wolf-sized dog that padded out from behind the counter to inspect her regarded her with an expression remarkably similar to Mason's. The animal wasn't just the size of a wolf — it looked like one as well. An aging wolf, she concluded. There was some gray around the muzzle. The beast's eyes were not the standard dark brown associated with most breeds. Instead, they were a disconcerting shade of hazel gold that was a little too close to the color of Mason's eyes.

"That's Joe," Mason said, nodding toward the dog.

She looked down at Joe and held out her hand. "Hello, Joe."

29

Joe stared at her for a moment longer, his gaze unflinching. Evidently concluding that she was neither a threat nor prey, he sniffed her fingers. Satisfied, he sat back. Gingerly, she scratched him behind his ears. Joe chuffed a bit and licked her hand.

"He likes you," Mason said. "Mostly he ignores people."

"I'm thrilled, of course, that he doesn't intend to rip out my throat," Lucy said.

"He hasn't gone for anyone's throat for at least a week." Mason tossed the gleaming wrench into the air and caught it with a barely noticeable twist of his wrist, making it look easy. "Heard you were in town to clean out your aunt's place and put it on the market."

"That's the plan." She stopped rubbing Joe's ears and straightened.

She was determined to remain as cool as Mason. It wasn't easy. She was still struggling to get past the shock of coming face-to-face with him. She had expected to see his uncle behind the counter when she walked into the hardware store.

The possibility that she might run into Mason while she was in Summer River had occurred to her, but she had dismissed it as extremely remote. According to the last update from Sara some six months ago, Mason was in Washington, D.C., where he and his brother ran a very expensive, very low-profile, very sophisticated private security consulting business.

"How long will you be around?" Mason asked.

She smiled. She couldn't help it. She made a show of glancing at her watch. "Less than three minutes into this conversation and already it sounds like an interrogation. In hindsight I may have made a mistake when I advised you to go into law enforcement all those years ago."

"You made the suggestion. I'm the one who made the decision."

What in the world was that supposed to mean? she wondered. Suddenly she got that faint, tiny little inner ping of knowing, the same sensation she experienced when she was closing in on a missing heir. Something bad had happened to Mason Fletcher. She would have bet good money that it was linked to his career path. And, being Mason Fletcher, he was taking full responsibility for the decision that had sent him down that road. Mason hadn't changed, she thought. He was the kind of man who would always take full responsibility — even for stuff that, technically speaking, wasn't his responsibility.

She sought a neutral topic of conversation.

"I'm glad to see that the hardware store survived," she said. "When did your uncle buy it?"

"A few months after he retired."

"It's the last store on the block that was here when I used to visit Aunt Sara. This town has really changed."

Most of the old, traditional stores on Main Street had been replaced with upscale shops and trendy eateries. Fletcher Hardware — bordered on one side by a wine shop and on the other side by an art gallery — was a stubborn anachronism.

Mason surprised her with a wry smile. "Welcome to the new, improved wine-country boutique town of

Summer River. But in case you're wondering, the old Summer River is still here, just beneath the surface."

"Meaning?"

"Meaning it's still a small town. News travels fast."

Lucy nodded. "Which is how you knew that I was here."

"A lot of people know you're here, Lucy," he said.

She raised her brows in polite inquiry. "Is that a warning?"

"Maybe. The fact that you are Sara's sole heir has stirred up some deep waters."

"Yes, I know."

She had been ignoring phone calls from lawyers and realtors for more than a month while she considered how to deal with her inheritance.

"That's why I asked you how long you plan to stay," Mason said.

"The answer to your question is that I don't know how long I'll be in town." She was determined not to let him intimidate her. "A couple of weeks, I think. I need to make arrangements to pack and move my aunt's belongings, and then I have to get the house ready to put on the market."

"The place should sell fast," Mason said. "It's a real nice little example of the Craftsman style, and one thing that has come out of Summer River going upscale is that property values have skyrocketed. Folks looking for a weekend house in wine country love that kind of architecture. But the real value is in the property."

"The old orchard?"

"It's prime vineyard land. Worth a bundle in this market. Every new Silicon Valley billionaire wants to open his very own winery and put his name on a label. It's a major status symbol."

"I noticed that most of the orchards and farms are gone."

"They've been disappearing for years. I'm surprised you didn't know that. But then, you never came back to visit Sara after you left thirteen years ago, did you?"

The comment, freighted as it was with stern disapproval, hit her like a bucket of cold water. Anger flashed through her.

"Okay, that answers one question," she said.

"What?"

"I knew the town had changed, but when I walked in here I wondered if *you* had changed. Clearly the answer is no. You are still in the habit of jumping to conclusions, assuming the worst and giving lectures."

He thought about that for a moment and then inclined his head half an inch. "You know what? You're right. Maybe I did jump to conclusions. So why didn't you come to visit your aunt for the past thirteen years?"

"What makes you so sure I haven't been back here?"

"Deke mentioned that you never returned."

"Your uncle implied that I ignored my aunt all these years?"

"He just commented that you hadn't come back, that's all." Once again Mason tossed the steel wrench casually into the air and caught it with fluid ease. "He said you never returned after that summer when I pissed you off by yanking you out of the party at Harper Ranch Park."

That stopped her. "The old Harper Ranch is now a park?"

"The town took it over a couple of years ago. Grass, picnic tables, a ball field, playground, dog-walking areas, the works. You wouldn't recognize the place."

"I see. Well, as it happens, your uncle is right. This is the first time I've returned to Summer River since that night."

"Why?"

She gave him a serene go-to-hell smile. "It's really none of your business, is it?"

"Nope, just curious."

Thirteen years ago everyone said you didn't want to mess with Mason Fletcher. Nothing had changed except that he was now the man she had known that he would become and then some. It was as if he had been tempered in fire like the steel blade of some ancient sword. Everything about him had gotten harder, stronger, more relentless. The sharp planes and angles of his face had become fierce. Time had added some sleek, solid muscle and endowed him with the confident air of a man who knows what he wants, what he will tolerate and where he draws the line.

The years had given him something else as well — the rare, invisible aura of quiet, inner power that was the hallmark of a man in full control of himself.

He did, however, look considerably the worse for wear around the edges. She had a feeling he'd learned the hard way what every professional guardian angel probably had to learn — that you couldn't save everyone. For a man as determined and unyielding as Mason, that would have been one very tough lesson.

In spite of her irritation, she felt herself softening. It was hard to stay mad at a man who was born to do the right thing when the chips were down. He really couldn't help it, she thought. He was what he was, and there was probably no force on the face of the planet that could change that.

"Oh, for Pete's sake," she said. "Just to clarify, Aunt Sara did not want me to come back here after that last summer. In fact, she didn't want anyone in the family to visit her in Summer River. We respected her wishes. And while I certainly don't owe you any explanations, I can assure you that I saw a lot of her. She and Mary stayed with me several times each year. Sara knew that I find the holidays stressful, so she made sure to spend them with me. After she and Mary sold the antiques shop, I joined them on some of their cruises. I can assure you that Sara was not neglected in any way." Lucy took a breath. "I loved her. And I loved Mary, too, because she loved Sara and Sara loved her. There. Satisfied?"

Mason had the grace to look apologetic. "Didn't mean to imply you had neglected your aunt."

She gave him her best fake bright smile. "Of course you did."

His jaw hardened. "I understand that family dynamics can be complicated."

"No kidding. Especially when viewed from the outside."

Mason exhaled slowly. "Okay, you've made your point. I liked Sara. Mary, too. I was sorry to hear that they had been killed."

"Thank you," Lucy said. She hesitated, wondering if it was too soon to probe for answers. "I suppose you heard it was a car accident?" she said.

"Yes. It's always a shock. Aaron and I lost our parents in a car accident."

"I know. I'm sorry."

"It's been a long time," he said.

"Doesn't mean it didn't happen and that it didn't leave some major wounds. You heal from wounds, if you're lucky, but there are always scars."

He looked as if the simple observation had caught him off guard. She got the feeling he was unsure how to respond.

"No," he agreed finally. "Doesn't mean there aren't scars."

She tightened her grip on the straps of the black tote she had slung over her shoulder. "Were you here in town when my aunt and Mary . . . ?"

"No, I arrived a couple of weeks ago. I'm taking some time off from work." He eyed her with sudden, sharp curiosity. "Why?"

"Nothing. Just wondered." She felt a little deflated. If Mason had been in town at the time of the accident, he probably would have asked any questions that needed to be asked. He had been a cop, after all. But he had not been in Summer River when Sara and Mary died. He didn't know any more than she did. "Sara told me that you and your brother run a security consulting firm back in D.C."

He looked first surprised and then amused. "Sara kept you informed of my whereabouts?"

"I gather that from time to time your uncle told her what was going on with you and your brother." Lucy smiled. "Sara said he is very proud of both of you."

"Deke and I always knew that Aaron would do something to change the world," Mason said. "He wound up with degrees in math and computer science."

"Impressive. What, exactly, do you and Aaron do as consultants?"

He gave her what was no doubt meant to be a charming consultant's smile. "We consult."

"Yeah, I get that. And for the record, the I'm-a-consultant-and-I'm-here-to-help smile needs an upgrade."

Mason stopped smiling. "I'll work on it."

"I'm serious," she said. "Who do you consult for?"

"We specialize in closing cold cases. Our clients are mostly smalltown police departments that lack the expertise, the technology and the manpower to handle major crimes that have gone stone cold."

"Do you go out into the field to investigate?"

"Sometimes. But our primary asset is a proprietary computer program we named Alice. Aaron created it to help identify patterns in an old case. If we can find a pattern, we've got a shot at helping the cops track down the perps."

"Sounds exciting."

"I'm not a cop anymore, I'm a consultant," he said coolly. "I don't see much action."

He probably wasn't lying, she decided. But he wasn't telling her the whole truth, either.

"What can I do for you today?" Mason continued. "I assume you came in here to pick up some of the things you need to get your aunt's house ready for the market?"

Whoa. Talk about hitting a stone wall, Lucy thought. Mason definitely wanted to change the topic of conversation.

"Actually, I stopped in to get some advice about local contractors from your uncle. I wasn't sure who else to ask. I know Sara trusted Deke when it came to that sort of thing."

"I can ask him for some names when he gets back. What kind of work are you thinking of doing?"

"The big-ticket item is the kitchen. It's badly outdated. Dad says that bringing it up to date will add a few thousand to the value of the house."

"He's right," Mason said. "Is your dad still a professor?"

"Yes. He's head of the sociology department at the college where he teaches."

"And your mother?"

"She's still teaching psychology."

Mason put the wrench down on the counter. "Both your folks remarried, didn't they?"

"Yes," she said, making the word very crisp. "About that contractor. I've got a limited budget."

"Right." Mason reached for a pad of paper. He pulled it close and picked up a pen. "Okay, you want someone who can update the kitchen without spending a fortune. Anything else?"

"The outside needs painting."

"That's another major job." Mason wrote a note on the pad of paper and then looked up. "You're starting to talk big bucks here. I'm not sure it's worth it, to tell you the truth."

"But everyone says those are the sorts of upgrades that add value to the house."

"That's true, but around here, it's the land itself that has the real value. Still, those old Craftsman houses go for a nice chunk of change, and there are always people looking for weekend places. I'm just suggesting that you don't pour a lot of cash into upgrades."

"There is one project I'd like to do inside that I think will make a big cosmetic difference in the living room."

"What's that?"

"I want to restore the fireplace to its original condition. It really was beautiful."

"I remember it," Mason said. "There was a lot of nice stonework around it. You don't see good craftsmanship like that anymore."

"Unfortunately, Aunt Sara covered the entire front of the fireplace with tile."

"Huh. Wonder why?"

"I'm not sure. She never mentioned it, so when I walked into the house yesterday I was surprised to see what she had done. I do remember that she complained from time to time. She said the fireplace sucked up almost as much heat as it put out. But she loved to sit in front of the fire in the evenings and read."

"She probably just got tired of hauling firewood," Mason said. "Can't blame her."

"No, but I wish she hadn't done such a poor job of putting in the tiles. The original fireplace would have been a huge selling point. Now it's a giant negative. It's the first thing you see when you walk into the house, and it's ugly. She must have done the job herself."

"Typical DIY disaster, huh?"

"Yes, and what's more, it feels unstable. I could take it down with a hammer and chisel, but I'm afraid of damaging the original stonework behind the bricks."

"Let's hope she didn't ruin the original. Tell you what, why don't I drop by after work and take a look at it? I'll bring some tools with me. Maybe I can take care of those tiles for you this evening and save you a few bucks."

The offer left her openmouthed for a beat, and then, for some inexplicable reason, her pulse kicked up. It took her a few seconds to pull herself together.

"That's very nice of you," she said, suddenly cautious.

"No trouble. It's not like I've got anything else to do this evening."

"I see." She gave him a chilly smile. It was always good to know where one fit into a man's list of priorities.

Mason did not notice the ice in her smile. "Why don't I drop by around five-thirty? Does that work for you?"

40

Cocktail hour. Interesting. She tried and failed to suppress the whisper of anticipation that sparkled through her.

"That will be fine," she said smoothly. "It's not like I've got anything else to do tonight, either."

"Ouch. Guess I didn't phrase my offer in the most diplomatic way."

"As I recall, you always had a very direct style when it came to communicating," she said.

"Yeah, my ex-wife used to complain about that a lot."

Lucy felt the heat rise in her cheeks. "Sara mentioned that your marriage did not work out."

"No."

Another wound, she decided. Not a giant blow, but he had definitely taken a hit. He probably blamed himself for the failure of his marriage. Typical Mason. At least he had been brave enough to give it a whirl. She was still hanging back, afraid to make the leap.

"I'm sorry," she said again.

"Heard you called off your engagement a while back."

"Yes."

"Sorry about that."

She smiled. "We seem to be saying sorry a lot to each other."

"Look on the positive side — my screwed-up marriage and your screwed-up engagement give us something in common."

"Two screwed-up relationships is supposed to be a positive?"

"You know me, I was always a glass-half-full kind of guy."

"Gee. That's not how I remember you at all. I always saw you as a worst-case-scenario kind of guy."

An unreadable expression lit his eyes. "And I always thought of you as a dreamer."

She wrinkled her nose. "Don't remind me. You were convinced that I needed someone to look after me and make sure I didn't get into trouble."

He hesitated, evidently sensing a trap. "Not exactly."

"Yes, exactly."

"Well, damn, I knew we would get back to the night that I pulled you out of the party at the ranch. You really know how to hang on to a grudge, lady."

"Nonsense." She sniffed. "I don't hold grudges."

"Yeah, right. You're never going to thank me for what I did that night, are you?"

"Probably not." She turned on her heel and started toward the door. "I'll be going now. I'm staying at the house, so I've got some grocery shopping to do."

"See you at five-thirty," he called after her.

She stopped short at the door. "I almost forgot, I need lightbulbs. A lot of them. Half the lamps and wall fixtures at Sara's place are burned out."

"We've got a fine selection of bulbs. You want the energy savers?"

"What I want are really, really bright bulbs. I swear that old house is as dark as a cave."

"Sounds like you need halogen for at least some of the fixtures." He came out from behind the counter and led the way to a display of lightbulbs. "I'll bring takeout with me tonight."

He intended to arrive at the cocktail hour, and now he was telling her he would bring dinner with him. Somehow her little home-improvement project had just been transformed into a date with Mason Fletcher.

A deer-in-the-headlights sensation made her go very still. They had been together for all of fifteen minutes and Mason was already taking charge.

On the other hand, she had to admit that she liked the idea of having company for a few hours that evening. Last night — her first night back in Sara's house — she had discovered that she did not like being alone in the place. Something about the atmosphere bothered her in ways she could not explain. Maybe it was because it held too many memories of Sara, or perhaps it was simply because the place was so dark, due to the lack of bulbs.

Nevertheless, she could not let Mason take full control of the situation. He meant well, but he needed some pushback. For his own good, of course.

"Forget the takeout," she said. "I've already got plans for dinner."

"Yeah?" His eyes darkened a little.

"Yeah." She smiled. "I'm dining in, and since you are going to be kind enough to take out those tiles for me, I will buy enough salmon for two."

"That works," he said instantly. "Thanks."

He looked pleased, she decided. Really pleased. Like he'd just won the lottery. She was feeling oddly energized herself. What had she just done?

"Okay," she said. "I'll see you at five-thirty. Bring your tools."

"I never leave home without them."

She hesitated and then made herself do the right thing. He was doing her a favor. The least she could do was be gracious.

"Thanks," she said.

He surprised her with a wicked smile. "For offering to deal with the fireplace or for rescuing you from that party out at the Harper Ranch thirteen years ago?"

She gave him polite bewilderment. "For the offer to help with the fireplace, of course. I don't recall being rescued from a party. What I remember is being humiliated beyond redemption. But, hey, that's all water under the bridge now. I forgave you a long time ago because I knew even then you just couldn't help yourself. In your own heavy-handed way, you were trying to protect me."

"Heavy-handed, huh? Is that by any chance your way of telling me that I'm a bad communicator?"

"No, it's my way of telling you that you obviously haven't shaken the take-charge attitude. But it's okay because I have been known to take charge once in a while myself. Now, if you don't mind, I'd like to get my bulbs and leave. There is a lot of stuff to do at the house."

"What sizes do you need?"

She took out the list she had made and went through it. When she was finished, Mason collected the various bulbs and headed back to the counter. She followed.

Mason rang up the sale, swiped her credit card and gave her the sack full of bulbs.

"Thanks," she said. "I'll see you later."

Once again she started toward the door.

"Don't change any bulbs that require getting on a ladder," Mason said behind her. "Not until I get there. It's too dangerous. People fall off ladders all the time. I'll take care of the ceiling and wall fixtures tonight."

She smiled, shook her head and kept walking. Really, the man did not know when to quit.

She paused with her hand on the doorknob and looked back. "I suppose you know that Sara's house and land weren't the only things I inherited."

"I heard. By some quirk in Sara's and Mary's wills, you got Mary's shares in her brother's company. It's all over town."

"I thought that might be the case," she said. "Hard not to notice the curious stares."

"I'm no financial guru, but even I can tell you that it would probably be in your best interests to sell those shares back to the Colfax family as soon as possible."

"That's what my parents told me. Turns out it's not going to be that easy. Two different lawyers representing various members of the Colfax family have been emailing me and leaving messages on my phone for the past month."

"Colfax Inc. is one of the few things that hasn't changed in the past thirteen years," Mason said. "It's still a tightly held, family-owned company, and according to Uncle Deke, there is one hell of a squabble going on at the moment. Something to do with a merger proposal."

"Yes, I got that much from the lawyers' messages."

"You don't want to get in the middle of that situation, Lucy. You know what they say about family quarrels."

"Right," Lucy said. "They are always the worst."

CHAPTER
FIVE

He could tell from the coolness in her voice and the resolute set of her very nice shoulders that she was not going to take his financial advice. The question was, why not? Evidently, it was the same advice her parents had given her. She stood to make a fortune selling the shares back to the Colfax family.

But she wasn't going to do it — not immediately, at any rate.

Mason waited until the door closed behind her before he went down an aisle to the big display window at the front of the shop. Joe padded after him and sat at his feet. Together they watched Lucy slip on a pair of dark glasses and walk briskly toward a small, silver-gray compact parked at the curb.

Mason took in a deep breath and let it out slowly. Something deep inside him that had been in a coma for the past couple of months had slammed into wide-awake mode the moment Lucy opened the door of the shop.

"Well, what do you know?" he said to Joe. "She's all grown up now. She sure looks good, doesn't she?"

Joe slapped his tail against the floor a couple of times and focused his attention on two crows that were amusing themselves by dodging vehicles in the street.

Lucy looked better than good, Mason decided. She looked like exactly what — until now — he didn't know he needed.

The weird part was that he had not even realized that he had been sleepwalking since the Gilbert Porter case until Lucy showed up. He reminded himself that there was a term for this kind of intense jolt. It was called sexual attraction, and it was merely a force of nature like heat lightning or wildfire — and just as dangerous.

Still, he could not remember the last time he had felt anything this powerful. What he knew for a fact was that there were only two options when it came to dealing with forces of nature. A man either ran for shelter or went straight into the storm and to hell with the risks.

He was not about to run.

Out in the street the crows abandoned the car-dodging game and flew off in search of another source of entertainment. Joe yawned, got to his feet and prowled back toward his favorite spot behind the counter.

Mason did not take his eyes off Lucy. He did not want to take his eyes off her. Yesterday, when he'd heard that she was back in town, he'd discovered that he was suddenly curious to see how she had turned out. But he had not been expecting the kick-in-the-gut shock of excitement that had hit him when he got his first look at her.

He had been surprised by her air of cool self-confidence and professional sophistication. So much for assuming she would follow in the footsteps of her aunt and become an adult flower child who ate organic, meditated and practiced yoga.

Instead, everything about Lucy told him that she'd learned a few hard lessons since leaving Summer River. She was no longer the sweet, lonely, too-trusting girl who could be easily deceived by a budding young sociopath like Brinker. The all-grown-up Lucy had claws.

Claws and some money to spend on clothes and a few discreet but expensive-looking accessories. The gray pullover, black trousers and sleek little flat-heeled shoes looked pricey. So did the big leather bag and the small gold studs in her ears. Her dark brown hair was precision-cut in a stylish, angled curve that ended at her jawline, framing her expressive face and knowing green eyes.

He watched her open the door of the compact and slip behind the wheel. There was something sleek and sexy about the way she moved. Maybe she had kept up with the yoga.

He realized he was not the only one watching Lucy. Some of the customers sitting at the sidewalk tables in front of the Sunrise Café were also paying attention. He recognized two of them from the old days — Nolan Kelly, the proprietor of Kelly Real Estate, and Jillian Benson, now Mrs. Jillian Colfax.

Jillian hadn't changed a lot since the summer that Tristan Brinker had mesmerized the local teens. She looked like what she was — a former cheerleader who had discovered the hard way that when you married for money, you earned every penny. Life in the Colfax clan had probably proved a lot more difficult than she had anticipated.

But at least she and Quinn Colfax were still together, he reminded himself. He was the one whose marriage had gone down in flames.

Jillian raised a hand to get Lucy's attention, smiled vivaciously and called out a greeting. The words were muffled because the door of the shop was closed, but Mason thought it sounded like "*Lucy. Lucy Sheridan. It's me, Jillian. I heard you were in town. Why don't you join us for a latte?*"

Lucy gave no indication that she saw or heard Jillian even though the café was just across the street. She closed the car door and pulled away from the curb.

"Nicely played, Lucy," Mason said aloud. "You really have learned a few things."

Anticipation about the coming evening crackled through him. He watched the snappy little car until it turned the corner and disappeared.

He stood there for a while, contemplating his prospects for the night. Then he remembered the closed-up fireplace and started making a mental list of the tools he might need.

Nolan Kelly finished his latte and got to his feet. He strolled across the street and opened the door of Fletcher Hardware.

"Hey there, Mason." He flashed his warm, easy smile. "How's it going?"

Thirteen years ago Nolan had exhibited all of the attributes that had destined him for a career in sales. Red-haired, blue-eyed and infused with a friendly, high-energy personality, he still radiated the earnest, honest air that had made parents trust him while their kids were buying pot and booze from him on the side. The only thing that had changed, Mason decided, was that these days Nolan sold real estate.

Joe got to his feet and wandered out from behind the counter to take a look at Nolan. Joe did not appear to be impressed. Bored, he went back behind the counter.

"Things are going fine," Mason said. "What can I do for you?"

"That was Lucy Sheridan I just saw coming out of here, wasn't it? Heard she was in town."

"So?"

"I thought I recognized her. She sure has changed. Who would have thought that she would turn out looking that good? She was here the summer that Brinker disappeared. Remember?"

Mason said nothing. He had discovered a long time ago that the old cop trick of staying silent actually worked very well in real life. It was amazing how people would try to fill in a conversational void, especially people like Kelly, who were constitutionally inclined to talk.

"She inherited her aunt's place, you know," Nolan continued. "I'd like to talk to her about putting it on the market. I sent her a couple of emails and tried phoning her, but she never responded."

Lucy had not answered Kelly's emails or calls, and she had made a point of pretending not to see him a few minutes ago, even though he had been sitting right across the street. It didn't take a detective to figure out that she was not interested in talking to Kelly. Not yet, at any rate.

Mason made his way back toward the counter. "I expect she's probably still grieving."

"Sure, sure, understandable. The house needs some work, but it's a nice piece of property, and that old orchard is worth its weight in gold. I can get her a very good price." Nolan headed back toward the door. "I'll drive out there now and see if I can catch her."

"Don't bother. She mentioned she was going to do some grocery shopping."

"In that case, I'll drop by later on this afternoon or early this evening, then," Nolan said.

"She told me that she has plans for this evening."

"How could she have plans?" Nolan frowned. "She just got into town yesterday."

"Sounded like personal business. Doubt she would appreciate having a real estate agent knocking on her door tonight. If I were you, I'd wait until tomorrow before trying to talk to her."

Nolan's clear blue eyes gleamed with a speculative expression. "What was she doing in here?"

"This is a hardware store," Mason said. "I sold her some lightbulbs. What did you think she was doing?"

Nolan's jaw tightened, but he obviously realized he wasn't going to get any more information.

"See you later," he said.

He did not actually slam the door on the way out, but something about the way he closed it made it clear he would have liked to have been able to slam it.

Mason watched him walk back across the street to join Jillian Colfax. Nolan sat down at the table and spoke briefly to Jillian. She did not look pleased.

Interesting, Mason thought.

CHAPTER
SIX

What was it about the beautiful old house that made her so uneasy? It wasn't just the general gloom, Lucy thought. That would soon be rectified with the new lightbulbs she had picked up at Fletcher Hardware.

She set the sack of groceries, the six-pack of beer and the lightbulbs on the ancient, scarred wooden table that occupied the center of the kitchen. She paused to look around, searching for whatever it was that was bothering her. She remembered the house as warm and welcoming, but now it felt cold. True, it was late in the day, but the place seemed darker than she remembered it.

The paneled walls, faded drapes, wooden floors and heavy, vintage furniture had always been atmospheric, but in a cozy way. Now the two-story house was saturated with shadows. She wasn't sure the new lightbulbs were going to help all that much.

Perhaps the problem was that while Sara was alive the house had reflected her bright, positive, spiritual personality. Now that she was gone, the old house was simply an old house. *Missing its owner*, Lucy thought.

"I miss her, too," she said into the silence.

54

Her phone chirped. She took the device out of her tote and glanced at the screen. The very pricey online matchmaking service with which she was registered had identified another match. All she had to do was log on for more information. Mr. Almost Perfect was waiting out there somewhere in the ether.

She deleted the message and dropped the phone back into the tote.

She put the baby bok choy, the fresh salmon, the white wine and a few other items, including a wedge of excellent cheese from a local artisanal cheesemaker, into the vintage refrigerator. Thirteen years ago the selection of cheeses available in Summer River had been limited to what the chain supermarket on Main Street carried. That afternoon she had spotted two specialty shops stocked with a dazzling array of exotically named cheeses, many made in the surrounding area.

She placed the loaf of crusty French bread on the counter and then turned to contemplate the six-pack. The brown bottles wore designer labels, but there was no getting around the fact that the stuff inside was beer. What had she been thinking? She didn't drink beer. She didn't know if Mason drank it, but she had a feeling he would prefer beer to white wine. Manly men drank beer, didn't they? Or possibly whiskey. She wasn't sure, because she hadn't met a lot of manly men. Mostly the thirtysomething guys she knew were still boys waiting to grow up.

Maybe she should have bought a bottle of whiskey instead of beer.

"You're an idiot, Lucy. It is probably not a good idea to get tangled up with Mason Fletcher."

But she was not getting tangled up with him. He had been gracious enough to offer to see if he could save her some money by tearing out the tiles that blocked the fireplace. The least she could do was give him a glass of wine and feed him. That did not constitute a date. A real date was having coffee or drinks with one of the string of possible matches the dating service had come up with in the past three months.

"Nice job rationalizing," she said. "Spoken like a true commitment-phobe. Dr. Preston would be proud."

Six weeks of cognitive therapy taught a woman a lot about herself.

She got busy opening up the packages of lightbulbs.

CHAPTER
SEVEN

"What the hell do you mean, you've got a date?" Deke demanded. "I've been trying to get you to go out with a woman — any woman — ever since you landed on my doorstep two weeks ago. You kept saying you weren't in the mood. I figured you were depressed or something."

"Or something," Mason said. He did not pause in the act of stacking rolls of duct tape on a shelf.

"And now, out of the blue, you announce you've finally got a date?"

"Breathe, Deke. Don't hyperventilate on me. You can deal with this."

Deke snorted. "Don't be too sure of that. It's a shock to the system, I tell you."

It was doubtful that anything, not even the apocalypse, would come as a stunning shock to Deke Fletcher, Mason thought. If any man could roll with the punches, it was his uncle. He'd sure as hell taken enough of them in his time. And delivered his share.

Deke Fletcher had run through three wives before he'd given up on marriage. All three women had filed for divorce claiming irreconcilable differences. Mason suspected that the term was a polite gloss for the real truth — none of them could take the demanding life of a military spouse married to a soldier who always chose deployment over hearth and home.

Mason and Aaron had had only limited contact with Deke when they were very young. They were vaguely aware that he spent a lot of time abroad fighting wars in far-off places. He was a larger-than-life figure in their vivid imaginations, and they were proud of him. But most of what they knew about him came from overheard conversations between their parents. Their mother had complained that Deke drank too much and that he was a womanizer, and said that it was no wonder he couldn't keep a marriage together. Their father said Deke probably had some form of post-traumatic stress disorder.

Once in a while Deke surprised everyone by showing up for Thanksgiving or New Year's, and when Mason turned ten he and Aaron had spent a memorable two weeks with Deke while their parents took a cruise. Deke had taken Mason and Aaron camping and taught them how to fish. Deke didn't drink much during that visit — a beer in the evenings or a glass of whiskey late at night was about it — so Mason couldn't tell if Deke had a drinking problem. Deke hadn't brought a woman along, either, so it was hard to gauge whether or not he was a womanizer.

The car crash had been caused by a drunk driver, and it had changed everything. Mason was thirteen at the time; Aaron, eleven. Rebecca Fletcher had died at the scene. Jack Fletcher had survived long enough to make it to the hospital — just long enough to say goodbye to his sons and give Mason his marching orders. *Take care of Aaron. You two stick together, no matter what happens.*

The authorities had put Mason and Aaron into foster care while they set out to track down next of kin. Everyone had an excuse. Rebecca's parents explained that they were living in a retirement community and could not bring in young children. Jack's parents had divorced and remarried years earlier. Neither of them wanted to start all over again with two young boys. An aunt on Rebecca's side refused on the grounds that she had never gotten along with her sister and, besides, she was a single mom with two kids of her own to raise. An uncle declined because he had recently remarried and his new wife refused to get stuck with someone else's children.

And so it went. Everyone expressed sympathy; everyone maintained that they wanted to stay in touch with Mason and Aaron — everyone presented a logical reason for why they could not take on the responsibility of raising two boys.

That left Deke.

No one, least of all Mason and Aaron, expected him to step forward and shoulder the responsibility of two boys. After all, he had the very best excuse of all. He was single, and he frequently deployed to war zones. Certainly no one thought that he was fatherhood material — just the opposite. The general opinion was that he would be a bad influence on impressionable youths.

At that point, Mason had understood with blinding clarity that he and Aaron were staring down the very real possibility that they would both end up permanently in the foster care system. If that happened it was likely that they would be separated. He would not be able to carry out his mission to protect Aaron.

He was making plans to disappear into the streets with Aaron when Deke Fletcher arrived, fresh from yet another war zone.

Mason and Aaron had been sitting in the office of their very nice, very kind caseworker, having the facts of foster care life explained to them, when a gleaming gray SUV rolled into the parking lot. Mason knew that neither he nor Aaron would ever forget the sight of Deke striding into their lives. He was pretty sure the very nice, very kind caseworker would never forget it, either.

Deke had not been in uniform that day, but one look at him and you knew that he was hard-core military. It was there in his ramrod-straight bearing — his clean-shaven face, the high-and-tight hair, the neatly pressed shirt, polished boots, sleek wraparound dark glasses and the you-don't-want-to-mess-with-me attitude.

When he walked through the door of the office, Mason and Aaron had stared at him, awed and thrilled. Mason knew in that moment that Uncle Deke had come to save them. For his part, Deke had taken one look at his nephews and nodded once, evidently satisfied with what he saw.

"Let's go home, boys," he said.

The very nice, very kind caseworker had given Deke close scrutiny, asked him a few questions, and then she had smiled. She, too, had been satisfied with what she saw.

Not everyone else in the office, including the very nice caseworker's boss, was of the same mind. There had been some hasty, behind-closed-doors conversations, but the caseworker had triumphed. She had blazed through the formalities with lightning speed — a warrior of another sort, Mason thought.

And then Deke had taken Mason and Aaron home.

Home had been a series of military bases for a few years. Deke stopped deploying, but he stayed in the Army. There was a lot of relocating, but none of them had a problem with that. They had one another.

In the end they wound up in Summer River. Deke deployed one last time the summer Mason turned nineteen. Everyone knew why. The family needed the extra money. Three divorces had wiped out what little Deke had managed to save, and Aaron was destined for college.

Living with Deke gave Mason a chance to discover the truth. In addition to taking a couple of beers or a glass of whiskey in the evenings, Deke did like women. But he treated both the alcohol and the women with respect. He taught Mason and Aaron to do the same.

Mason concluded that Deke was neither an alcoholic nor a womanizer. But he was pretty sure that Deke had possessed another secret. Deke had been more than a little addicted to war. He had given up that addiction to take on another mission — raising his nephews.

He had gone to war one last time to help pay for Aaron's education, but when he came home that time he hung up his shield for good. He bought the old hardware store and settled down to live a different life. As far as Mason could tell, Deke was content now. Either the old addiction had burned out or Deke had changed.

"Who are you seeing tonight?" Deke asked. "You might as well tell me, because we both know it will be all over town by tomorrow morning."

"It's no secret," Mason said. "I'm going to drop by Sara Sheridan's old place."

Deke did look genuinely shocked now. "You've got a date with little Lucy?"

"She's not so little anymore."

Deke chuckled. "Gained a little weight, has she? Generally speaking, that's a good thing in a woman."

Mason turned and looked at him. "I meant she's not sweet sixteen anymore. She's still little, though. Sort of. But she's all grown up."

Deke grinned. "Yeah, I hear that happens. That was quick work on your part. She just got into town yesterday. How'd you manage a date so damn fast?"

"She's planning to do some repairs before she puts the house on the market. Her first priority is to open up the fireplace in the front room. She says her aunt blocked it with a lot of tile because it was inefficient. I told Lucy I'd see if I could handle the job and maybe save her a few bucks. She's going to need the name of a reliable contractor, by the way."

"Hang on here, you call tearing out some old tiles a date?"

"I'm going over to her place at approximately five-thirty in the evening. I'm doing her a favor, and she is going to repay me by cooking me dinner. What do you call it?"

Deke pondered that briefly and then smiled his slow smile. "You could call that a date."

"Certainly struck me that way. As long as you're here, I'll let you close up by yourself." Mason took his keys out of his pocket. "I need to go back to the cabin and clean up."

"Don't use all the hot water. Remember, I've got a date tonight, too. Becky and I are going to shoot some pool and do some dancing out at Hank's."

Mason shook his head. "You've got a pool game lined up and I'm taking out some old tiles. We're a couple of real wild guys, aren't we?"

"Definition of *wild* changes as you get older."

"I'm starting to notice that."

CHAPTER
EIGHT

Lucy took a sip of her white wine.

"What do you think?" she asked.

"You were right," Mason said. "Whoever did this job was a world-class DIY amateur."

"That pretty much describes Aunt Sara. She had a lot of talents, but home repair was not among them."

They were standing in front of the big fireplace, contemplating the tiles that walled up the front. A short time earlier, Mason had replaced the last of the burned-out bulbs in the ceiling fixtures that she had been unable to reach. After examining the wobbly stepladder in the hall closet, she had concluded that he'd had a point about the dangers of ladders.

The lights were on throughout the first floor now, but it seemed to Lucy that the house was as gloomy as ever and no room was darker than the front room, with its cold, closed-up fireplace. Things would be different when she would finally be able to get a real fire going.

Mason swallowed some of his beer, leaned down and used a chisel to poke at one of the tiles. Some of the grout that secured it to the backing crumbled into fine dust.

He straightened and set the beer on a side table. "The grout is in bad shape. I could probably take this down with my bare hands."

"I wonder why she didn't call in a professional to install the tiles," Lucy said.

Mason shook his head and studied the raggedly arranged tiles with the expression of a doctor surveying a doomed patient. "We in the hardware business see this type of mistake over and over again. Someone insists on a do-it-yourself job to try to save a few bucks. The result is that it ends up costing more to fix the bad workmanship than the project would have cost if it had been done right in the first place."

Lucy smiled. "Luckily, I can afford dinner. How long do you think it will take to remove the tilework?"

"Not long — maybe a couple of hours, start to finish. I'll want to go slow so I don't do any damage to the original fireplace surround."

"A couple of hours." Lucy glanced at her watch. "Why don't we have dinner and then tackle those tiles?"

"Good idea."

Mason looked remarkably cheerful, she thought. No, not cheerful, more like filled with keen anticipation. She could see it in his eyes.

It was just dinner. So why was she feeling a little rattled?

"How does pan-seared salmon sound?" she asked.

"Very good," he said. "Terrific."

"Follow me."

She walked through the wide opening that divided the living room and the front hall and crossed into the old-fashioned kitchen. Mason followed hard on her heels.

"Can I do something?" he asked.

"You can set the table. Dishes are in that glass-fronted cabinet. Silverware is in the drawer next to the refrigerator."

He went to work, looking extremely satisfied with himself.

"Nolan Kelly came to see me right after you left the store this afternoon," he said.

"Did he?" She opened the refrigerator and took out the salmon that she had marinated in olive oil, lime juice and soy sauce. "I saw him sitting at a table in front of the café."

"Figured you did," Mason said. "He was with Jillian Colfax."

"Yes, I saw her, too."

Mason tore off a chunk of the bread and took a bite. "Thought so. Your aunt told you that Jillian married Quinn Colfax?"

"Sara mentioned it. No surprise there."

"No," Mason agreed. "She always had her eye on the prize. And the big prize in Summer River was the son of Warner Colfax."

"How long have they been married?"

"Deke said they married a year or two after they both graduated from college."

"I'm surprised they haven't had kids."

Mason folded a paper napkin with origami-style precision. "I don't think things are turning out the way Jillian hoped they would."

Lucy set the strainer filled with washed baby bok choy on the counter next to the stove. "Meaning?"

"Deke says everyone thought that when Warner Colfax took it into his head to fire up his very own winery here in the valley he would turn the job of running Colfax Inc. over to his son."

"That didn't happen?"

"Nope. Word is the old man brought in an outsider as CEO."

"That had to hurt."

"Probably." Mason adjusted the handles of the knife and spoon so that they were perfectly aligned at the bottom edge of the folded napkin. "Quinn got stuck with a marketing job at the winery."

"Jillian can't be thrilled with that. Maybe it explains why they haven't had children."

"Maybe." Mason placed the fork into position with great care. "You do know that Colfax bought out his partner's share of what was then Colfax and Brinker, right?"

"Yes. Aunt Sara mentioned it. She said that Brinker was so devastated by the death of his son that he lost all interest in Colfax and Brinker. He sold his half to Colfax and a few months later died of a heart attack."

"The first thing Warner Colfax did after buying out his partner was change the name of the company to Colfax Inc., which should tell you something."

She smiled. "He wanted the world to know the company was his and his alone."

"It's natural. First thing Deke did when he bought the old hardware store was change the name. Aaron and I call our consulting firm Fletcher Consulting."

"I get that. What surprises me is that Warner Colfax overlooked his own son when it came to selecting a CEO."

"I'm guessing Quinn didn't prove to be management material."

"Think Jillian will leave him?"

"Beats me." Mason positioned a glass. "But I've got a hunch that if she does, she'll wait until after the merger is settled one way or the other. Too much money involved. Deke says the company is structured so that spouses, like Jillian, own a noncontrolling block of shares, but if there's a divorce, the spouse loses those shares. According to Deke, that's what happened to Warner Colfax's first wife, Quinn's mother. Warner dumped her for a woman who is less than half his age. The former Mrs. Colfax probably got a nice settlement, but she had to forfeit her shares in the corporation." Mason paused for emphasis. "The idea is that all shares remain within the Colfax family."

Lucy looked through the kitchen window, watching the evening light fade from the old orchard. "But now the rules have been broken because I inherited Mary Colfax's shares."

"Yes."

Mason went quiet. She turned around and found him watching her with an intent expression.

"What?" she asked.

"I meant what I said earlier today, Lucy. You don't want to get into the middle of the Colfax family feud."

"Thank you for your advice," she said very formally.

"But you're not going to take it. You want to explain why not?"

"Not yet. I'm still thinking about it."

"Then let's try another subject. What are you going to do about Nolan Kelly? He's after the listing on this place, and he's not going to stop coming at you."

"I know."

"He was planning to drive out here to see you this afternoon."

She went back to the frying pan. "Was he?"

"I told him you were busy shopping. Then he said he would drop by tonight. I told him you had other plans."

She stilled in the act of picking up the bottle of olive oil. "You did?"

"Yeah. Figured I'd head him off at the pass for you."

She turned deliberately toward him, one hand braced on the old tile counter. "Excuse me?"

"You know he's just going to pressure you into listing the house with him."

"So you took the liberty of informing him that I was busy all afternoon and evening?"

"Sure. Why not? You said yourself you didn't want to talk to him about the property yet."

"You took it upon yourself to inform him that I was unavailable."

Mason's brows scrunched together in a wary expression. "You look mad."

"Annoyed. Irritated. But lucky for you, I am not yet mad. You've never seen me mad, and it's probably best that way. But let's get something straight here. You are not my personal secretary. I'm a big girl now. I can take care of my own business. I do not need anyone to schedule my life and my appointments while I'm in town. Are we very clear on that?"

Mason managed to look both crushed and bewildered. "I was just trying to do you a favor."

She aimed a finger at him. "When I want a favor from you, I will request said favor. Do I make myself clear?"

"No favors." He held up a hand, palm out. "No problem."

Great. Now she had probably hurt his feelings. Or not. It was hard to tell with Mason Fletcher.

She smiled.

"I'm glad we have an understanding," she said. "You can finish setting the table now."

"Yes, ma'am."

He completed the process with his usual efficient, competent ease. Memories of the night he had driven her home from Brinker's last party floated through her mind. She remembered how in control he had been that night — not only of the old truck but of himself. And she remembered something her aunt had said about Mason. *Someday that young man will either learn to bend or he will break.*

Thus far it did not appear that Mason had done much bending, and he certainly was not broken. But she could see shadows deep in his eyes, not depression or despair — at least she did not think that was what she saw. It was more like a kind of world-weariness mixed with resignation, as if he had spent the past few years searching for something he wanted or needed and was now beginning to accept that he might never find it.

"What brought you back to Summer River?" she asked. "Was it something that happened on the job, or was it personal?"

He looked at her across the table. "You said you didn't need an administrative assistant to organize your life. Fine. I don't need a counselor."

She flushed. "Right. Sorry." She tossed the bok choy into the pan with the salmon. "I do have a couple of questions about the night of Brinker's last party. Can I ask?"

"Ask," he said.

"I've never been able to buy the story that you took me away just because you thought I couldn't handle myself in a crowd of hard-partying teens."

"It wasn't a story," Mason said.

"You really thought that I would get stupid drunk? I may have been sixteen, but I wasn't into drinking or drugs."

"Your aunt never told you the truth, did she?"

She looked at him. "Guess not, since her story remained the same as your own — that I was too young, in over my head, blah, blah, blah."

Mason picked up his beer and propped one shoulder against the refrigerator. "Okay, then, seeing as how you're all grown up, here's the truth. On the evening of the party I heard a rumor that Brinker had plans to target you that night."

"What?" She felt like the wind had been knocked out of her. "I don't understand."

"What part about the word *target* don't you get? He intended to drug you, rape you, film the rape scene and post the video online."

"Good grief." She leaned back against the counter and gripped the edges with both hands. *Thunderstruck* would not have been too strong a word to describe her reaction, she thought. "You *knew* that?"

"All I had to go on was the rumor, but I didn't think it would be smart to take any chances. So, yeah, when I couldn't get hold of your aunt, I went looking for you."

"Every kid in town knew that I was going to be Brinker's target that night?" she demanded, voice rising.

"I doubt it. Brinker kept his secrets close. But he did tell one person."

"Who?"

"Jillian."

"Jillian," Lucy repeated, numb with the shock of it all. "I didn't think she even knew who I was back in those days. She was the local prom queen and a cheerleader. I was just a kid from out of town who was spending the summer with her aunt."

"She knew who you were, trust me."

Lucy frowned, thinking it through. "Because she wanted Brinker, and Brinker wanted to target me."

"Something like that. Whatever Brinker wanted, he got."

"Why would he want me? I wasn't his type. Jillian was his type."

"It was just a horrible game to Brinker. The guy was a sociopath. If he'd lived, he probably would have become a serial rapist or maybe a serial killer. Who can say? You represented what he could never be — a sweet, decent kid. So he wanted to destroy you."

She took a deep breath. "That's very . . . insightful of you."

"You learn a few things about human nature when you track bad guys for a living."

"Yes, I suppose so."

She suddenly smelled the bok choy and salmon. Seizing a hot pad, she whirled around and yanked the pan off the heat. For a moment she stood there, staring at the contents of the skillet.

"You were right," she said. "I really do owe you my thanks for saving me that night."

"No."

"Yes." She met his eyes. "If Brinker had succeeded with his evil act, I would have been seriously traumatized. My life would probably have gone in an entirely different direction, and it most likely would not have been a good direction. So . . . thanks."

CHAPTER
NINE

Lucy sat on the sofa, one leg curled under herself, and watched Mason take apart the wall of tiles that blocked the front of the big fireplace. It dawned on her that she liked to watch him, regardless of the task at hand — driving, flipping a wrench into the air, setting a table, removing tiles. She just liked to look at him.

It was weird to think that nothing had changed since he had dropped her off at her door the night of the party thirteen years ago. It wasn't as if she'd spent the intervening years thinking about him or missing him. Her life had been fulfilling and, with the glaring exception of her love life, satisfying. She had a career she found interesting and challenging. She had good friends.

The point was that she had not been lonely since leaving Summer River and she had not been pining for Mason Fletcher. When she had thought about him at all, it had been with a mix of amusement and sympathy for the sixteen-year-old kid who'd had a crush on an older, out-of-reach male who, she now knew, had saved her from a vicious sociopath.

The bottom line was that Mason Fletcher had been a treasured memory of her youth, but she certainly had

74

not obsessed over him. She was an adult now. She no longer viewed him from the perspective of a shy teen with a crush on an older boy. Now she saw him as an equal. The age difference between them was no longer an obstacle. And she found him even more fascinating than he had been all those years ago.

"How long do you plan to stay in Summer River?" she asked.

Mason used a small hammer to tap the end of a chisel. Another tile fell free. He caught it and placed it on top of the growing stack.

"Depends," he said.

She let it go. Mason would talk only when he was ready, and that might be never.

"You know, I never would have envisioned you working in a hardware store," she said.

"Why not? I like selling hardware. Hardware is real. Hammers, saws, drills, screwdrivers — they're useful. When you think about it, civilization as we know it depends on stuff like that."

"I hadn't considered screwdrivers and hammers from that perspective, but I see what you mean. Personally, I've always considered good indoor plumbing the basis of civilization. It's the reason I never saw the appeal of camping."

"You can't put a toilet or a shower together without good tools."

"Good point."

"What happened to your engagement?"

The question came out of nowhere, catching her off guard.

"It ended after about a year when I found him in bed with his administrative assistant," she said.

Belatedly, she wished she'd kept her mouth shut.

"You were engaged for nearly a year?" Mason gave her a severe look. "That should have told you something was seriously wrong."

Now he had put her on the defensive.

"Why do you say that?" she asked, going for a little chill in her tone. "A lot of engagements last a year or longer. A long engagement gives two people an opportunity to make sure they are right for each other."

Mason looked unconvinced. "I say if it takes you a year to decide whether or not you can make a commitment, something is missing."

"Yes, well, turns out something was missing in the case of my engagement."

He pried off another tile. "What?"

"Me, I think."

He raised his brows. "Meaning?"

"I have commitment issues, according to my therapist. Something to do with being a child of divorce — all that shuttling back and forth between two feuding parents. Add in the fact that I didn't like my mom's second husband or my father's second wife and they didn't like me, and things get complicated."

He smiled. "No shit?"

She smiled, too. "No shit."

"Got a plan?"

"Absolutely. I finally decided to go the scientific route to finding the right partner. I registered at a very reputable, very expensive online matchmaking site. I've had thirty dates in the past few months. All of them were excellent matches, at least according to the computer algorithms that matched us."

"But?"

She exhaled slowly. "But I've still got those darn commitment issues. What about you? Made any progress on the relationship front since your divorce?"

"Well, I probably still have communication problems." He dropped another tile onto the stack. "But tonight I had dinner with a very interesting woman who has commitment issues, so things are definitely looking up."

She laughed. "You're right. You really are a glass-half-full kind of guy."

"You miss your ex-fiancé?"

She stopped laughing and went with the truth. "Nope. The dirty little secret is that I was relieved when it was all over. Miss your ex-wife?"

"Nope. I was relieved, too, when I came home one day and discovered that she had walked out. It meant I could stop trying to fix myself. Lucky for me, she left before Fletcher Consulting started to make some money."

He removed the last of the tiles and studied the wooden frame and backing for a moment. Then he reached for another tool.

A few minutes later, he eased the frame and backing out of the fireplace, revealing the dark opening.

"Looks like there is something inside," he said.

Lucy uncoiled and sat forward on the sofa, trying to peer into the darkness. She could make out a large lumpy shape.

"Why on earth would Aunt Sara —" She stopped.

"Got a flashlight?" Mason asked. "If you don't, I can get one from my truck."

"Sara kept one in the kitchen. I'll get it."

"I think I'm going to need a clean towel, too."

Lucy jumped up and went into the kitchen. When she returned, Mason took the towel and used it to remove a poker that had been lodged inside the fireplace.

"What is it?" she asked.

"I can't be positive yet, but I've got a feeling that this is not going to be good."

He set the poker aside and took the flashlight from her. He aimed the beam through the opening. She moved closer and looked into the deep fireplace.

"Looks like a copy of an old newspaper," she said. "It's sealed in a plastic bag."

"Look closer."

A cold chill iced her blood. "Is that a black garbage bag? Don't tell me Sara stuffed the fireplace with trash before she covered it with tiles. That would be just too weird."

"Garbage bags don't have zippers," Mason said. "It's a body bag."

"Good grief." Lucy stepped back reflexively. "I can't believe it."

Mason used the towel again to reach into the fireplace. He removed the bag containing the newspaper. Lucy glanced at the banner.

"It's a San Francisco paper," she said. She glanced at the date and did the math. "Oh, crap. It was published in August, thirteen years ago. That's the summer when Brinker was in town. Someone circled the headline, *Scorecard Rapist Strikes Again.*"

Mason turned the plastic bag over to view the other side of the newspaper. "There's a driver's license in here."

Lucy stared at the photo of the young, astonishingly good-looking man. He was blond and blue-eyed, with a charismatic smile that promised dark thrills.

"Tristan Brinker," she said.

CHAPTER
TEN

"She killed him because of what he had planned to do to me, didn't she?" Lucy said.

"There are still a lot of questions to be answered here, but yes, I think that scenario is the most likely one," Mason said.

He watched Lucy out of the corner of his eye as he removed two bottles of water from the refrigerator. She probably needed something stronger than water, but she had declined another glass of wine. He could not tell how she was handling the shock of the discovery. She appeared surprisingly calm — maybe *somber* was a better word. Then again, it was possible she was simply exhausted. It had been a very long night, and it wasn't over yet.

They were back in the kitchen of the old house. Lucy was slumped in a chair at the table. It was after midnight. Chief Whitaker and the two officers who had accompanied him had finally departed after taking a lot of pictures and bagging up some samples of the debris in the fireplace. The unpleasantly droopy body bag had been loaded into an ambulance and driven off into the night.

A yellow crime scene tape had been strung across the wide doorway into the living room. Whitaker had warned Lucy against building a fire in the newly opened fireplace. She had assured him in a sharp tone that she had no plans to do so. In any event, the chimney would need to be thoroughly cleaned and inspected first.

"Dear heaven." Lucy shook her head slowly, awed. "My dear, sweet little aunt who practiced yoga, meditated every day and ate a strict organic vegan diet murdered the son and heir of one of the richest men in Northern California and stuffed his body inside her fireplace. It's unbelievable."

"There's still some question about the identity of the body," Mason reminded her. "The decomp process has been going on for thirteen years."

"Who else could it be? The date on the newspaper, the timing of Brinker's disappearance all those years ago, the driver's license — it all fits."

"Can't argue with that," Mason said.

Chief Whitaker's last words had been exactly what Mason had expected. *I want you both to come to the station in the morning. I'll need statements.*

Mason sat down at the table. He opened the bottles of Summer Springs water and placed one in front of Lucy.

Lucy contemplated the bottle as if she had never seen one before. Then she picked it up and drank some of the water.

"It looks like we accidentally closed the only known cold case in the history of Summer River," she said.

"You never know what you're going to find when you start down the DIY remodeling road."

She blinked, brows crinkling in a frown. "That is probably a very inappropriate remark."

"Probably."

"So why do I want to laugh?"

"Don't worry, it's a nervous reaction."

"Oh, I see." She paused. "Aunt Sara would have laughed."

"If it had been anyone other than Brinker, I wouldn't have made an inappropriate remark," he said. "But it was Brinker, and to tell you the truth, it's a relief to find out that he's been sealed up in that fireplace all this time. The bastard was one of the monsters. Assuming your aunt was trying to tell us something by leaving that newspaper with the body, Brinker may have been the Scorecard Rapist. Regardless, it's good to know he hasn't been out in the world doing bad things to good people for the past thirteen years."

"There is that." Lucy hoisted her bottle of water in a small salute. "Here's to Aunt Sara."

"To Aunt Sara." Mason raised his own bottle of water.

"Just think, if I had sold the house in as-is condition, the buyer would have gotten a heck of a shock when he took out that tilework," Lucy mused. "Because sooner or later someone would have opened up the fireplace."

"Yes."

Lucy shuddered. "No wonder I couldn't get to sleep last night."

Mason leaned back in the chair. "Are you going to tell me that you think this house is haunted by Brinker's ghost?"

"No, of course not, but this place felt very weird to me last night. I got that icy vibe people get when they walk across graveyards and battlefields."

"People get that vibe only when they happen to know that they are walking across a cemetery or a battlefield," Mason said. "The imagination is a powerful thing."

She shot him a quick glare and then wrinkled her nose. "Never mind the reasons for my insomnia last night. The real question is how could Aunt Sara sleep here in this house knowing that there was a dead body in the fireplace, one she had put there herself?"

Mason shrugged. "Maybe it was all that meditation and yoga she practiced. Could be it endowed her with some Zen-like ability to ignore the body in the fireplace." He paused for a beat. "Or it could be that she was okay with it because she felt justified in killing Brinker — which she was, in my book, by the way."

"I wonder if she told Mary?"

"I doubt if we'll ever know. But in situations like the one your aunt was facing, the smart thing to do is to follow the Three-S Rule. Got a hunch Sara would have figured that out for herself."

Lucy frowned. "What's the Three-S rule?"

"Shoot, shovel and shut up."

Lucy turned the water bottle between her palms. "Yes. I see what you mean." She hesitated. "But I doubt if Aunt Sara actually shot Brinker. She didn't approve

83

of guns, and she didn't own one. She must have used some other method."

"I think the ME will conclude that Brinker was killed with one or more blows to the skull."

"The poker?"

"Uh-huh." Mason drank some of his water. "There was some stuff sticking to the end of it."

"Stuff?"

"Hair, I think."

Lucy sighed. "Well, finding the body in the fireplace tonight certainly explains why Sara and Mary started doing a lot more traveling after that summer. It also explains why she didn't want me coming back to Summer River to visit her. To her way of thinking, inviting me to stay here in the house with a dead guy would have been very bad karma."

"I apologize, again, for jumping to the conclusion that you had ignored her for the past thirteen years."

Lucy gave him a faint smile. "Apology accepted. You're right, though, there are a lot of questions. The first one that comes to mind is, why hide the body here in the house?"

"Can you think of a better way to make sure it wasn't found and subjected to a forensic autopsy? Take it from me, it's hard to hide a body. Over time they have a way of showing up. They wash ashore. They get uncovered by a heavy rain. Developers stumble onto them when they start building houses on previously unused land."

"I see what you mean," Lucy said. She shuddered. "No wonder she stopped doing major repairs and renovations."

"Bringing in a contractor or a handyman or a painter would have been too risky," Mason said. "Any halfway decent craftsman would have taken one look at that fireplace and started asking questions. He would have offered to give her the name of a good tile man. Sara would have declined. The contractor or the painter would have wondered why she didn't want it repaired."

Lucy contemplated that for a moment. "Were you ever a suspect in Brinker's disappearance?"

"The leading theory at the time was that Brinker was the victim of a drug deal gone bad, but Brinker's father didn't want to hear that. If you'll remember, Hobbs was the chief of police back then, and Brinker senior was pushing him hard. A lot of people saw you leave the party with me that night, and at least one other person, Quinn Colfax, knew there was some bad blood between Brinker and me. So, yes, Hobbs came around asking questions."

"What happened?"

"Thanks to your aunt, I was able to tell Hobbs the flat-out truth — I had no idea what had happened to Brinker. Hobbs had no proof to the contrary. I told him what Brinker had planned to do to you that night. But I couldn't prove it, and Hobbs knew that Brinker's father wouldn't want to hear that news, either, so I doubt if Hobbs ever told him."

"Did Hobbs talk to Jillian?"

"Sure. He talked to her, Quinn Colfax, Nolan Kelly and several other people who were known to hang around Brinker. But everyone denied knowing anything about the plan to drug you and rape you."

"Including Jillian?"

Mason finished the water and set the bottle aside. "Including Jillian."

Lucy's mouth twisted into a grim smile. "She lied."

"Yes."

Lucy studied him intently. "You said that there was bad blood between you and Brinker. What happened?"

"After I drove you back here that night, I went out to the ranch and waited for the party to break up. It didn't take long, because someone phoned in a complaint. I had a talk with Brinker — told him not to go anywhere near you again. He made a run at me and slammed into the fender of his car instead."

Lucy's brows rose. "I see."

"Quinn Colfax was a witness to the conversation."

"I should have known." Lucy shook her head. "My guardian angel couldn't let it go. In addition to allowing Brinker to bruise himself on his own vehicle, did you by any chance make threats?"

"More like promises. I let Brinker know that if anything happened to you, he would have to deal with me."

"He would have believed you," Lucy said. She was silent for a beat while she absorbed that information. Understanding darkened her eyes. "You thought that if you threatened him he would go after you first. He would have been obsessed with rage because you dared to get in his way."

"I wanted to distract him."

"You deliberately made yourself a target. What on earth did you think was going to happen?"

Mason said nothing. He watched as another shock of comprehension struck her. Tension coiled inside him. He had no clue how she would react.

"Dear heaven," she whispered. "You intended to kill him if he came after you."

Mason let the statement seethe in the atmosphere between them. There was nothing more he could say.

Lucy took a deep breath and let it out slowly. "I need a moment here."

Mason sat quietly, waiting for the verdict. Thirteen years ago he had been willing to cross the line. Lucy had to know that he probably hadn't changed all that much over time. He would do a lot for Lucy, but some things he could not do. He could not pretend that he was all that different from the nineteen-year-old he had been that summer. Given the same set of circumstances, he would be willing to cross the line again.

"I don't know what to say except thank you," Lucy said. "And I'm very, very glad you didn't have to do it."

It was not the reaction he had been expecting, Mason realized. Then again, he hadn't known what to expect.

"I don't want your thanks," he began.

"You were only nineteen. It would have been a heavy burden for you to carry. Aunt Sara understood that. She also knew that Brinker was a monster and a threat both to me and to you. She considered herself to be the adult in that situation. She knew she couldn't go to the police because Hobbs wouldn't have paid any attention to her. She took care of Brinker so that you wouldn't have to do it."

Mason looked through the kitchen doorway at the crime scene tape strung across the entrance to the living room. "You sound very sure you know what was going through Sara's mind at the time."

"I am sure, now that I know her secret and the facts. People tell me that I'm a lot like her, you know."

"Yeah?"

"Oh, not the eccentric, flower-child, student-of-enlightenment thing. But deep down I understood her better than anyone else in the family did. And she understood me. So yes, in hindsight I can imagine her thought processes and her logic."

Mason nodded. "I get it."

Silence stretched between them.

"Did you search for him?" Lucy asked suddenly.

"Brinker? Oh, yeah, from time to time over the years. After Aaron got the program up and running I plugged in everything I knew about Brinker. Alice came up with a high probability that he had been murdered the summer he disappeared."

"Well, it looks like that conclusion may be right."

"Alice also estimated that there was an eighty-nine percent probability that Brinker had been killed by someone who knew him and that the motive was personal. He wasn't the victim of a drug deal gone bad."

"A reasonable conclusion. Brinker was too smart to get caught in that kind of scenario."

"Yes."

Lucy regarded him with an expression that could only be classified as one of professional interest.

"Did Alice offer up a list of possible suspects?" she asked.

"I fed in all the names of the people I could remember who had been associated with Brinker that summer. The program spit out only one serious suspect."

Lucy winced. "You?"

"Me."

"Whew. Good thing Fletcher Consulting was not called in by the local police to consult on the Brinker case at some point during the past thirteen years."

Mason smiled. "Yeah, that could have been awkward."

"What about Aunt Sara? Did her name come up in any way in your program?"

"No. But Alice did offer up a couple of other low-probability suspects."

"Who?"

"Quinn Colfax, for one."

"Motive?"

"Jealousy. Quinn and Brinker were both in line to inherit their fathers' financial fund empire, but it was clear to everyone — including Quinn, I'm sure — that Brinker would end up as the guy in charge. If that happened, sooner or later Quinn would have been eased out of the company altogether."

"Think so?"

"Absolutely," Mason said. "Brinker wouldn't have wanted a partner. He would have found a way to get rid of Quinn."

"Well, that didn't happen, did it? Who was the other suspect?"

"Nolan Kelly."

Lucy frowned. "That's hard to imagine."

"Not if you were aware that Nolan was the local go-to guy for pot and booze back in the day. He catered to the teen crowd."

"Okay, I didn't know that. Why would he have killed Brinker?"

"Where there are drugs, there are guns, and sometimes people wind up dead." Mason drank some of his water and put the bottle down. "There were always rumors of drugs swirling around Brinker."

"Do you think Nolan was Brinker's connection?"

"For the pot, probably. Not so sure about the hallucinogens. It's hard to picture Nolan as a high-end dealer who had the kind of contacts it takes to get the expensive, exotic stuff that Brinker apparently made available at the parties. Kelly always struck me as a small-time operator. I can't see him risking a murder charge. And if he was Brinker's connection, why would he want to get rid of his best client?"

"Good question."

"Deke says Nolan has really cleaned up his act, by the way. He's sure that the only thing Kelly is selling these days is real estate."

"That's good to know." Lucy made a face. "Still, I may want to consider giving the listing to another agent." She looked at the crime scene tape across the hall. "We can now say for certain that all of the prevailing theories about Brinker's disappearance were wrong. By morning everyone in town will know that Aunt Sara murdered him. I wonder how it all went down."

"I don't know, but I can tell you one thing: Sara did some very careful planning, and she did it fast."

"What makes you say that?"

"The body bag."

Lucy swallowed hard. "Yes, I see what you mean. Where does a person go to purchase a body bag, anyhow, if she isn't in the medical or law enforcement field?"

"Where else? Online. Probably paid extra for overnight shipping."

Lucy winced. She set her water aside and dropped her head into her hands. "One thing is for sure. I can't sleep here tonight. Or tomorrow night, either, for that matter. It was bad enough last night without knowing there was a body in the fireplace. But now that I know this place has been a crypt for the past thirteen years, there's no way I can stay here. I'm going to check into a motel."

Mason checked his watch. "It's midnight."

"So? Motels are open twenty-four hours a day, aren't they? Wasn't there an old inn on the square in town?"

"The Harvest Gold Inn. It's showing its age, but it's clean and the location is convenient."

Lucy pushed herself up out of the chair. "I'll go upstairs and pack."

She crossed the kitchen and went out into the hall. There she paused and looked at Mason, her eyes shadowed. "You know, it's pretty amazing when you think about it, isn't it?"

"That your aunt got away with murder for thirteen years? Yes, it is."

"But now she's dead and the truth is going to come out."

"So what? There's nothing the law can do to her now."

"No."

Lucy did not move. She just stood there, watching him with her knowing eyes.

He got a cold feeling in his gut. "What are you thinking?"

But he was pretty sure he knew exactly what she was thinking.

"You're in law enforcement," she said quietly. "I thought cops didn't like coincidences."

"No, but they happen. And so do car accidents. I don't like where you're going with this."

"Sounds to me like you're already there. Here's the thing, Mason. We forensic genealogists have a few things in common with other kinds of investigators — we are a suspicious lot. Probably something to do with all those fake heirs who come out of the woodwork when a wealthy person dies. Makes us ask questions. And guess what? We also know a little something about investigation techniques."

"No," Mason said. He tried to make it sound nonnegotiable. "You are not going to start investigating Sara's and Mary's death. It was ruled an accident."

Lucy gave him a brilliant smile.

"In that case, where's the harm in asking a few questions?" she said.

"Damn it to hell, Lucy —"

"The way I see it, there are two possibilities. The first is that there is someone who cared enough about Brinker to avenge his death. That person decided that Sara killed Brinker and took revenge."

"No."

"What makes you so sure?"

"Think about it, Lucy. Brinker's body was stuck in the fireplace for thirteen years. No one knew it was there until tonight. There is every reason to believe that Sara took her secret to the grave. Therefore, there's no logical reason to conclude that after all this time someone suddenly decided that your aunt was the one who killed Brinker and that said individual took revenge by murdering Sara."

"I agree with you," Lucy said.

He took a breath. "Okay. Good."

"Which leaves only one other motive — those Colfax shares."

"Damn." He didn't say anything else, because there was no denying that money was always a logical motive.

"Everyone assumed those shares would go to Quinn upon Mary's death," Lucy said. "Mary certainly led everyone to believe that. She was Warner's sister, but she always had a special fondness for her nephew, Quinn. However, she changed her will without telling anyone, leaving the shares to Sara instead. Sara, in turn, left them to me."

"That theory would make Mary the target of a staged accident."

"Yes," Lucy said. She swallowed hard. "Sara was collateral damage."

"Lucy —"

"I'll be down in a few minutes."

She rushed up the stairs.

"Damn it to hell," Mason said again. But this time he said it to himself. Because he could see the writing on the wall.

Lucy was going to ask questions, and there was no way he could stop her. The only thing he could do was watch her back.

CHAPTER
ELEVEN

The following morning Lucy was sitting at a table in Becky's Garden, the cheerful café next door to the Harvest Gold Inn, sipping a cup of freshly brewed organic green tea and munching a slice of toast that was also guaranteed to be organic and baked locally, when she heard her named called out.

"*Lucy*. Lucy Sheridan. I thought that was you I saw coming out of the hardware store yesterday."

There was no mistaking a former cheerleader's voice — bright, vivacious and downright perky. Lucy looked toward the door and watched Jillian Colfax sweep toward her through the crowded café. Jillian hadn't changed much in thirteen years. Her blond hair was shorter now. She wore it in a stylish shoulder-length bob instead of a ponytail. Some of the natural radiance of youth had been replaced by an expensive spa glow, and she looked as if she had put on some weight. But she was still a remarkably lovely woman. She would look good at ninety. She had the bones.

She also wore clothes very well. Today Jillian was a model of what Lucy had concluded was the local look — an expensive, laid-back style that was meant to convey the mystique of wine country. The clothes were designed to indicate that the wearer was at home toiling in the vineyards.

The reality, of course, was that the real work in the vineyards was done by the same hardworking people who picked all the other crops on the West Coast — migrant laborers. Lucy suspected that very few of them wore designer jeans, silk shirts and Prada sandals into the fields. She was willing to bet that they left the diamond and emerald rings behind as well.

Jillian arrived at the table and sat down without waiting for an invitation.

"It's wonderful to see you again," she said. "Can you believe it's been thirteen years?"

"No problem at all," Lucy said. She put down the pen she had been using to make notes on a pad of yellow paper.

Jillian looked briefly baffled by the response, but she barely broke stride.

"Time goes by so quickly," she said. "You look fabulous, by the way. You've really changed. I wasn't even sure at first that it was you when I first saw you yesterday. Love the haircut. It really suits you."

"I'm so glad you approve," Lucy said in her most exquisitely polite tones. She picked up the pot and poured more tea into her cup.

Jillian regrouped and tried another approach.

"I'm so sorry about the circumstances that brought you back to Summer River," she continued. "We were all shocked to hear about the car crash. Your aunt was a fixture of the community. Everyone liked her. I know you were close to her — at least you were when you were in your teens."

"I loved her," Lucy said. She set the pot down. "I was very fond of Mary, too."

"I know. We will miss them both."

"Will you?"

"Of course." Jillian's full lips tightened ever so slightly, and her eyes lost a few degrees of warmth and several carats of sparkle. "As I said, we were all shocked. But everyone knows that stretch of the old road to the coast is very dangerous. I don't know why they took that route."

"They always took Manzanita Road when they drove to the coast. They were very familiar with it. They liked to stop and eat a picnic lunch at the site of the old commune where they met. It was something of a weekly ritual for them."

"Yes, well, I must admit the biggest stunner came this morning when Quinn and I heard that you and Mason Fletcher found Tristan Brinker's body in the fireplace of Sara's house. Absolutely unbelievable."

"It was something of a surprise."

"All these years everyone has wondered what happened to him."

The attractive, middle-aged woman who had welcomed Jillian to the café a short time earlier cruised purposely through the crowd. She had introduced herself as Becky Springer, and it was clear that she was the proprietor. Becky was a robust, full-figured woman endowed with the unflappable personality and the kind of bubbly energy it took to run a small business. She came to a stop at the table where Lucy and Jillian were seated.

"Coffee, Jillian?" she said with a polite smile that did not quite reach her eyes.

Jillian glanced up impatiently. "Hi, Becky. Yes, coffee, please."

"I'll be right back," Becky said.

Somehow she made it sound like a warning. Lucy hid a smile. Reading between the lines, she was quite sure that Becky was not a big fan of Jillian Colfax's.

As soon as Becky was out of earshot, Jillian leaned in a little closer and lowered her voice.

"Do you have any idea why your aunt would have murdered Brinker?"

There was a thread of anxiety in her voice, and if you looked closely, you could see the evidence of strain around her eyes, Lucy thought.

"We don't know for certain that she did," Lucy said calmly. "For that matter, we don't know yet that it's Brinker's body we found."

"But they're saying Brinker's driver's license was with the body, and also a newspaper with a headline about the Scorecard Rapist, who was terrorizing college campuses that summer."

"I did see the driver's license and the newspaper, but I'm sure the authorities will want to do a bit more investigating before they close the case."

"It must be him," Jillian said. "It has to be him. It explains why he suddenly vanished. I don't think there will be an extensive investigation. Brinker's only close relative was his father. Jeffrey Brinker died a few months after his son. There's no one left who will push to reopen the case. After all, it looks very open-and-shut."

"Does it?"

Tension tightened the corners of Jillian's mouth and eyes. "Don't tell me you want the police to start asking a lot of questions. It will make everything so much more complicated."

It was half command, half plea.

"Define *complicated*," Lucy said.

"You know what I'm talking about. You don't want to dredge up the past."

"What is there to dredge up?"

"Brinker hurt some people — maybe more people than we knew, if he really was the Scorecard Rapist. His victims won't thank you for bringing the ghost out of the closet, trust me."

"I didn't know that much about Tristan Brinker. The closest I ever got to him was the night of his last party out at the old Harper Ranch. You may remember the occasion. You invited me to go with you."

Jillian flushed slightly, and her eyes hardened, but she gave no other indication that the mention of the party brought back uncomfortable memories or twinges of guilt. Probably because they didn't, Lucy thought. In Jillian's mind the events of that long-ago evening no doubt came under the heading of teenage fun and games.

"What I remember about Brinker's last party was that you left early with Mason Fletcher," Jillian said.

"Yes." Lucy made a note on the yellow pad.

Jillian watched uneasily. "What are you doing?"

"Just jotting down a few reminders to myself. I've got a lot to do while I'm here in town."

"How long will you be in Summer River?"

"I have absolutely no idea," Lucy said. "I had intended to spend a couple of weeks getting the house ready to sell, but you're right, a murder investigation could complicate things. Why do you ask?"

"I know this isn't a good time to talk about business, but you need to know that Colfax Inc. is in the middle of a very important business negotiation. A lot of money is on the line."

"I heard something about a possible merger."

"Yes. Raintree Assets has approached Colfax with a very lucrative offer. Quinn and I recently found out that due to a quirk in Mary Colfax's will, you inherited her shares in Colfax Inc."

"It wasn't a quirk at all," Lucy said. "Mary was a very shrewd businesswoman. In exchange for the rather large sum of money that she invested in Colfax Inc. back at the beginning, she insisted that she have full control of her shares. She chose to leave them to Sara, who, in turn, left them to me."

"All of the shares are supposed to remain in the family. Warner insisted on it."

"He made an exception when he and Brinker founded the company. He needed Mary's cash, so he met her terms. It's all quite legal, I assure you. And rock solid. Mary and Sara handled their legal affairs with a trust. You know what lawyers say — wills are broken all the time, but trusts are almost impossible to take apart. I

100

can vouch for that fact. In my work, we see plenty of examples of the strength of a well-designed trust."

Jillian placed her perfectly manicured fingertips on the table and lowered her voice.

"According to Quinn, that wasn't the way it was supposed to work," she said.

Lucy laughed. "I can't begin to tell you how many times I hear that in my profession."

Jillian sat back, anger and confusion flashing across her face. "What, exactly, do you do for a living?"

"I'm a forensic genealogist."

"What on earth is that?"

"I spend my days tracking down lost heirs and connecting them with their inheritances."

"I didn't know there was such a profession."

"I get that a lot."

Jillian's eyes glittered with suspicion. "Did you know that you were in line to inherit those Colfax shares?"

"It came as a complete surprise. I knew I was Sara's heir, of course, but I never had a clue that she was one of Mary's heirs."

"Neither did anyone else in the known universe, damn it," Jillian shot back.

Becky Springer chose that moment to arrive at the table with a graceful porcelain coffeepot decorated with yellow flowers. She poured the coffee into Jillian's cup.

Two dark shadows fell across the bright café.

Becky glanced over her shoulder.

"Oh, look," she said, affecting mild surprise. "Two latecomers for breakfast. I'd better make another pot of coffee."

Jillian was sitting with her back to the door. She did not turn her head to see who had entered the room. It was obvious she couldn't have cared less. She was completely focused on Lucy and the shares of Colfax Inc.

But Lucy watched, fascinated, as Mason and Deke prowled through the maze of delicate tables and chairs. She was not the only one paying attention. With the exception of Jillian, everyone else in the room glanced either surreptitiously or in outright curiosity at the men. In the pretty, sunlit space they stood out like a couple of Old West gunslingers traversing a flowered meadow.

Mason looked like he had gotten some sleep. The midnight shadow of a beard that she had noticed late last night was gone. He was dressed in jeans, a denim shirt and low boots.

Sara and Mary had often remarked that Mason resembled his uncle. Thirteen years ago, Lucy had not agreed. This morning the family link between the two was starkly clear. Deke's once dark hair had gone steel gray. But the shared genetic heritage was there in the wolf-gold eyes, the fiercely etched features and the tough, lean lines of the two men.

"Something tells me Deke and Mason will want to join you two ladies," Becky said. She winked at Lucy. "I'll get two more cups."

Jillian did turn around then. She shot a quick, uneasy look at Mason and Deke and then switched her attention back to Lucy.

"We can't talk here. We need privacy."

"I don't have any problem chatting here," Lucy said. Deliberately, she gave Mason and Deke a bright, welcoming smile. Deke nodded in acknowledgment. Mason looked amused.

Becky moved away from the table and greeted Mason and Deke.

"You two have a seat," she said. "I'll be right back with more coffee."

"Thanks, honey," Deke said.

He leaned over and gave Becky a quick, affectionate kiss as she went past him on the way to the coffee bar. It was the kind of easy good-morning kiss that two people who have been lovers for a long time exchanged.

Well, Lucy thought. *So that's how things stand in that quarter.*

Mason must have noticed her reaction, because he flashed her a quick grin and winked.

And then both men were at the table. Neither of them was especially big, but between the two of them they managed to block out most of the sunlight pouring through the windows behind them.

"Well, well, well, little Lucy Sheridan," Deke said. He gave Lucy a once-over and smiled approvingly. "Didn't you turn out just fine? Figured you would."

"It's nice to see you again, Mr. Fletcher," she said.

"Real sorry to hear about Sara and Mary."

"Thank you," Lucy said quietly.

"Good morning, Lucy," Mason said. "Jillian. Mind if we join you?"

Jillian opened her mouth in what Lucy was pretty sure was going to be a no.

"Please do," Lucy said.

Neither man hesitated. They each grabbed a chair from a nearby table, snapped it into position and sat down.

Jillian looked seriously irritated, but she was trapped and she knew it. The table was Lucy's, after all.

Deke inclined his head at Jillian in a crisp, military-style acknowledgment of her presence that gave away nothing of what he was thinking.

"Jillian," he said. "Surprised to see you here this morning."

"I heard Lucy was in town," Jillian said. Each word was chipped from ice. "She and I have some private business."

"Is that so?" Deke looked at Lucy, brows raised.

She smiled. "Trust me, it's nothing that can't wait."

Jillian got a pinched look and rose quickly.

"You'll have to excuse me," she said. "I've got an appointment. Lucy, I'll get in touch with you later to set up a private meeting."

"I'm going to be quite busy for the next few days," Lucy said. "But I'll check my calendar and see if I can free up some time for you."

"You might want to do that," Jillian said evenly. "There is a considerable amount of money at stake, and you stand to do very well out of the deal if you manage to find the time to discuss the details."

"Sounds good," Lucy said. "I like to talk about making money as much as the next person. But right now I'm a little busy."

Jillian looked torn. Then she appeared to come to a major decision. She smiled.

"I understand," she said. "Listen, Quinn and I are having a reception at the winery to celebrate Warner's birthday this evening. We'll be opening the first bottles of the Colfax Reserve. Everyone at the winery feels it will set the wine world on fire. I know it's awfully short notice, but I would love it if you could join us."

"Wow, déjà vu all over again," Lucy said. She smiled. "Got a surprise in store for me this time, too?"

"Good question," Mason said.

Jillian looked blank. "I'm afraid I don't get the joke."

"The last party you invited me to wasn't intended to end well for me, was it?" Lucy said. "I was just wondering how this one is slated to finish."

Jillian's eyes went very cold. "That was a long time ago."

"And Brinker is dead," Lucy finished quietly.

Jillian's hand tightened around the strap of her purse. "Yes. I doubt if there is anyone who will mourn him."

An acute silence descended on the table. Lucy knew they were all waiting for her reaction.

"Thank you for the invitation to the reception," she said. "But I'd feel very awkward attending alone. Okay if I bring someone with me?"

Jillian was almost pathetically relieved. "Yes, of course. You're more than welcome to bring a date. But I thought you were here in Summer River on your own. Is someone joining you?"

"My date for the evening will be Mason." Lucy looked politely at Mason. "Assuming he's willing."

Mason watched her with a steady, calculating expression. "He's definitely willing. I've never been invited to one of those classy winery receptions. This should be interesting."

Jillian did not look thrilled, but she managed a determined smile. "Fine. We'll see you both tonight, then. Seven-thirty." She paused to give Lucy one last bright smile. "Dress code is the usual — wine-country casual."

"I'll make sure to clean my boots," Mason said.

Jillian ignored that. She adjusted her shoulder bag and walked briskly toward the door.

Lucy looked at Mason and Deke. "Wine-country casual?"

Deke chuckled. "Don't look at me, I've never been invited to any of those shindigs at the wineries."

Becky appeared at the table. "Neither have I, but I can give you one piece of advice, Mason: Whatever you do, don't wear a suit and tie. You'll stand out like a tourist."

"Wouldn't want to do that," Mason said.

Becky took herself off to seat two more customers who had appeared in the doorway.

Mason looked at Lucy and lowered his voice. "Just out of sheer curiosity, what the hell were you thinking by accepting Jillian's invitation?"

"I'm thinking that a Colfax family gathering is an excellent place to start asking a few questions," she said.

106

"Damn," Mason said. "I was afraid of that."

Deke looked interested. "What kind of questions do you plan on asking?"

Mason exhaled slowly. "She doesn't think that the car crash that killed Sara and Mary was an accident."

"Well, hell," Deke said. He said it very, very softly.

"I was willing to accept that verdict at first," Lucy said. "Accidents happen. But now I'm working on the theory that Sara's and Mary's deaths are linked to the shares of Colfax Inc. that I inherited."

"Huh," Deke said. He looked intrigued.

"Must be something about being back in Summer River," Lucy said. "Brings out my suspicious side."

"Yeah, mine, too," Mason admitted.

Deke looked at him. "Hell, you've been suspicious your whole life."

"Same with you," Mason said. "Probably in the blood."

"Probably," Deke agreed. He turned back to Lucy. "Got any evidence of this theory of yours?"

"Three dead people, all of whom are in one way or another connected to Colfax Inc."

Mason picked up his coffee cup. "As the only professional investigator present, I feel obliged to point out yet again that one of the deaths occurred thirteen years ago and in all probability is unrelated to the deaths of Sara and Mary."

"I'm aware of that," Lucy said. "And as I told you, I agree with you. But still, there are three deaths."

"Are you going to mention your theory to Chief Whitaker when we talk to him this morning?" Mason asked. His tone was neutral, but there was a sharp, watchful curiosity in his eyes.

"No, not yet," Lucy said. "He'll want proof. In my experience, the cops and the courts prefer a nice chain of evidence."

"In your experience?" Deke asked.

"A large part of my job with Brookhouse Research consists of gathering solid evidence to prove or disprove the claims of a lost or missing heir. Trust me, that requires a clear trail, because there is usually a lot of money at stake. People are always willing to fight very hard in court to get their hands on hard cash."

"I don't doubt it," Deke said. "Folks get killed on the street for a few bucks or a little dope. No telling what they'd do for a cut of a multimillion-dollar inheritance."

"It's true I don't deal in gunshot residue and blood-spatter patterns," Lucy said. "But I have to track down things like birth, marriage and death certificates that can be used to build a family tree that might go back several generations. I use immigration and census records. Draft registration records. Military service papers. Property records and wills and trusts and so on. Believe me, I know what it takes to build a case."

Mason glanced at the yellow pad. He did not look impressed. "And that's what you're going to try to do here in Summer River?"

"Yes." Lucy pulled the yellow pad closer in a protective gesture. "In my line, it always comes down to the family."

Deke narrowed his eyes. "Given that the family you're dealing with controls a fortune — not to mention a lot of what goes on in this town — it might be a good idea to keep your little theory just between the three of us, at least for now."

"Don't worry, I intend to do just that." Lucy collected the yellow pad and her tote. "Now, if you'll excuse me, I've got things to do."

"Where are you going?" Mason asked.

"Got a big day today. First I have to get ready for our interview with Chief Whitaker, and then I go shopping."

"You want to *shop*?"

"For something to wear tonight. I didn't bring any evening clothes with me. I need to find out what wine-country casual means. Enjoy your coffee, gentlemen."

She went briskly toward the door, but she was not quite out of earshot when she heard Mason's low-voiced comment to Deke.

"Damn," he said softly. "This is going to get complicated."

"No kidding," Deke said. "I think we just got stuck with the check."

CHAPTER
TWELVE

"It's impossible to describe wine-country casual," Teresa Vega announced. "But around here you know it when you see it. The look covers a lot of territory, especially when it comes to women's wear. Think elegant, laid-back chic — *expensive* elegant, laid-back chic. You want to look as if you were born to the vineyard life, as if your family has been in wine for generations."

"You know the rule," Lucy said. "You can't go wrong with a little black dress. I've got several in my closet at home. Too bad I didn't bring one with me."

"There's an exception to every rule. Wine-country casual happens to be the exception to the little-black-dress rule."

"I am putting myself into your hands, Teresa."

Lucy studied the artfully displayed clothes that filled Teresa's Closet, a small, colorful boutique just a block away from the inn. Teresa had recognized Lucy the minute she walked through the door. Her delight at the reunion had been genuine. Her condolences had been sincere.

Lucy had been surprised by the little burst of warmth that she had experienced when she and Teresa exchanged hugs. It had, after all, been thirteen years since they had last seen each other. Teresa had been Teresa Alvarez in those days.

Part of the bond between Teresa and herself that last summer had hinged on the fact that both of them had been excluded from the cool-kids list. But they had other things in common as well. Teresa's parents had also separated. Although Lucy's folks had split up three years earlier, she had still been grappling with the fallout. Teresa had been able to offer some pragmatic teenage advice. The first and most useful bit had been *Don't waste your time hoping your folks will get back together. That's just a fantasy for little kids.* The second Teresa saying had proven equally valid: *Don't bother asking them why they got divorced. They'll tell you everything but the truth.* Lucy remembered asking, "*What is the truth?*" To which Teresa had replied with clear-eyed wisdom, "*One of them got tired of being married to the other and started sleeping with someone else.*" That, too, had proved to be true.

Thirteen years ago, Teresa had been a shy teen with big brown eyes and glasses. She'd had an obsession with fashion and design, and had spent hours online studying the latest trends and style blogs. Even on the limited allowance her struggling single mother had provided, she'd had a knack for looking put-together. Today she appeared effortlessly chic and casually elegant in a way that was somehow just right for the proprietor of a clothing boutique in wine country.

"The wine country doesn't do little black dresses," Teresa said. "If you show up at the Colfax reception in a black dress you'll stand out like a tourist."

"I'm getting the impression that is not considered a good thing."

"Well, it does imply you are not a local. And while it's true that you were not born and raised here, you've still got deep roots in Summer River."

"Those roots are not in the wine industry. Aunt Sara owned an apple orchard, remember?"

"So what? It's not like the Colfaxes have several generations of wine-making in the blood, either. Their money comes from a hedge fund. Everyone around here knows the winery is just a hobby for Warner Colfax."

Lucy smiled. "You don't think Quinn and Jillian have an interest in making fine boutique wines with the Colfax name on the label?"

"Good question, actually. They don't care about the wine, but they do enjoy playing the role of wine-country socialites. So does the second Mrs. Warner Colfax, by the way. You did hear about the divorce, didn't you?"

"Mason mentioned it."

"Rumor has it that Quinn was furious when his father dumped his mother for a woman who is younger than Quinn," Teresa said.

"Second and third marriages usually don't sit well with the offspring of the first marriage. I can personally testify to that truism. Also, I see a lot of family drama based on that dynamic."

"Sara told me about your job with an investigation agency that specializes in finding lost heirs." Teresa's expression brightened with curiosity. "It sounds fascinating."

Lucy recalled the scene in the bar when the Grieving Widow had tossed the contents of a glass of beer in her face. "It has its moments. Well, if the little black dress is out, what do you suggest?"

Teresa moved around the end of the counter. "I've got a couple of things, either one of which will be perfect for tonight."

"Great. I certainly didn't come prepared for this kind of party — or any party at all, for that matter."

Teresa took down a summery, cap-sleeved, knee-length dress in a shade of blue that had summer sky written all over it. "Something along these lines with a light sweater or wrap will work. It turns cool after sundown."

"I'll need shoes as well."

"Absolutely no heels. Wine-country casual means flats or wedges or sandals. Parties at wineries are often held at least partially outdoors or on a terrace, especially at this time of year. You're supposed to look like you are prepared to tramp around the vineyards or go do some work in the tank room at any given moment."

"Got it." Lucy glanced at the ring on Teresa's left hand. "Sara mentioned you were married."

Teresa laughed. "Two kids, a couple of dogs, a mortgage and a husband — not necessarily in that order, I might add."

"Congratulations. I'm glad it worked out so well for you."

Teresa gave her a commiserating look. "Your aunt told me that your engagement had ended."

"As everyone keeps reminding me, better to find out things weren't going to work before the marriage than afterward."

"True. Was he a total jerk?"

"I found him in bed with someone else."

"Right." Teresa nodded. "Total jerk. Think of it as an experiment that didn't go well."

"It was a mistake, not an experiment."

"Uh-uh." Teresa wagged her forefinger. "You know what they say, it's only a mistake if you don't learn from it."

"I learned a lot from it," Lucy said. "Saw a very expensive therapist for about six weeks afterward."

"And?"

"Turns out I've got commitment issues."

"Bullshit."

"The implication was that it was probably my fault that the engagement ended. My inability to commit drove the total jerk to another woman."

"I repeat, bullshit. A total jerk is a total jerk. Total jerks are incapable of change. On some level you must have sensed the total jerkiness of your fiancé, and that is why you couldn't commit. So either consciously or unconsciously you tested him, and sure enough your suspicions proved to be correct."

"Wow." Lucy was impressed. "That is deep, Teresa."

"Yes, I know." Teresa smiled a smug little smile. "You should have consulted me instead of a very expensive therapist. I would have sold you the right clothes and sent you out to look for a replacement for the total jerk."

Lucy laughed. "You're right. I needed retail therapy after my engagement ended, not psychological counseling. What was I thinking?"

"I can tell you that your taste in men has already taken a quantum leap forward."

"Meaning?"

"Mason Fletcher is taking you to the ball, Cinderella. How cool is that?"

"It's not exactly a date," Lucy said quickly.

"Yes, it is a date, your second one, according to my calculations. Mason was with you when you found Brinker's body in your aunt's fireplace, wasn't he?"

"Well, yes, but I'm not sure finding a dead body together constitutes a date."

"So dates with Mason are a little different than dates with other men. That's a good thing, if you ask me." Teresa took down a second breezy dress in the muted colors of twilight. "Have they figured out for sure if it was Brinker's body in your aunt's fireplace?"

"The verdict isn't final, but there's really not much doubt. When Mason and I gave our statements to Chief Whitaker this morning, I could tell that he was going on the assumption that the body was that of Tristan Brinker. They have determined that it is the body of a male about Brinker's age. Whitaker said he couldn't find any record of another man going missing in the vicinity of Summer River that year."

"It's Brinker. Has to be him." Teresa shook her head. "Hard to imagine your sweet little aunt killing anyone,

115

but as long as she did get into the mood, I can't say I'm sorry she chose Brinker as her target. In hindsight, it's clear he was a real sociopath. I don't have any trouble at all picturing him as the Scorecard Rapist."

"I agree."

"Wonder why Sara did it, though. Do you think he attacked her? Maybe she defended herself and was afraid to call the cops because she had just killed Jeffrey Brinker's son. Brinker senior would have made her life a living hell if he found out that she was responsible for the death of his precious heir. In his eyes, Tristan could do no wrong."

"We may never know why she did it," Lucy said. She was not prepared to divulge the conclusions that she and Mason had come to regarding Sara's reasons for committing murder — not yet, at any rate.

"It certainly has the locals talking, that's for sure," Teresa said. "And now I'm dressing you for a party out at the Colfax Winery. No offense, but just between you and me, mind satisfying my curiosity and tell me how you got the invitation?"

"Jillian Colfax invited me personally," Lucy said.

Teresa clutched the hanger and dress to her bosom and widened her eyes.

"Holy crap. *Jillian* invited you? Okay, didn't see that coming. Last I heard, you and Jillian did not move in the same social circles."

"Nothing has changed in that regard." Lucy grasped a handful of the dress fabric, enjoying the soft, fluid, lightweight feel. "However, in case you weren't aware of it, I inherited a nice little chunk of Colfax Inc."

"Oh, yeah, that news is all over town, too, trust me. Which is why it is a very good thing that Mason is going with you tonight. You may need someone to watch your back, and I don't know of anyone better qualified to do that. You know what they always said about him."

"You don't want to mess with Mason Fletcher," Lucy quoted softly.

"Right. Just so you know, the Colfaxes as a clan are said to have been both horrified and furious when they found out that Mary left her shares to Sara and that those shares are now in your hands. You do know there's a major merger or acquisition deal in the works, don't you?"

"I've heard that," Lucy said. "I think I like the twilight dress. I'll need a wrap to go with it, and shoes, of course."

"Maybe you should accessorize with a pistol and a holster," Teresa said. "You and Mason might as well be walking to the gunfight at the O.K. Corral."

"Not to worry, I'll be wearing wine-country casual."

CHAPTER
THIRTEEN

This isn't a date.

Mason stood at the foot of the inn's staircase and watched Lucy come down to meet him. Silently, he repeated the litany he had been saying to himself all day. *This isn't a date. You're taking her to the reception because you can't talk her out of going and you can't let her walk into that gladiator ring alone. This isn't a date.*

But it sure as hell felt like a date, the second one he'd had with Lucy. A prowling anticipation had heated his blood all day. Night could not come too soon. And now it was here and he was here, waiting for Lucy.

She seemed to float down the stairs in a little dress that stopped just above her knees. The neckline was modest. The very short sleeves showed off her nicely rounded arms. A narrow belt defined her small waist. She wore cute little wedge sandals and a tiny cross-body purse that looked barely large enough to hold a cell phone and a credit card. Her jewelry consisted of a pair of dainty gold earrings and a small bracelet composed of gold links. She carried a white shawl over her arm. There was nothing flashy or showy about the outfit, but somehow it all went together to give her an aura of cool, feminine confidence.

"Yeah, that works," Mason said. He smiled.

"Thanks." Lucy did a little pirouette. "I had help from Teresa Vega at Teresa's Closet. She used to be Teresa Alvarez. Remember her?"

"Sure. Nice kid. Glasses. Always wore weird clothes like work boots and long black dresses."

"That was her Goth phase. She's over that now."

"Probably just as well. Hard to picture a combination of Goth and wine-country casual."

Lucy laughed and started briskly toward the door. "We can take my car." She reached into the tiny purse and produced her keys.

He caught up with her, managed to wrap his fingers around her arm and deliberately applied the brakes, forcing her to stop in the middle of the lobby.

"Thanks for the offer," he said. "But since I'll be driving, we'll take my vehicle."

She blinked, but she did not argue. He opened the door and steered her out into the summer evening. The anticipation that had been riding him hard all day was suddenly infused with a deep knowing. This was exactly where he wanted to be tonight — with this woman.

He popped the locks on the sleek black car sitting in front of the entrance.

Lucy looked at him, not bothering to conceal her amusement.

"You mean we're not taking the truck?" she asked.

"Not tonight. Some other time, maybe."

"Nice car," she said. Genuine appreciation edged the words. "Security consulting must pay well."

"One thing about the crime business — it's steady."

"This isn't a rental, and Fletcher Consulting is located back in D.C. Don't tell me you drove all the way across the country."

"You're good at this detecting thing. Yes, I drove across the country. I wanted some downtime to do some thinking. Those long stretches on the interstate are a good place for that."

She shot him a quick, curious glance, but she did not ask any more questions.

He opened the door on the passenger side and watched her slip into the front seat. Everything inside him stirred. What was it about women in little summer dresses? Scratch that. What was it about Lucy in a summer dress?

What was it about Lucy?

Oh, shit. I've got it bad.

And he didn't give a damn, he realized. A man did not get a lot of evenings like this one in his lifetime. It was a real shame that he was going to have to waste a chunk of it at a party watching over Lucy while she played detective. Unfortunately, she was playing with fire.

So was he.

He made an effort to tamp down the heat and closed the door very firmly. He walked around to the driver's side and got behind the wheel.

"What did you think about during your long drive from D.C.?" she asked.

"Stuff." He fired up the engine and reversed out of the parking slot.

He heard Lucy's phone chirp. He breathed a small sigh of relief, grateful for the interruption. He had a feeling that once Lucy got on a man's case and started asking questions she wouldn't let go easily.

She took the device out of the tiny purse and checked the screen. She inserted the phone back into the small bag.

"It's just the agency," she said.

"Brookhouse Research?"

"No, the online matchmaking agency. They notify me whenever their computers kick out a possible match."

Suddenly, he was no longer feeling so grateful for the interruption.

"Is that so?" He realized he was speaking between set teeth. "Get a lot of notifications?"

"That's my second one today."

He willed himself to remain calm.

"No luck?" he asked.

"So far nothing has clicked."

"Oh, yeah, the commitment-issues thing."

"Yes. But my profile looks good. Single, reasonably well educated, never married, no kids to support, good job, excellent health. The good job has been a big asset for me, by the way."

"Is that so?"

"They say that women prefer men who make a lot of money. But it turns out the reverse is true, too. You'd be amazed by the number of men who are looking for wives who make high salaries."

Time to change the subject.

"Do we have a plan for this evening?" he asked.

"Not exactly." Lucy glanced at him. "I consider this party to be an intelligence-gathering mission."

"*Intelligence* is not the first word that comes to my mind. By all accounts, the Colfaxes bear a striking resemblance to a nest of snakes. If we had any sense we would steer clear."

"Look at it this way," Lucy said. "It's an opportunity to gather additional information on the family dynamics of the Colfax clan."

"You really think one of them killed Sara and Mary, don't you?"

"I'm not absolutely positive about that yet, but they all have motive, and the fact that Sara and Mary died just as the merger wars broke out within the Colfax family strikes me as too much of a coincidence."

"Those Colfax shares are motive, all right," he agreed. "But there's something you need to keep in mind here — if there is a killer in this situation, he will be very pissed off right now. He miscalculated. He couldn't have known that the shares would end up in your hands."

"Or she," Lucy said.

"What?"

"You referred to the killer as he. Women kill, too."

He tightened his hands on the wheel. "Believe me, I'm well aware of that fact. The point is that in my experience, violent sociopaths who happen to be pissed off are dangerous people."

122

"I know," Lucy said. "But I owe this to Aunt Sara. She did what she believed she had to do to protect me thirteen years ago. I need to find out the truth about that car accident now."

He did not say anything for a long moment. Then he exhaled slowly.

"I understand," he said.

She smiled faintly. "I know you do."

She sat quietly, watching the road through the windshield. He could feel the determination coming off her in waves. Nothing was going to stop her. There was no point arguing with her.

He drove through the center of town, passing the little boutiques and the small, crowded restaurants that fronted the tree-shaded square.

"I did a little research of my own today," he said after a while.

"What kind of research?"

"I looked into the Scorecard Rapist case. One of the theories at the time was that Brinker was not working alone."

"He had an accomplice?"

"Maybe someone he brought in to watch. Maybe someone who filmed the rape."

"Oh, crap. I never thought about the actual filmmaking," Lucy said. "I suppose I just assumed that Brinker set up the camera ahead of time to record the rape."

Mason shifted gears for the turn onto River Road.

"According to the reports I read, one of the detectives who worked the case and later retired left some notes saying that he was convinced he saw indications in at least some of the videos that there was another person in the room. Shadows, for the most part. The videos have all been taken down, so there's no way to check."

"What about the victims?"

"They were heavily drugged with some kind of hallucinogen. Their memories were unreliable. But a couple of them stated that they believed there was someone else present at the scene."

Lucy folded her arms tightly beneath her breasts. "Brinker was creepier than anyone realized. Did the cops ever pursue the second-person angle?"

"Yes, but they got nowhere. After Brinker disappeared, the videos stopped showing up online. The case got very cold very fast."

"Do you think Chief Whitaker will reopen it?"

"No. The Scorecard Rapist operated down in the Bay Area, not here in Summer River."

"Maybe Brinker intended me to be his first victim here."

"If that's true, his pattern was changing slightly. The other victims were all college age. You were still in high school at the time."

"He wanted younger, even more vulnerable girls."

"It's possible. Serial rapists tend to escalate in terms of violence, just like serial killers. Whatever the case, I think Whitaker is satisfied with the scenario I gave him for Brinker's death."

"Brinker attacked Aunt Sara. She fought back, killed her assailant, and then hid the body because she was afraid that she would be arrested for murder."

"There's only one thing wrong with that theory of the crime. Sara definitely did not fit the profile of the other victims. Whitaker knows that, but I doubt he'll push it. There's nothing to be gained. It's easier to take the credit for closing an old cold case."

"But what if there was a second person involved?" Lucy said.

"Whitaker has more urgent cases to worry about."

"And so do I," Lucy said. "I need to find out what really happened to Sara and Mary."

"We," Mason said.

"What?"

"We need to find out what really happened to Sara and Mary. You're not working that case alone."

Lucy gave him a long, considering look. Then she smiled faintly.

"Thank you," she said.

CHAPTER
FOURTEEN

The Colfax Winery was an artful reproduction of an old-world Mediterranean villa. It sat on a tree-studded hillside and commanded views of the vineyards and the river. The birthday reception was held in the tasting room, a richly paneled space decorated in sunburnt hues of ocher and dark red. A wall of French doors had been opened to allow the party to spill out onto a broad terrace.

Lucy was not surprised by the size of the crowd. Warner Colfax and his family moved in elite wine-country social circles. An invitation to an event at his winery was a status symbol in the valley.

They were greeted by a smiling Jillian, who immediately steered them toward a middle-aged man dressed in a hand-tailored short-sleeved sports shirt and polished, country-club-style slacks. Wine-country casual for the male of the species, Lucy concluded.

"Have you met my father-in-law?" Jillian asked.

Her vivacious smile did not falter, but the tension that Lucy had detected that morning seemed to be permanently etched into the corners of Jillian's eyes and mouth.

"No," Lucy said.

"We move in different circles," Mason added.

Jillian ignored his dry tone of voice and forged a path through the crowd. Warner Colfax was on the short side, bald and somewhat thick through the shoulders, chest and belly. But whatever he lacked in glamor was more than compensated for by the far younger, decidedly taller and quite beautiful woman at his side.

"That must be the new Mrs. Colfax," Mason observed.

"Yes," Jillian said. Her tone was glacial. "Ashley."

Jillian brought them to a halt at the fringes of the small group gathered around Warner. She gave her father-in-law a brilliant smile.

"Warner, I'm so sorry to interrupt," she said, not sounding sorry at all, "but I wanted to make sure you knew that Lucy Sheridan and Mason Fletcher had arrived. We're all so pleased they could make it tonight."

Warner turned, and for the first time Lucy got a good look at him. He did not appear to be the suave, slick, sophisticated salesman that she had been expecting. Instead, he greeted her with an easy, disarming warmth. His gray eyes seemed to brighten at the sight of her, as if he was genuinely pleased to meet her.

You had to look closely to see the cold assessment that was taking place behind the scenes, she thought. No doubt about it, Warner Colfax was trying to figure out how he could manipulate her.

Maybe this was what a really good salesman looked like, after all.

She gave him her best "Congratulations, you are a long-lost heir" smile.

"Lucy Sheridan," he said. "A pleasure." His expression turned abruptly somber. "I was so sorry to hear of your aunt's death. I did not know her well, but we met a number of times because of her connection to my sister. She and Mary were very close, both personally and professionally."

"Thank you," Lucy said. "Please accept my condolences on Mary's death. I will miss both of them."

"Thank you." Warner's warm smile returned. He switched his calculating gaze to Mason. "I don't believe we've met, but I do know your uncle. We run into each other from time to time in town."

"Small town," Mason said.

Warner chuckled. "It certainly is. So glad you could both make it tonight."

The two men shook hands. And then Warner touched his wife's shoulder in a cool, possessive manner.

"My wife, Ashley," Warner said.

"Lucy." Ashley smiled in acknowledgment of the introduction.

Unlike her husband, Ashley came across as coolly polite and reserved. Once you got past her long, elegant jaw and patrician nose you could see something that resembled anxiety in her beautifully made-up brown eyes. Ashley and Jillian had a couple of things in common, Lucy decided. They were both on edge, perhaps even scared.

128

But when Ashley turned her attention to Mason — which happened pretty much in the blink of an eye — the icy veneer vanished beneath a gracious charm.

"Mason, what a pleasure," she murmured. She smiled again, this time managing to include Lucy. "Come with me, both of you, and I'll make sure you get some of Warner's incredible Reserve that we're pouring tonight."

She led the way through the crowd toward the long, polished bar. Lucy followed. Mason fell into step directly behind her, staying close. There was something both intimate and protective about the way he made it clear that he was with her tonight.

She got a little thrill from knowing that he was close enough to touch. She had liked it earlier when he had wrapped his powerful hand around her arm to walk her to the car. She had liked it a lot. She liked the scent of him as well. The clean, masculine tang was infused with just a hint of aftershave.

He stood out in the crowd — at least he stood out to her. It was a good bet that many of the other male guests in the room wielded the kind of power that came with money and social and political connections. But Mason possessed a different kind of power. It wasn't just physical, she thought. It was the kind of strength that you could depend on at crunch time. The steel in Mason had been infused with old-fashioned virtues such as honor and courage and determination. He was the kind of man who would always take full responsibility for his actions. Even as a teen she had been able to sense that inner fortitude in him. What was true back then was even truer now.

She knew from the manner in which some of the other guests surreptitiously studied him that most of them had gotten the message. You did not want to mess with Mason Fletcher.

Several of the men surveyed him with a calculating air. She suspected that they were busily assuring themselves that in spite of what their instincts were telling them, their money and connections ensured that they held a superior status in the room. The women in the crowd viewed Mason in an entirely different manner. Lucy caught expressions that ranged from curiosity to discreetly veiled sexual interest.

It was a lot easier to analyze the reactions of others to Mason than it was to understand her own disturbing response to him. In the course of her recent whirlwind dating spree, she had met some very nice, very interesting men. A few of those introductions should have worked out for her. At the very least, she ought to have felt some regret when the relationships failed to coalesce into something that could go the distance. But every time she closed the book on another arranged date she experienced a sense of relief, not despair. True, she had cried a few times, but mostly because she knew deep down that it was her fault that the relationships always fell apart.

Commitment issues.

But tonight she was experiencing a revelation. She had been looking for a man like Mason.

130

Maybe she should contact Dr. Preston and tell her about the breakthrough that had occurred in the middle of a possible murder investigation. On second thought, that was not a good idea, she decided. In Preston's world a patient who became a conspiracy theorist was probably a lot more worrisome than one who was an ordinary commitment-phobe.

Lucy smiled to herself.

Mason gave her a sharp look. "What?"

"Nothing," she whispered. "Just a fleeting thought. Forget it."

Ashley stopped at the long bar and spoke to one of the two women who was not wearing a catering uniform.

"Beth, would you pour two glasses of the Reserve for our very special guests?" she said.

Beth turned around. Her curly brown hair was cut in a short style that framed her strongly etched features. She looked out at the world through a pair of black-framed glasses. Lucy thought she looked familiar.

When Beth saw Mason, her polite smile was transformed into glowing delight.

"Hey, Mason," she exclaimed. "Remember me? Beth Crosby. It's been a while. Heard you were back in town."

Mason smiled. "Good to see you again. Looks like the wine-making degree you were going for worked out well."

"It certainly did. I'm the winemaker here at Colfax." Pride warmed Beth's voice. She picked up an open bottle and moved to stand across from Mason and

Lucy. "I heard you were back in town, Mason. I keep meaning to stop by the hardware store and say hello, but I've been insanely busy lately. It's great to see you again. How are things going?"

"Good," Mason said. "Do you know Lucy Sheridan?"

"Hi, Lucy," Beth said. Smiling, she poured two glasses of the red wine. "I wouldn't have recognized you. We passed each other in town a few times back in the day, but that was about it."

"I remember," Lucy said. "It's nice to see you again."

"I got to know your aunt fairly well. I collect antique wine-making equipment. Sara found some wonderful pieces for me. Mr. Colfax let me put some of the objects on display in the tank room. Tourists love the old things. I was so sorry to hear about the accident."

"Thank you," Lucy said. She wondered how many more times she was going to have to say that. "Congratulations on the great position here at the winery."

"Thanks." Beth smiled proudly. "I wouldn't be here if Mr. Colfax hadn't taken a chance on me. He hired me right out of school and gave me everything I asked for in terms of state-of-the-art equipment. He says he always trusts his gut when it comes to hiring talent."

"Warner was not mistaken in his choice of winemakers," Ashley said. Impatience edged her words, but she kept her smile in place. "The Reserve is Beth's finest creation to date. Warner is convinced it will make Colfax famous in the wine world."

"Try it," Beth said. She put the bottle down and waited with an expectant air.

Lucy picked up the long-stemmed glass.

"I'm no connoisseur," she warned.

"Neither am I," Mason said. "Now, when it comes to beer —"

Beth laughed. "Go on, try the Reserve."

Lucy dutifully went through wine-tasting protocol. She swirled the Reserve gently in the glass, inhaled the essence and took a tentative sip. The wine was lush and dark on her tongue.

"Very nice," she said.

"It's a little young yet," Beth said. "But it's got everything. It's impressive now, but just give it a couple of years."

"The magic of wine," Lucy said, smiling.

"It's not magic," Beth said. "Modern wine-making is a science. If you like, I would be happy to give you both a tour of the winery sometime."

"Thanks," Lucy said. "Sounds interesting."

Ashley had evidently had enough. "Let's go out onto the terrace. It's easier to talk out there. Too much background noise in here."

Once again Lucy and Mason followed her through the crowd. There were a number of people gathered in small clusters on the spacious, lantern-lit terrace, but Ashley did not pause to make introductions. Like a guided missile locked onto a target, she kept going until she found an unoccupied corner. She halted at last and fixed Lucy with a penetrating look.

133

"I'm sure you know by now that discovering that you got those shares of Colfax Inc. came as a shock to the whole family," she said.

"I was more than a little stunned myself," Lucy said. "But I was a good deal more shocked by Sara's and Mary's death."

Ashley's elegant jaw tightened. "Such a tragedy. I'm new to the family, as I'm sure you're aware. I married Warner less than a year ago. I'm sorry that I never got the opportunity to know your aunt. I'm not into antiques. I met Mary, of course, but I only saw her on a couple of occasions."

A tall man walked out of the shadows. "Which is why no one knew that she left her shares to Sara Sheridan," he said.

The observation was made in a rich, resonant voice. The newcomer sounded ruefully amused.

"Cecil," Ashley said. She looked relieved to see him. "Let me introduce you to Lucy Sheridan and her friend Mason Fletcher. Lucy, Mason, this is Cecil Dillon. He's the CEO of Colfax Inc."

"A pleasure," Cecil said.

He could have played the part of a CEO in a film, Lucy decided. He had the height, the dark hair, the chiseled features, the gym-toned body and the savvy, nothing-gets-past-me eyes.

He smiled warmly at Lucy and held her fingers a beat longer than necessary.

When he turned to Mason, his expression switched to a coolly polite, businesslike look. The handshake between the two men was brisk and short. One alpha

134

acknowledging another and also doing some sizing up, Lucy decided.

"Is it common to bring in an outside CEO to run a family business?" she asked, in an attempt to ease the subtle tension that seemed to have infused the atmosphere.

Cecil smiled at her. "A lot of family businesses hire an outsider to run the firm, just like any other corporation. Sometimes it's because no one in the family is qualified to take on the responsibilities. Sometimes it's simply because no one in the family wants the job. The personal dynamics can be tricky to navigate. Often it's easier on everyone if the person making the day-to-day decisions is not a relative."

"Okay, that makes sense," Lucy said.

"But now, for the first time, there's going to be an outsider on the board," Ashley said. She gave Lucy an appraising look. "That should certainly make for some interesting family dynamics. Are you aware that there's a merger offer on the table?"

"I heard something about it," Lucy said.

"I might as well take this opportunity to warn you that the Colfax family is deeply divided on the wisdom of going through with the merger," Ashley said. "You appear to hold the deciding shares."

"Whoa." Cecil held up a hand. "This is a birthday party. No business talk tonight. I can go over the pros and cons of the merger with Lucy some other time."

"You're right," Ashley said. "Wrong place, wrong time. It's just that the merger has been on everyone's mind for the past few weeks. It was supposed to be a done deal. And now everything's in chaos."

Cecil took charge. He touched Ashley's arm in a small, telling gesture. He was warning her to calm down, Lucy realized. Ashley's tension was palpable.

"I think that's enough for now, Ashley," Cecil said. "Why don't you go back to your other guests? You know Warner likes to have you by his side at events like this. I'll explain the situation to Lucy at some other time."

"Yes, of course," Ashley said. She pulled herself together with a visible effort and gave Mason a glowing smile. "I'll see you both later. Enjoy yourselves."

She turned quickly and disappeared into the crowd.

"I apologize for Ashley," Cecil said to Lucy. "There's a lot of tension in the family — always has been. The merger offer is bringing things to the surface. Mary's death and finding out that her shares went to someone outside the family has added another level of complexity. She left everything else in her estate to Quinn. Most of it was in the form of property in the area that she bought years ago, when land in wine country was cheap."

"Any idea how Mary felt about the merger?" Mason asked.

"She never paid much attention to the business," Cecil said. "But when there was division on the board she always voted with Quinn. For the most part, Quinn backs his father."

"But not this time?" Lucy asked.

136

"No. Warner is still opposed to the merger for sentimental reasons. Colfax Inc. is his creation. He built it from the ground up. But he no longer takes an active interest in it. His passion now is this winery. I'm afraid that without him at the top it's only a matter of time before Colfax Inc. loses its edge. It was Warner's intuition for investments that made the firm so successful. Unfortunately, there's no one in the family who can replace him. No one has his gut instincts for the market. Everyone involved realizes that."

"What about you?" Mason said.

"I'm good," Cecil said. He raised one shoulder in a confident, self-effacing shrug. "I'm very good. That's why Warner put me in charge. But when it comes to surfing the markets long-term, Colfax is a genius. The problem is he's just not that interested anymore, and that's the sad reality. Without him at the helm on a day-to-day basis, the wheels will eventually come off. He's a stubborn man, but he's a realist. In the end, I know he'll do what's best for the family."

"Which is to accept the offer?" Lucy asked.

"Right. The merger will allow Warner to get out on top of his career. His legend will remain untarnished. And everyone in the family — and you as well, Lucy — will walk away with a very nice profit. We're talking multimillion-dollar payouts for each stockholder. But I'm breaking my own rule here, talking business at a party. If you wouldn't mind, I'd like to sit down with you sometime at your convenience and walk you through the spreadsheets. That way you'll have all the facts before you make up your mind."

"All right," Lucy said.

Cecil took out his phone and tapped it a couple of times. "Would ten tomorrow morning work for you?"

Lucy did not bother to take out her own phone. "No, I'm afraid I'm very busy at the moment." She smiled. "The body in the fireplace has complicated things."

Cecil winced. "I understand. Maybe later this week? I don't keep an office here in Summer River. I'm staying in one of the guesthouses on the estate. But that doesn't matter. All I need is my computer. Ashley mentioned that you are at the Harvest Gold Inn. We can meet there, if that's convenient."

"No," Mason said before Lucy could respond. He looked at Lucy. "You won't have any privacy there, not unless you use your room."

He let that hang in midair. There was no need to fill in the blanks, Lucy thought. She did not need a reminder that it would not be a good idea to meet with Cecil alone in her room. She doubted that Cecil needed a lecture on the subject, either.

He cleared his throat. "I was thinking we could have coffee together in the square."

She stifled her irritation and gave Cecil a bright smile. "That sounds fine. I'll get in touch when I've got some free time to sit down with you and look at the numbers."

Mason looked even less pleased. Cecil, on the other hand, was clearly satisfied.

"That will be ideal," he said. He dropped his phone into his pocket. "A pleasure to meet you, Lucy." He nodded, ever so slightly, to Mason. "And you, Fletcher."

138

He turned and waded into the crowd with casual ease, pausing to chat here and there before disappearing into the tasting room.

"Don't," Lucy said firmly, "ever do that again."

"What?" Mason asked. He was watching the doors through which Cecil Dillon had just vanished.

"Do not step in while I'm making a business appointment."

"He intended that business appointment to take place in your bedroom," Mason said.

"I doubt that very much. You leaped to a dumbass conclusion, admit it."

"Dumbass?"

"Oh, for Pete's sake. He's the CEO of Colfax Inc. You heard him, there are millions of dollars on the line. He wants to talk me into voting for the merger. That's all he has on his mind."

"How do you know that?"

"Because of the money, of course. Trust me, when there's that much cash involved, money is usually all anyone is thinking about."

"Usually?"

"What?"

"You said when there's a lot of cash on the line, money is *usually* all anyone is thinking about. Are there exceptions to the rule?"

She hesitated and shrugged. "Sometimes people will let emotions overrule their own greed. Doesn't happen often, but it does happen. Not in this case, though."

"What makes you so sure?"

"Dillon is not a member of the family. The only thing he has at stake here is money. I'm sure the merger offer includes a very fat bonus for him."

"So all he cares about is seeing that merger go through?" Mason asked.

"Yes. But I suspect he cares a *lot* about that."

"So he'll lean in hard to convince you to either sell the shares back to Quinn or vote in favor of the merger."

"I can handle myself. I've been in high-pressure situations before. I have testified in court as an expert witness, and I have been confronted with irate heirs who didn't think they got their fair share of an estate. Trust me, no one gets angrier than an heir who feels he's been stiffed. I'm not sixteen years old anymore."

Mason winced. "Sorry."

"I know, you just can't help yourself." She patted his arm. "I realize you mean well."

He looked down at her fingers on his arm. When he raised his head, his eyes were charged with a dark warning. "In exchange for not setting up the venues for your business appointments, I'd appreciate it if you didn't pat me like a dog."

She yanked her fingers off his arm. "Right. Sorry. Does it strike you that we are snapping at each other?"

"I noticed," Mason said.

"We're both a little tense tonight. The last thing we should be doing is quarreling."

A man's low, derisive laughter interrupted Mason before he could respond. Quinn Colfax strolled out of the shadows of a vine-draped trellis.

140

"You call that quarreling?" he said. "That's nothing compared to what goes on in my family. You haven't seen a family feud until you've witnessed a Colfax family fight."

The words were ever so slightly slurred. Lucy knew the glass of wine in his hand was not the first or second one he'd had that evening. He'd started early. But Quinn managed to walk a fairly straight line.

He had not changed much in the past thirteen years, she thought. Everyone said he took after his mother, not his father. The first Mrs. Colfax had bequeathed him dark brown hair, brown eyes, and a narrow, fine-boned face that made Lucy think of an early-nineteenth-century portrait of an artist. She remembered something else that people had said about Quinn Colfax — he wasn't made for the cut-and-thrust of the business world.

Mason glanced at the half-empty glass in Quinn's hand. "How long have you been eavesdropping?"

Quinn shrugged. "Long enough to hear Cecil and the bitch make their pitch." He grinned. "Hey, that rhymes, doesn't it?" He looked at Lucy. "Dillon will try to close the deal with you as soon as possible, you know."

"Do you have a problem with that?" Lucy asked. "I got the impression from Jillian that you and she were both in favor of taking the offer."

"Just to clarify — when Jillian speaks, she speaks for herself, not me. Same with Cecil and the bitch. We've all got our own agendas."

"What's your agenda look like?" Mason asked.

Quinn smirked. "Do you really think I'm going to tell you, Fletcher?" He turned and started to walk away, but he paused and looked back over his shoulder. "Tell you what. For old times' sake and because you seem to be concerned with Lucy's well-being, I'll give her a little free advice."

"What's the advice?" Lucy asked.

"Sell those Colfax shares back to the family as fast as you can and put Summer River in your rearview mirror. You do not want to get involved in what is going down inside Colfax Inc."

"Is that a threat?" Mason asked.

"No, it's not a threat," Quinn said. He sounded unutterably weary. "Just some free advice. Take it or leave it."

"Thanks," Lucy said.

Quinn looked at Mason. "You know, I always figured that you were the one who got rid of Brinker. Always wanted to thank you. And now it turns out that I should have thanked Sara Sheridan instead. I'm sorry I didn't do that while she was still alive."

Quinn walked off again. This time, he did not look back.

There was a short silence. Lucy set her barely touched wine down with great care on a nearby table. For some reason, her fingers were trembling ever so slightly.

"You know," she said, "I think I've had about all the fun I can stand at this party tonight. I'm ready to leave now."

"So am I."

CHAPTER
FIFTEEN

Lucy was still shivering a little when she slipped into the car and fastened the seat belt. Adrenaline, she thought, and nerves. She clasped her hands together very tightly in her lap and waited until Mason got behind the wheel and drove out of the winery parking lot.

"Quinn was scared of Brinker, too," she said.

Mason turned onto River Road. "I'm starting to wonder who wasn't scared of him."

Her phone chirped. Absently, she took it out of her purse, deleted the message about the latest match and returned the phone to the little evening bag. She snapped the bag shut.

There was a long silence from the other side of the front seat.

"Think you'll ever give marriage a try?" Mason asked after a while.

There was something odd about his tone of voice, but she couldn't put her finger on it.

"I don't know," she said. "The older I get, the less I'm willing to compromise. I've been told I'm becoming way too picky."

"Who told you that?"

"The last guy I dated," Lucy said. "And Dr. Preston, my therapist."

"The last woman I dated said I was too dictatorial and that I didn't share my emotions very well."

That surprised a small, tight laugh out of her. "We sound like a couple of real losers, don't we?"

The corner of his mouth edged upward. "Gives us something in common."

"You may be right."

"Moving right along: what's your take on the situation back at the Colfax den?"

She considered that briefly. "Quinn may have a drinking problem."

"I'd say that's a good bet."

"I'm sure he expected to take his father's place at the head of the company, but that never happened. Instead, Warner Colfax hired an outside CEO who may or may not be sleeping with the second Mrs. Warner Colfax."

"Ah, you got that impression, too?" Mason asked.

"Something in the atmosphere between Dillon and Ashley."

"Not a lot to go on," Mason said.

"No."

"But I'm inclined to agree with you." Mason changed gears, slowing the car. "Anything else?"

"There appears to be a certain amount of desperation among those in favor of the merger. But as I told you, that's not uncommon in these situations. The older generation builds the empire and rakes in millions. The younger generation wants to take the money and run." She broke off in surprise when she

144

realized that Mason was turning onto a side road. "Where are we going?"

"Someplace we can talk."

He eased the sleek car along the narrow gravel road. They drove through the trees until they reached a small clearing. The car's headlights revealed the dark river. Mason killed the lights. The almost full moon took over.

"I spent a lot of time in Summer River when I was young," Lucy said. "But I don't remember this spot."

"Deke found it years ago. He brought Aaron and me here to teach us how to fish."

She was not sure what to say next, so she let the silence lengthen. With each passing beat of her heart, the aura of intimacy in the darkened front seat grew stronger. She wondered if she was the only one who felt it.

She was trying to think of a way to break the tension when Mason opened the door.

"Let's get out," he said. "It's not cold."

She opened her own door, unfastened her seat belt and slid out of the front seat. Mason was right, the night air was not cold, but there was a chill. She pulled the wrap around her shoulders and went to join Mason at the front of the car. Together they made their way to the bank of the river.

"What did you want to talk about?" she asked.

"Damned if I know," he said. "I'm not a good communicator, remember?"

"Oh, right, I keep forgetting. Well, I'll give you a hint. You probably brought me here because you want to give me my marching orders."

"Marching orders?"

"You think I should sell the shares back to the Colfax family and stop trying to find out if the car accident that killed Sara and Mary really was an accident, don't you?"

He took so long responding that she finally turned her head to look at him. In the darkness she could not read his expression, but she sensed that he was coming to a decision.

"Logic and common sense tell me that dumping those shares and leaving town would be the smartest thing you could do," he said eventually. "If you keep going along the path you're on now, you're going to make some enemies in the Colfax clan."

"I think I've already got a few. What can they do to me?"

"I don't know. That's what has me worried. If you're right about Sara's and Mary's death, you could be in danger."

"Do you really think that whoever killed them will come after me now? But that wouldn't do him or her any good. I've got a trust, and believe me, it's tight. In my profession, you find out real fast that a badly drawn-up will or trust can be a disaster for the heirs. I've left everything to my parents. The murderer can't just go on getting rid of everyone in my family one by one in hopes of eventually getting hold of the shares. Someone — you, probably — would be bound to notice."

"Oh, yeah," Mason said, his voice lethally soft. "I'd notice if anything happened to you."

146

She shivered again, but not from the chill in the night air. Mason's vow scared her, but it also gave her a strange confidence. If anything happened to her, he would tear the Colfax family apart.

"So I think I'm relatively safe, at least for now," she said.

"Maybe," Mason agreed. He sounded reluctant. "If someone did murder Mary and Sara, he or she miscalculated. But that doesn't mean the killer won't try other tactics."

"Such as?"

"Intimidation? An offer you can't refuse? Hell, I don't know. But if you sold the shares back to the family, you would take that issue off the front burner."

"The shares are the only cards I have to play."

He watched the moonlit surface of the water, not speaking. The leaves overhead rustled.

"I have to do this," Lucy said finally.

"I know." This time he sounded resigned to the inevitable. "In your shoes, I'd be doing the same thing."

"Well, actually, you are doing the same thing," she pointed out. "In a way."

"Guess it's just who we are."

"Yes," she said. "But I'm sorry for dragging you into the situation."

He moved then, one hand closing around her shoulder. Deliberately, he turned her to face him. He gripped her other shoulder and tugged her closer.

"Whatever you do, do not say you're sorry," he said. "I'm doing this for my own reasons."

She managed a misty smile. "I know. You're doing it because you can't help yourself. You're a guardian angel by nature."

"No, I'm doing it at least in part because I've got a few questions about what really happened to Sara and Mary, too. But I think I should make something very clear."

"What's that?"

"Mostly I'm doing this because of you."

She was not sure how to respond to that, but it didn't matter, because he kissed her then, and she was stunned into speechlessness.

The kiss was not a teenage girl's fantasy come true. It was so much more, because she was a woman now and she knew something about kissing — enough to judge Mason's kiss. It was not the kiss of her girlish dreams. There was nothing sweet or romantic or gently seductive about it. This kiss was all about primal masculine desire and fiercely controlled passion. This was the kind of kiss a man gave a woman when he set out to make it clear that he wanted her.

She knew intuitively that there were only two possible responses to such a kiss: she could return it with interest or she could break free and walk back to the car. There was no middle ground. There never would be, not with Mason Fletcher.

For the first time in her life she realized that there was no middle ground for her, either. She went all in, wrapping her arms around him and kissing him back with a sensual hunger she had never before experienced. Excitement sent adrenaline sparking through her.

By the time he freed her lips and moved his mouth to her ear, she was hot and cold, breathless and a little shaky. She clutched him, savoring his scent and the hard feel of his unyielding body. When she kissed the warm skin of his throat, he exhaled deeply. It could have been a sigh of pleasure or surrender or exultation. She could not be sure. But his breathing was harsher now.

He used one finger to raise her chin. His mouth came back down on hers in another intense kiss. She could feel the heat of the fire that smoldered just beneath the surface.

He shuddered, took a deep breath and held her slightly away from him. In the moonlight his eyes were darkly brilliant. Fascinated, she touched the side of his jaw. He turned his mouth into her hand and kissed her palm.

"Don't tell me you didn't see this coming," he said, his voice rough and edgy. "Because I sure did."

"I saw it coming," she admitted. "But it still caught me by surprise."

"Same with me," he said. "I didn't think I could still get surprised like that."

She smiled. "Thirteen years ago, I had a terrible crush on you. But you were barely aware of my existence."

He speared his fingers through her hair, pushing it back from her face. "You were just a kid."

"Who needed rescuing. Yes, I know. But I'm not a kid anymore."

"I noticed." He brushed his mouth lightly across hers. "Definitely not a kid. I'd give a hell of a lot to take you to bed tonight, but it's probably too soon and there's no bed."

It wasn't a statement, she realized. It was a question.

"I'm sure the problem of a bed could be handled," she said. "But you're right, it's too soon." She slipped lightly out of his embrace and started back toward the car. "Which makes it time to leave."

"Hey, you could have at least argued with me about the timing thing," he said behind her.

She laughed, suddenly feeling more lighthearted than she had in a long while. She was awash in a delicious sense of anticipation. Mason laughed, too. He caught up with her, kissed the tip of her nose and opened the car door.

"I've got to tell you, all things considered, this date turned out a lot better than it looked like it would when we started out tonight," he said.

"Yes," she said. "It did."

He closed the door, went around the front of the car and got behind the wheel. He did not start the engine immediately. He sat quietly for a while, watching the river, very intent, very serious now.

"How will you know when the time is right?" he asked.

She smiled, serenely confident in her newfound feminine power.

"Don't worry, I'll tell you," she said.

He flashed her a wicked grin and fired up the engine.
"Promise me you won't forget," he said.
"I won't forget."

CHAPTER
SIXTEEN

Mason drove back into town, aware that in spite of extreme sexual frustration, he was feeling good — better than he had felt in ages. Years, maybe. He walked Lucy into the lobby of the inn and watched her climb the stairs. When she disappeared, he went back outside, got into the car and drove to the cabin.

The lights were still on. Joe was stretched out on the front porch. He got to his feet to greet Mason.

"Hey, there, Joe."

Mason gave Joe a greeting rub behind the ears and opened the front door. Joe followed him inside and padded into the darkened kitchen.

Deke was still awake, lounging on the sofa. He was watching a movie on television. Mason heard Bogart speak the familiar last line of the film: *"Louis, I think this is the beginning of a beautiful friendship."*

Mason headed for the kitchen. *"Casablanca* again?"

"Best movie ever made." Deke pushed himself up off the couch. "About time you got home."

"It's a little late to tell me I've got a curfew," Mason said. He went into the kitchen, flipped on the overhead light, opened the cupboard and took down the bottle of whiskey that was always there. "Probably should have done that fifteen years ago."

Deke made his way into the kitchen. "You never got into any trouble you couldn't handle, so why bother giving you a curfew?" He sat down at the table. "How did things go tonight?"

"Beats me." Mason took two glasses out of the cupboard and splashed a little whiskey into each. He put both glasses on the table and sat down across from Deke. "Lucy and I both think that there is some real instability inside the Colfax empire. Got a hunch Warner's second wife is sleeping with the CEO, Cecil Dillon, and it looks like Quinn is drinking — maybe a lot. As for Jillian, you saw her yesterday. She looks desperate."

"Maybe scared."

Mason thought about that. "Maybe. One thing's for sure: Everyone with a vested interest in the merger wants it to go through — except Warner. He owns the largest block of shares, but if the others combine their shares, they can outvote him."

"Unless Lucy sides with him."

"Unless."

Mason drank some of the whiskey.

"Lucy is going to take a lot of heat from both sides," Deke said. "She ought to sell those shares back to the family and get out of Dodge while the getting is good."

"She won't — not until she's got some answers."

Deke drank some whiskey and exhaled heavily. "Figured as much. Sounds like she turned out a lot like you. Stubborn as hell."

"Yeah." Mason smiled. "Yeah, she's a little on the stubborn side."

Deke cocked a brow. "You really think that car accident that took Sara and Mary might have been murder?"

"I don't know." Mason leaned back in his chair and drank a little more whiskey. "I pulled up the accident report this morning. There was nothing in it to indicate that it was anything other than an accident."

"Manzanita Road hasn't been well maintained in years. It's used mostly by motorcyclists and bicyclists who are into off-road riding. But Mary and Sara both knew it well. They drove it countless times. Everyone knows they liked to stop off at the old commune and have a snack."

"The accident occurred early in the afternoon. There was no fog. No indication that either of them had been drinking."

Deke sipped some whiskey. "Accidents happen."

"Sure. But there's something else I don't like about this one."

"What?"

"The timing. Lot of money in play because of the Colfax merger. Lot of tension in the family."

"There's always been tension in that family. Warner is a tough SOB. Got to hand it to him, he built himself a real empire. But he paid a price."

"And now all he wants to do, apparently, is make wine."

"I wouldn't be too sure of that," Deke said. "The company still means a hell of a lot to him."

154

Mason raised his brows. "You don't think he'd murder his own sister to try to get his hands on those shares, do you?"

"Mary wasn't his sister — not by blood, at any rate. She was his step-sister. Her mother was a widow with a little girl when she married Warner's father."

"I didn't know that."

"A lot of people don't know that," Deke said. "Or they've forgotten about it."

"How did you find out? You didn't grow up here. We didn't move here until Aaron and I were in our teens."

"Got the info from Becky. She was born in Summer River."

Mason nodded. "Did Becky tell you anything else?"

"She did, and it's something you might find interesting. She told me how Mary got those shares and why they are wild cards. When Mary turned twenty-five she came into an inheritance from her mother's side. That's where she got the money to invest in Warner's company. Mary believed in the company because she knew that Warner had a talent for making money. But she and Warner were never close. For Mary, it was a business investment. Warner was desperate for the cash infusion, so he gave her the shares on her terms."

"Okay, that changes things up a bit. Any idea why the partnership between Colfax and Brinker broke up?"

"I heard the same story everyone else heard. After his son disappeared, Jeffrey Brinker lost interest in Colfax and Brinker. He became obsessed with trying to discover what had happened to Tristan." Deke wrapped both hands around the whiskey glass and looked straight at Mason. "Only natural. I'd have done the same if you or Aaron had gone missing."

Mason felt a little whisper of warmth, the kind that didn't come from the whiskey.

"I know," he said. "If you suddenly vanished without an explanation, Aaron and I would never stop looking for you."

"That's how it is with family. At any rate, the story goes that Colfax took advantage of Brinker's depression and more or less pushed Brinker into selling out." Deke paused. "There were some who hinted that Colfax didn't give Brinker a fair price, that he knew at the time that Brinker wasn't really thinking straight. Whatever the case, the deal was made. A few months later, Brinker was dead of a heart attack."

Mason wrapped one hand around his glass of whiskey and lounged back in his chair. "Even if Colfax took advantage of Brinker, the buyout still would have been a big deal. Lot of money involved."

Deke looked intrigued. "Sure. Those two were both multimillionaires by the time they arrived in Summer River. Warner's worth a lot more now. Where are you going with this?"

"Not sure yet. You wouldn't happen to know who Brinker's heirs were, would you?"

"No. I wasn't paying that much attention. The only thing I can tell you is that whoever they were, they didn't live here in Summer River. Word would have gotten around real quick if that had been the case."

"I'll ask Lucy to follow the money from Brinker's estate," Mason said. "That's her area of expertise."

156

"What do you think the information will tell you?"

"I have no idea."

"Huh." Deke pondered that. "Is this how you usually work one of your old cold cases?"

Mason swallowed some whiskey and lowered the glass. "Pretty much. I keep asking questions — turning over rocks — until I get some answers."

"You must have some sense of direction."

"In my experience, you usually can't go wrong if you follow the money. Thirteen years ago a lot of cash changed hands. It would be interesting to know who got it. And who didn't."

Deke studied him with a piercing look. "You could be opening a real can of worms here."

"Or not. Thing is, it's become clear that Lucy is going to open that can one way or the other. I don't want her doing it alone."

"That would not be a good idea," Deke said.

They drank a little more whiskey in a companionable silence.

"I found something interesting in the old files on the Scorecard Rapist," Mason said after a while. "At least one of the investigators believed that there was a second person involved in the assaults, possibly the photographer."

"Son of a bitch. If that's true, he's still out there."

"Or she," Mason said.

"Hard to imagine a woman helping some bastard do something that vicious to another woman."

"You and I both know that both sexes are capable of cruelty and violence."

"Yeah." Deke ran his fingers through his buzz-cut hair. His eyes darkened with memories. "I know. But even after some of the stuff I saw over there, it still amazes me when a woman does something downright evil and unforgiveable."

"You were raised in different times," Mason said.

"Maybe. Think that if there was a second person involved in the rapes he or she might still be here in town?"

"It's a possibility. And that's what has me really worried. If the second perp is still here, he or she will be running scared now that Brinker's body has been found along with some proof that he was the Scorecard Rapist. Hell, even if the other perp doesn't live here now, odds are he or she will hear about the discovery of the body soon and start sweating."

Deke raised his brows. "Because there's a chance that the case will be reopened?"

"Right, although I don't think that's very likely. Whitaker isn't interested in doing that. The real problem is Lucy. If there is someone else out there and if Lucy starts asking too many questions in the wrong places —" Mason stopped talking.

"Got it," Deke said. "What do you want me to do?"

"You meet a lot of folks at the store. Sooner or later, Becky sees everyone in town come through the front door at her café. Between the two of you, you've got the town covered. People talk. I want you to listen closely to anyone who brings up the subject of Brinker's body."

"Hell, that will be everyone in Summer River. But Brinker was only nineteen when he ended up in Sara's fireplace. Seems to me that if there's any useful intel to be had on him, it would come from people who were closer to his age at the time. You, for instance."

"Lucy and I will cover that angle. But I'd like to know if any of the locals who were adults back then take an interest in the news of the discovery of Brinker's body that goes beyond the normal curiosity factor."

"I'll see what I can do," Deke said.

He knocked back the last of his whiskey.

"Thanks." Mason stood and collected the glasses. "I need some sleep. Got to put a plan together in the morning before Lucy starts opening too many closets. No telling what might fall out."

"Summer River is like any other small town," Deke said. "Lot of secrets. Lot of closets."

Mason headed for the stairs.

CHAPTER
SEVENTEEN

Joe lumbered to his feet and crossed the room to rest his head on Deke's knee. He watched Deke with his wolflike eyes. Deke put his hand on the dog. They communed together in silence as they often did at night. Just a couple of aging warriors, home from the wars, Deke thought. He and the dog understood each other as no one else except another warrior could.

He contemplated the conversation he'd just had with Mason. One thing was clear: Mason was looking a lot better than he had a couple weeks ago when he had shown up on the front porch, a duffel bag slung over his shoulder. His eyes had had the same look as the eyes of the thirteen-year-old kid who had been waiting for him in the offices of the child protective services agency all those years ago — like he'd witnessed the end of the world and nothing the future held would surprise or astonish him.

That thirteen-year-old kid had looked like he'd never laugh again or trust anyone again except his younger brother. But raw determination had burned in the kid. His dying father had given him a mission to complete. That mission had a single objective — to protect Aaron.

One look at Mason and Deke had known that the kid would carry out that mission or go down trying.

According to the child protective services people, Mason had anger-management issues. They claimed that he had acted out in the three foster homes he and Aaron had been placed in over a period of three months. There were reports of fights with other boys in the homes and one incident in which Mason was accused of attacking an adult male relative of one of the foster parents. The well-intentioned child services folks strongly suggested counseling.

But Deke had been pretty sure that regardless of what had occurred in the foster homes, Mason had just been doing his job, taking care of his younger brother. He could tell by the relief in the caseworker's eyes that she knew that, too. That's why she had pushed through the paperwork so damned fast it had made everyone's heads spin.

Within an hour Deke had stowed Mason and Aaron and their few belongings in the SUV and hit the road.

Life had changed for all three of them that day.

When Mason grew up he had not gone off to a war zone on the other side of the world. Instead, he had become a soldier in another kind of war, the never-ending battle against the bad guys at home. He had taken on a new mission. When Deke had found him at the front door two weeks ago, it was obvious that Mason hadn't come back to Summer River because he needed a break, as he claimed. He needed some healing.

Deke had recognized the shadows in Mason's eyes because, in spite of the counseling and the meds, he saw similar shadows when he looked in the mirror.

Mason had returned to Summer River carrying the heavy weight that only a man who believes that he has failed to complete the mission could know.

CHAPTER
EIGHTEEN

Lucy's phone rang just as she opened the closet in Sara's bedroom. She glanced at the familiar name on the screen, took a deep breath, braced herself and answered.

"Hi, Mom. I'm fine. Everything's under control."

"What in the world is going on there in Summer River?" Ellen demanded.

The academic world had its own accent, a cool, assured "I just published another peer-reviewed paper — what have you done lately?" edge that never failed to irritate ever so slightly those who lived outside the bubble that was the college environment. This morning, however, Ellen's usually well-modulated tones were laced with genuine alarm.

"Sounds like you've heard the news," Lucy said.

"They found Tristan Brinker's body inside *Sara's fireplace*?" Ellen's voice rose slightly on the last two words. "I can't believe it. The media is saying that the authorities think he was that serial rapist who was in the news at the time."

Lucy studied the row of exotically printed dresses, long skirts and flowing tops that had been crushed against one side of the closet. No wine-country casual for Sara. She had been heavily into the New Age look.

"There is definitely some indication that Brinker was the Scorecard Rapist," she said. "Sara seems to have been certain of it. There was a newspaper with a headline about the rapist sealed up alongside the body. Nothing has been proven yet, but the local cops are going with that theory."

"I can't begin to imagine the shock of having a body fall out of the fireplace. And your aunt's fireplace, at that. She was a vegan, for heaven's sake."

"She killed him, Mom. She didn't eat him."

Ellen sailed right past that. "Sara was antiwar. Antiviolence. Antiguns."

"She didn't use a gun. It looks like her weapon of choice was the business end of a poker. We found it inside the fireplace as well."

"It's just so hard to imagine your aunt killing someone — especially in what sounds like a premeditated act."

"They say that most people can and will kill under the right circumstances."

"Yes, I know," Ellen said. "There was a notorious case a few years ago in which a female academic murdered a few of her colleagues because she didn't get tenure, of all things."

"Imagine that," Lucy said. Having been raised by academics, she did not have any problem at all envisioning such a scenario.

"Still, it's hard to wrap my head around the idea of Sara killing someone."

164

"It was somewhat disconcerting," Lucy said. "Fortunately, I wasn't alone when I found the body. Mason was with me."

"Who is Mason?" Ellen asked. "The contractor you brought in to do the upgrades?"

Lucy smiled. "Not exactly. Remember Mason Fletcher?"

"No."

"He was the person who brought me home on the night of Brinker's last party."

"Now I remember the name. He was the young man who convinced Sara that you should leave town immediately. She was quite sure he knew what he was talking about. I had to cancel a conference to pick you up at the airport in San Diego."

"Whoa. Mason told Sara that I had to leave Summer River? He's the reason she hustled me out of town the next day? Well, damn. I should have guessed that."

"All I know is that Sara called me the next morning. She said a young man named Mason had talked to her a short time earlier and claimed that you were in danger. She said that she was going to drive you to the San Francisco airport and put you on the first plane to San Diego. She told me to meet the plane on the other end and not let you out of my sight until she called to tell me that everything was okay."

"So that's how it went down. I never got the whole story from her." Lucy paused, thinking about the timing. "Did she ever call you to confirm that everything was all right?"

"Yes, about a week later. But she sounded odd — not like her usual self. That was when she told me that you were safe but that you could not stay with her again there in Summer River. She never explained her decision, but she was adamant."

Lucy closed the door on the jumbled contents of the closet. "She didn't want me to have to sleep in a house with a dead man in the fireplace. Bad karma."

"Good grief. She killed him that same week, didn't she?" Shock and disbelief shuddered through Ellen's voice.

"The timing fits. Do you remember anything else about Sara's reaction to the events that week?"

"I'm not certain — it's been thirteen years. To tell you the truth, I thought at first that Sara might have been overreacting. I knew you would never be so stupid as to get sloppy drunk at a party and put yourself in danger. Then Sara explained that the bastard had intended to drug you."

"They think the Scorecard Rapist used a date-rape drug."

"Yes, well, the possibility that drugs were involved explained Sara's panic. I panicked, too. So did your father. That's why I canceled the conference and why Richard and I made sure that you were never alone that week. We didn't relax until I got the call from Sara saying that Brinker was believed to be dead and that you were safe."

"I remember," Lucy said. "You and Dad never let me out of your sight. You even made me sit in on your classes so that I was never alone."

"We were both very worried. We talked about going to the police, but we had nothing but Sara's suspicions to go on. Let me tell you, Richard and I were never so relieved in our lives as we were when we got the call from Sara telling us that Tristan Brinker was believed dead."

Memories of that week floated through Lucy's mind. She had not really understood what was going on. But she had sensed that somehow her parents were united that week, bound together by their mutual love for her. In her teenage naiveté she had even dared to hope that they would dump their new spouses and remarry each other. That little fantasy had, of course, been shattered once the call from Sara had assured Ellen and Richard that the danger was past.

"The only other thing I can remember is that, in addition to being worried about your safety, Sara was also concerned for the young man who brought you home that night," Ellen said.

"Mason. His name is Mason Fletcher."

"Mason Fletcher, yes."

"She was afraid that he might be in danger?"

"I got that impression. I think what alarmed her was the possibility that he might try to deal with Brinker himself. She said she did not want him to do that."

"Aunt Sara was worried about both of us."

"So she got rid of the source of the problem. Permanently. Who knew your aunt had such a fierce side? It must have been incredibly traumatic for her. And it does explain the changes in her behavior. She was never quite the same after that summer."

Lucy opened a drawer and studied a tumbled array of yoga tops. "The shadow."

"What?"

"There seemed to be a shadow around her after that summer. Even when she was enjoying herself, you could feel it."

"I don't know what you mean by a shadow, but given what we now know, it's highly probable that she suffered some post-traumatic stress. Perhaps that's what you detected."

"Yes." A thought struck Lucy. "But I never noticed the same shadow around Mary."

"What do you mean?"

"I think Sara kept her secret even from Mary. Sara probably didn't want to burden her with the knowledge. Or, as Mason suggested, maybe she didn't want to take the risk that Mary might accidentally let the secret slip. Whatever the case, Sara carried the full weight of killing Brinker to her grave."

"Evidently." There was a short silence on Ellen's end of the connection. "Speaking of Mason, I'm a little sorry to hear that he is there in Summer River."

"For heaven's sake, why?"

"Sara always felt that Mason had a lot of potential and would someday make something of himself. I take it that didn't happen."

"Mason never had to *make* something of himself." Lucy crossed the room to the dresser and yanked open a drawer. "He is now what he was intended to become."

"Dear, you know it annoys me when you talk like Sara. I can't translate that New Age jargon. What on earth are you trying to say?"

There was no explaining Mason, Lucy decided. "Never mind. Mason doesn't live here in Summer River. He's just visiting, spending some time with his uncle. Mason went into law enforcement."

"I see." There was a faint, significant pause. "He's a cop?"

It wasn't disapproval in her mother's voice, Lucy decided — more like a tinge of disappointment, as if Ellen had hoped to hear that Mason had obtained a Ph.D. in quantum physics or chemistry. Lucy knew that note well. She had heard the same regret in the voices of both of her parents when she had informed them that she was going to work as a forensic genealogist. *"Are you sure you don't want to go to grad school?"* Ellen had asked. *"You have so much potential, dear."* Her father had been more blunt: *"You're wasting your education. Genealogy isn't a profession, it's a hobby. You don't need a degree to draw up a family tree. Any sixth-grader with a computer can go online and find out where her great-great-grandparents were born."*

"Mason was a homicide detective for a few years," Lucy said. "Now he and his brother run a security consulting company."

"Do you mean one of those companies that supplies guards for shopping malls and office buildings?"

"More like one of those companies that solves old murder cases."

169

"It sounds very macabre." Ellen paused. "Is there any money in it?"

"Evidently, there is if you're good at it. Mason and his brother are very good. But I don't think Mason does it for the money. He finds the work . . . satisfying, I think."

"That doesn't sound healthy, psychologically speaking."

Lucy closed one drawer and opened another. "We need people like Mason. And I'm pretty sure he was born to do that kind of work. Look, I've got to run, Mom. Lots to do today."

"What, exactly, are you doing? I thought I heard a door close a moment ago, and now it sounds like you're opening and closing doors."

"I'm in Sara's bedroom, getting things organized so I can pack up her belongings and dispose of them. She certainly accumulated a lot of stuff. Not to mention the antiques she kept after she and Mary closed their shop."

"She lived in that house all her life. I don't think she ever threw anything away. And do be careful when it comes to disposing of those antiques. Most of them will no doubt be valuable."

"Dad said to bring in an estate appraiser."

"Good idea. How long are you planning to stay in Summer River?"

Lucy opened another drawer and looked at a tangled heap of cotton and flannel nightgowns, most embroidered with flowers.

170

"I'm not sure," she said. "I took two weeks of vacation time from Brookhouse. It may take me that long to sort things out here. I need to do some work on the house to get it ready to put on the market."

"Are you staying at the house?"

"No, a local inn. The thought of spending the night here, knowing there had been a body concealed downstairs all these years, was just too creepy. Got to go, Mom. Love you. Bye."

"Good-bye, dear. I love you, too."

It was true, Lucy thought, ending the call. She loved her mother, and her mother loved her. The same was true of her relationship with her father. Their version of family would never be the subject of a Norman Rockwell painting, but still, it was a family.

She wanted something different for herself, though, something more glued-together. But she was not a romantic at heart. She knew the risks and the lousy statistics all too well. She was commitment-shy for a reason.

She went to the bed and dropped the phone into her tote. She had not discussed her suspicions about Sara's and Mary's death with her mother or her father for a very good reason. Both would have been seriously alarmed. There would have been long lectures on the phone. She could hear her father now: *Leave that sort of thing to the police.*

One thing you learned as an adult was that it was not necessary to tell your parents every little detail of your life.

She opened a few more drawers, assessing the contents. When she was finished, she walked out into the hall and entered the second bedroom, the one that she had used when she had stayed with Sara.

She opened another closet door. The sight of the jumbled pile of storage boxes and old clothes told her all she needed to know. It was not her imagination.

Her phone chirped.

She went back into the other room and got her cell out of the tote. She was in the process of deleting two more messages from the match-making agency when the device rang. She glanced at the screen. *Mason.*

"Good timing," she said. "I was just about to call you."

"Why?" he asked.

Just like that he had gone into cop mode, she realized.

"We really need to work on your phone etiquette," she said. "For the record, it's best not to treat a perfectly normal conversation as an interrogation."

"What the hell is wrong?"

She abandoned the attempt to instruct him in proper phone manners. "I'm at Sara's house." She heard a car pull into the driveway. "Hang on, there's someone here."

"Try to focus, damn it."

"I'm focusing on whoever just arrived." She went to the window and watched a black luxury sedan glide to a halt in front of the house. A familiar figure climbed out. He had a computer case in one hand. "It's Nolan Kelly. Got to go. I'll call you later."

"Wait," Mason ordered. "Do not hang up on me. Why were you trying to get hold of me?"

"*Please* do not hang up on me," she said.

"Lucy, I swear —"

Lucy went out into the hall and started down the stairs.

"I came here today to get a better idea of how much stuff I'm going to have to pack up before I put the house on the market," she said. She reached the foot of the stairs and walked quickly toward the front door. "First, you should know that although Aunt Sara rarely threw anything away, she was a very orderly person. She did not just toss things into the closets or drawers."

"What are you getting at?" Mason said.

"I spent my first night in town here at the house. I opened a few closets and drawers. Everything inside was neatly arranged in typical Sara style. But today the clothes and the storage boxes look like someone went through them in a hurry."

"You're saying you think someone searched the house?" Mason's voice went dangerously flat.

"Yes. It must have happened last night while we were at the winery party."

"What the hell would the intruder be looking for?"

"I have no idea. All I can tell you is that it doesn't look like anything was stolen. I'll get back to you when I finish talking to Nolan."

She ended the call before Mason could order her not to hang up again. Nolan was crossing the porch, preparing to ring the bell. She opened the front door.

"Hi, Lucy." Nolan's smile was warm and friendly, but it did not quite cancel out the slight sheen of anxiety in his eyes. "I thought we could take a look at some comps."

"Come on in, Nolan," she said. "We can talk in the kitchen."

CHAPTER
NINETEEN

Mason clipped the phone to his belt and moved out from behind the counter. He went down an aisle framed by ranks of gleaming nails and screws on one side and an assortment of plumbing fixtures on the opposite side, heading for the front door.

"Got to go, Deke," he called over his shoulder.

Deke emerged from the back room. "Where the hell are you off to in such a damn rush?"

"Sara's house. Lucy says she thinks someone searched the place last night."

"Son of a —" Deke stopped. He looked more puzzled than alarmed. "Why would anyone do that?"

"An interesting question, in light of the theory that the Scorecard Rapist may have had an accomplice who would now have some concerns about a reopened investigation."

"Damn."

"Exactly." Mason opened the door. "All I know is that I don't want Lucy alone with anyone who is even remotely connected to this case, and right now she's alone with Nolan Kelly."

"Kelly's a realtor. All he'll want is the listing."

"Let me rephrase that. I don't want Lucy alone with anyone who was at the party at the Harper Ranch thirteen years ago. Kelly was there that night. He was one of the regulars in Brinker's circle."

Mason went through the doorway into the warm sunlight. He didn't realize that Joe had followed him until he was halfway down the street. He looked down at the dog trotting close at his heels.

"You want to come along?" he said. "Fine. But don't go for Kelly's throat unless I give the okay. Understood?"

Joe looked at him briefly as if to say, *Give me a break. I know my job.*

A middle-aged woman came toward them on the sidewalk. She had a small, fluffy white dog on a pink leash. Her eyes widened in horror when she spotted Joe. She snatched up her little dog and tucked it under her arm out of harm's way.

Safe on its high perch, the small dog yapped at Joe, who paid no attention.

"Summer River has a leash ordinance," the woman announced to Mason. "All dogs in town are supposed to be on a leash."

She pointed to a nearby sign emblazoned with the silhouette of a dog on a leash.

Mason glanced at the sign and then jerked a thumb at Joe. "Take it up with him."

He kept walking. Joe paced at his heels. When they reached the small parking lot, Mason opened the rear door of his car. Joe jumped up onto the backseat and sat.

"Try not to embarrass me like that again," Mason said. "If we get arrested for violating the leash law, I'm not going to take the fall for you."

Joe appeared unconcerned. He sat at attention, ears pricked, gaze focused on the view through the windshield. He was on duty, riding shotgun in the rear seat.

Mason shut the door, went around to the other side of the car and got behind the wheel. He was pulling out of the parking lot and turning onto Main Street when he saw the familiar figure entering Fletcher Hardware.

It was hard to imagine Warner Colfax engaging in a little DIY home-repair work. Odds were Colfax intended to try to apply pressure to Deke.

"Good luck to him, is all I can say," Mason remarked to Joe.

If anyone in town could handle Warner Colfax, it was Deke.

It was still early. The daily tourist rush was not due to start for another few hours. The light traffic enabled Mason to make good time through town. He made even better time once he was on the road that would take him to Sara's house.

Ten minutes later, he turned onto the narrow lane that cut through the old apple orchard. The Gravensteins had not been picked that summer because Sara and Mary were gone. The apples hung heavily from the trees.

There was a long black car parked in the drive next to Lucy's compact. If Nolan Kelly had intended any harm to Lucy, it seemed unlikely he would leave his vehicle parked in front of her house. Still, like a lot of other people these days, Nolan wanted something from Lucy.

Mason shut down the engine, got out and opened the rear door for Joe. They went up the front steps together. Mason hit the doorbell, but he did not wait for Lucy to respond. When he tried the knob, he discovered that the door was open, so he let himself into the front hall.

"Lucy?" He resisted the urge to add, *"I'm home."*

"We're in the kitchen," she called.

She sounded fine. Mason told himself to relax. He had overreacted. It occurred to him that he had developed a disturbing tendency to do that a lot when it came to Lucy.

He went into the kitchen, Joe at his heels. Lucy and Nolan were at the table, huddled around a computer. There was a photo of a house on the screen.

Nolan managed a smile, but he did not look pleased by the interruption.

"Hello, Mason," Lucy said. She gave him a severe stick-to-my-script look. "Nolan is showing me some listings for other, similar houses in the area so that I can get an idea of the value of this place."

"I told you, the house is nice, but it's not nearly as valuable as the land," Mason said. He pulled out a chair, turned it back to front and straddled the seat. He folded his arms on the back of the chair. "But I'm sure Nolan has already explained that to you."

"Yes, as a matter of fact, I did explain that to Lucy." Nolan's jaw was clenched, but he managed to keep the smile going. "The property will certainly appeal to someone who wants to establish his own winery."

"I hate to think of all those lovely old apple trees being destroyed," Lucy said, "but I'm not a fanatic about saving the Gravensteins like Sara was." She smiled. "After all, I like wine, too."

"Glad to hear that," Nolan said. "Because I've got just the buyer for you."

"The thing is, my father insists that the house should be given a bit of a face-lift in order to get the best possible price."

"I agree the house is a fine example of the Craftsmanship style," Nolan said patiently. "I'm just trying to point out that you don't need to sink a lot of money into it before you put it on the market."

"Don't worry, I'm not planning anything major," Lucy said. "I don't have a lot of cash to pour into the house. I appreciate your time, Nolan. I'll think about these numbers and get back to you when I've made some decisions."

Nolan hesitated. but the salesman in him must have concluded that it would not be wise to press for the listing.

"Excellent," he said. He shut down the computer, got to his feet and took out a small silver case. "Here's my card. Call me if you have any questions, night or day."

"Thanks." Lucy gave him a warm smile. She rose. "I'll see you to the door."

"Thanks."

Mason watched the two of them walk across the kitchen and go into the hall. He got out of the chair and followed at a leisurely pace. Lucy glanced back and shot him a warning look. He widened his hands and gave her a polite I'm-not-trying-to-interfere look in return. He was behaving himself.

He stopped in the kitchen doorway and propped one shoulder against the jamb. He watched Nolan glance uneasily into the living room.

"Hard to believe Brinker's body was in that fireplace all these years," Nolan said.

"I don't think there's any need to mention that in the listing," Lucy said smoothly.

"No, no, of course not," Nolan said quickly. "But talk about weird. I don't suppose you have any idea why your aunt, uh, did that?"

"She must have had her reasons," Lucy said.

Nolan winced. "A lot of people may have had reasons to get rid of Brinker."

"Really?" Lucy said.

Mason had to hand it to her. She did innocent very well.

Nolan tightened his grip on the handle of the computer case. "He'd smile at you one minute, as if you were his best friend in the world, and the next minute he would stick a knife in your back. It's not hard to believe that he was the Scorecard Rapist. I don't even want to think about what this town would have been like if he had hung around any longer than he did that summer. He was smart, he was rich and he was a total sociopath."

"A real bad combination," Mason said.

Nolan nodded grimly. "A lot of folks were damned relieved when he disappeared. If you ask me, Sara did everyone a favor by getting rid of him."

Lucy cleared her throat gently. "As I recall, you were part of the crowd that hung around him that summer."

"Yeah." Nolan grimaced. "I was thrilled at first. But the big thing you learned sooner or later about Tristan Brinker was that there was always a price to pay for the privilege of being on his A-list."

Nolan did not wait for a response. He opened the door and let himself out onto the front porch. Lucy waited until she heard the big car start up in the drive before she turned around and looked at Mason.

"Are you thinking what I'm thinking?" she asked.

"I'm thinking that if Kelly is so happy to know that Brinker has been dead all this time, why does he seem so nervous?"

"Maybe it's just about the listing. After all, there's a big commission at stake, and he's not the only real estate agent in town."

"Maybe," Mason said. "But I think there's more to it than a commission."

"Something about the way he looked around the house when he got here bothered me, but I can't put my finger on it."

"Think he might have been the person who searched the house last night?"

"I have no idea."

"You're absolutely sure someone tossed the place?"

"Positive," Lucy said. "Whoever it was tried to be neat and orderly about the job, but I could tell that someone had gone through the closets and drawers and the desk. The question is, what was the intruder looking for? And why search for it now? The house has been sitting here, unoccupied, ever since Sara's death. There was plenty of opportunity for someone to break in and steal something."

"Obviously, the discovery of the body triggered the search."

"Yes."

"Lots of questions here." Mason straightened away from the doorframe. "We need to start finding some answers. How do you feel about doing a little genealogical research?"

"What's the name of the family?"

"Brinker."

CHAPTER
TWENTY

"Jeffrey Brinker and I were on top of the financial world back in those days," Warner said. "Oh, we were still small compared to the big outfits, but we were the smartest guys in the business, and we knew it. Brinker had a way with the clients. My job was to assess the markets and pick the investments. I always did the math before making a buy, but when decision time came, I went with my gut. My instincts were damn near infallible. Jeffrey and I were making money hand over fist."

Deke kept silent. He eased his rear down onto the stool that he kept behind the counter and watched Colfax contemplate a display of screwdrivers.

He had been surprised to see Colfax come through the front door almost immediately after Mason left. For reasons that were not yet entirely clear, Warner had started talking about the past as if they were longtime friends. That was about as far from reality as it was possible to get. In Deke's world, a man made a few extra bucks by deploying multiple times to war zones. If he survived, he came home and bought the local hardware store. In Colfax's world, a man played the markets, got rich and founded a boutique winery.

Deke was pretty sure that the only thing he and Warner had in common was their age.

Colfax was carrying on about the legendary accuracy of his apparently golden gut, but Deke had learned to trust his own gut a long time ago. It hadn't come in handy for making money, but it had kept him alive in some nasty situations. It was telling him now that there were only two possible explanations for Colfax's visit this morning. Either Warner wanted information or else he intended to try to apply some pressure. Probably both.

One thing about conversations like this, Deke thought: The best thing to do was just listen.

"But what good does it do to build an empire unless you can pass it on down to future generations?" Warner asked the screwdriver display. "Brinker and I were both cursed when it came to our sons. His died an early death. Mine turned out to be soft and weak."

Deke shrugged, trying for noncommittal. There was no good answer, even if he had wanted to supply one.

"I used to envy Brinker, you know," Warner said. "My boy was soft right from the start. I admit I have to bear some of the blame for the way he turned out. I was busy building Colfax in those days. I left Quinn to his mother to raise, and she turned him into a weak-willed mama's boy with no spine."

Deke said nothing.

"I had some hope when he married Jillian a few years ago. That girl had spirit and ambition. I knew she was marrying him for his money, but I figured the least Quinn could do was give me a grandson I could raise up to take over the reins of Colfax Inc. But he can't even manage that much. Jillian has never gotten pregnant."

Maybe Jillian wasn't interested in getting pregnant, Deke thought. But he didn't say it.

"Brinker's boy, Tristan, on the other hand, was whip-smart, and he had his old man's guts." Colfax made a fist. "A little reckless, maybe, but that's a good quality in a man, don't you think?"

"Don't know about that," Deke said, judging it was time to say a few words to keep the conversation going. "The kid ended up dead."

"Murdered, you mean."

"Yeah, well, dead is dead."

"Brinker's son would have been a man's man if he had lived."

More likely a serial rapist or possibly a serial killer, Deke thought.

"Do you know, I was damn glad when he and Quinn became friends that summer?" Warner continued. "I hoped some of Brinker's nerve and ambition would rub off on Quinn. But as usual, Quinn played the follower."

Deke folded his arms. "I wouldn't say that Brinker's boy was a leader. More like a first-class bastard. As far as I could tell, no one, except maybe his father, was sorry when he vanished."

"Strong men are feared, not loved. They don't have friends, they have rivals. They have people who take orders from them. They make their own rules."

"That works until you need someone you can trust to watch your back."

185

Warner snorted. "You don't have a clue about what it takes to be a success, do you? All you've ever done in life is spend enough time in the military to make sure you got your pension, and then you came back to Summer River to open a hardware store. Never mind. That's not important. It sure as hell isn't why I came here this morning."

Deke glanced at his watch. "Speaking of the store, I've got to open it in a few minutes. Mind telling me what this is all about?"

Warner's jaw tightened. Anger heated his eyes. He was not accustomed to having other people hustle him along. But he managed to keep himself under control.

"By now you know that the Sheridan woman got my sister's shares of Colfax Inc.," he said.

"Heard something about that."

Warner snorted. "Of course you did. The whole town is talking about it. Your nephew Mason appears to have attached himself to her."

Deke stilled, took a breath and let it out halfway, the way he did before he took the kill shot.

"What are you saying, Colfax?" he asked. "Are you implying that Mason is seeing Lucy because he wants to get his hands on those shares?"

Warner blinked a couple times. He went very still, too, but it was a deer-in-the-headlights kind of stillness. He stared at Deke for an instant before he recovered his nerve. He even managed a chuckle, but it was a little shaky.

"Take it easy, Deke," he said. "No offense intended. But we both know there's a lot of money involved here. Those shares that Lucy inherited represent a

186

controlling interest in Colfax Inc. A man would have to be a fool not to be aware that she could be a very wealthy woman if she decides to sell those shares."

"So?"

"So I'm offering to buy the shares," Warner said evenly. "Lucy can name her own price."

"Expect she knows that."

"Make sure Mason knows it. If he really has feelings for Lucy, he can do her a favor by encouraging her to sell."

"Maybe she doesn't want to sell."

Warner's mouth thinned. He shook his head. "That would be a poor decision."

"Is that a threat?"

"No." Warner exhaled heavily. "Just some good advice. You see, Deke, things are going to get real messy, real soon. Certain members of my family think I've gotten soft in my old age. They think I can't protect myself and everything I've built. They're wrong. Lucy Sheridan is swimming in the shark tank. If she doesn't sell those shares as soon as possible, she's going to find herself in the middle of a feeding frenzy. We both know she isn't one of the sharks. That makes her the prey."

"Sure appreciate the helpful advice, Colfax. I'll give you some in return."

"What's that?"

"Couple of minutes ago, you made it clear you didn't think friends were of much use."

Warner shrugged. "I've got all the friends I want, and I wouldn't trust any of them any farther than I can spit."

"Something you should keep in mind. Lucy also has friends here in Summer River. Unlike you, she can trust them."

He didn't have to spell it out. Warner got the message.

"Have it your way," he said. "But my advice is the same. As long as Lucy is holding those shares, she's asking for trouble. If she has any sense, she'll take the money and run. Tell her I said that."

"I'll tell her."

Warner nodded. He walked to the front door and stopped, one hand on the knob. "You know, it's kind of ironic, when you think about it."

"What is?" Deke asked.

"Brinker and I gave our sons all the advantages a man can give his boy — money, a good education, the right social connections and the opportunity to inherit a business worth millions. But you're the one who raised up a boy to be a real man. Everyone around here knows you don't mess with Mason Fletcher. Son of a bitch, Deke, I can't think of the last time I envied anyone, but I envy you."

CHAPTER
TWENTY-ONE

"There was nothing unusual about the terms of the Brinker estate." Lucy studied the data on her computer screen. "He left everything to Tristan. The trust stipulated that if Tristan predeceased his father, the assets were to be divided equally among some distant relatives."

"How distant?" Mason asked.

Lucy flipped to another screen full of data. "Some cousins on the East Coast. We're not talking enormous sums of cash, by the way, at least not when you consider what half the company must have been worth. Still, the total amounted to a few million."

Mason lounged back in his chair and sipped his coffee. His eyes were half closed. He was in some kind of Zen zone, Lucy thought — running scenarios and contemplating possible outcomes. Aunt Sara would have appreciated the aura of deep focus.

They were sitting at the kitchen table. She had made another pot of coffee after Nolan Kelly had left. She knew Mason had not been happy to see Nolan in the house. When he came through the door, his eyes had borne an uncanny resemblance to those of the dog. But he'd had the good sense not to lecture her about the dangers of allowing real estate agents through the front door. The man was learning.

Mason emerged from his contemplative state and fixed her with an intent look. "You said that none of the distant relatives got a huge amount of money out of the Brinker buyout."

She glanced at the screen. "I've worked on a lot of big family estates. I'm not an expert on hedge funds, but it looks like Brinker sold his half of the company to Colfax for a surprisingly small amount of money."

"Wonder why Brinker gave up his half for less than it was worth?"

Lucy looked up from the screen. "Maybe, like people say, with his son and heir dead, Brinker just didn't care anymore. But there's another possibility. Maybe by then Brinker knew he was dying."

"A fortune doesn't look so interesting if you know you're not going to live long enough spend it and if you don't care much about any of the people you're leaving behind. Wonder if he realized he'd fathered a sociopath?"

"Knowing Tristan was a psycho wouldn't necessarily lessen a father's grief."

Mason folded his hands behind his head. "I'll bet Jeffrey Brinker knew that he was ill."

"Why are you so sure of that?" Lucy asked.

"Because otherwise he probably wouldn't have taken the low offer. He was still in his prime. He could have remarried and maybe tried for another heir."

"Huh." Lucy picked up a pen and tapped the point lightly against the table.

"What?"

"It occurred to me that everything you just said about Brinker could apply to Warner Colfax. I'm not saying Quinn is a sociopath, but evidently he isn't management material. For whatever reason, his father has never given him anything except a token position in marketing, and that job is here in Summer River at the winery, not in San Francisco at the headquarters of Colfax Inc. Warner obviously doesn't consider Quinn to be a fitting heir to the throne."

"What are you thinking?"

"Just wondering if Warner dumped the first Mrs. Colfax in an effort to try for another heir."

Mason whistled softly. "Wow. That's cold. And I thought I was a tad cynical."

"I'm sure cops see it all, but I can guarantee you that when it comes to Machiavellian-style scheming and manipulation, nothing beats the warfare that goes on inside families when a large estate is at stake. I take that back. There doesn't even have to be a lot of money involved. There are plenty of stories of siblings not speaking to each other for years because one of them got Mother's antique hutch and the other one got the gilt mirror in the living room."

"Well, as we both observed going into this thing, there's no feud like a family feud."

"The infighting is supposedly over money or property, but deep down it's always the result of the underlying family dynamics." Lucy tapped the tip of the pen on the tabletop a couple more times. "And there's nothing like throwing a second wife into the pot to stir things up. If the objective is for her to be more than just arm candy — if her job is to produce a second heir to the throne — things get really, really messy."

Her phone rang, startling her. She glanced at the screen and winced, but she took the call.

"Hi, Dad," she said.

"I just got an email from your mother," Richard Sheridan said. "What's this about a body in Sara's fireplace?"

She knew her father was in his office. She could tell by the brusque tone. He was probably preparing for yet another academic meeting. But he was very good at compartmentalizing. She could tell that she had his attention for the moment, so she gave him a quick rundown of events.

"Sara was more than a little eccentric, but it's hard to imagine her murdering anyone, let alone concealing the body in her fireplace," he said when she had finished.

"Well, when you think about it, it's not that easy to get rid of a body — not if you want to be absolutely certain it won't be found, at least not in your lifetime," Lucy said.

"I'll admit I haven't given the problem a lot of thought," Richard said dryly. "But it's just damn weird. And it will probably have a negative effect on the asking price of the house. Any way you can keep the information off the listing form?"

"Believe me, I don't plan to mention it. Doubt if the real estate agent will want to make a note of it, either."

"Thirteen years ago, Ellen and I were very relieved to find out that Brinker came to a bad end. You do know he's the reason Sara sent you back to us that summer, don't you?"

"Yes, I know."

"The son of a bitch had it coming, is all I can say. When I found out what had almost happened to you, I wanted to go straight to the police. But Sara was convinced that wouldn't do any good. I was consulting with a lawyer about our legal options — restraining orders, that sort of thing. Then Sara called your mother and me, and said Brinker was believed to be dead. She sounded very, ah, positive about that."

"Now we know why." Lucy paused. "Thanks, Dad."

"For what?"

"For consulting with the lawyer and . . . and everything. I appreciate that you were looking for a way to protect me."

"I'm your father. What the hell else would I do?"

Lucy felt tears gathering in her eyes. "Thanks." She cleared her throat. "About the house —"

"Have you found a real estate agent?"

"I've, uh, interviewed one."

"Like I said, make sure you keep the business about the body off the listing form if at all possible."

"I'll be careful." She hesitated and then decided to update her father. "There's another problem. The police told me that the house is no longer a crime scene, but it appears there was an intruder last night. Someone searched the place."

"Were you there?" Richard's voice was laced with alarm.

"No. I'm staying at an inn in town."

"Good." The sudden alarm faded from Dick's voice. "Did you inform the police?"

"No, because I can't prove anything. Nothing was taken, as far as I can tell. You know how the cops are when it comes to chasing down suspects in a burglary — especially when nothing was stolen."

"Empty houses are magnets for vandals and burglars — everyone knows that. The news about the body in the fireplace no doubt drew plenty of attention in the area. Maybe some kids broke in to have a look around."

"Except that there was no sign that anyone forced his way into the house."

"According to the media, the average thief can get through the average household lock in about sixty seconds."

Lucy met Mason's eyes across the width of the table. "Yes, I've heard that, too."

"Look, there's no need to hang around Summer River. Get Sara's things packed and have a charity pick them up. Call in an appraiser to give you some advice on the value of the furniture and those antiques. Get a local contractor to do the touch-up work and get the house on the market."

"Sure thing," Lucy said. "Thanks for the advice, Dad."

Mason looked amused. Probably something about the way she had thanked her father, she decided.

"Have you contacted Warner Colfax about selling those shares you inherited back to him?" Richard asked.

Lucy took a deep breath. "We haven't discussed price yet."

"I told you, let the lawyer for the estate handle the negotiations."

"I understand," Lucy said dutifully.

Mason raised his eyebrows.

"Got to go," Richard said. "I have a meeting in a few minutes. Let me know if you need any more help."

"Thanks for the advice, Dad. Bye."

"Bye."

"Love you," Lucy added.

She was always the one who said it first. But Richard always responded, even if he did need prompting.

"Love you, too, Lucy girl."

Lucy ended the call, squelching the old wistfulness that always whispered through her when she talked to her father. She put the phone back into her tote. When she looked up, she saw that Mason was watching her with a thoughtful expression.

"*Thanks for the advice, Dad?*" Mason repeated, brows slightly elevated.

"He gave me a long list of instructions. Get the appraisal on the furniture and the antiques, hire a mover, hire a contractor. He means well."

"And you're used to listening politely and then doing exactly what you want to do."

"It works for both of us. It's not that he's wrong. Eventually, I will get around to doing all the stuff on the list. But at the moment, I'm more interested in finding out what happened to Aunt Sara and Mary."

"I notice you didn't mention your suspicions to your father."

Lucy sipped some coffee and lowered the glass. "Didn't tell Mom, either. They would only worry if they knew."

A knowing look illuminated his eyes. "You're used to telling both of them what they want to hear and then going your own way."

"I never lie to my folks, but I often proceed on the philosophy that what they don't know won't hurt them."

"Unless things blow up in your face."

"Unless that happens, right. But I've got a secret weapon in this case."

"What?" he asked.

"You. I'm sure Dad would approve. He's always very keen on hiring the best. He says it pays in the long run. And as it happens, I am working with one of the preeminent cold case consultants in the world."

"And that's what you plan to tell your folks if the wheels come off this little project of yours — that you were working with a consultant."

"A *preeminent* criminal investigation consultant."

"*Preeminent* is a big word," Mason said. "Does it mean not too smart, by any chance?"

"Nope, it means outstanding." Her phone rang again, an unknown number this time. She took the call. "This is Lucy."

"Lucy, it's Teresa. I called to see if you would like to have dinner with my husband and me this evening. My niece says she'll watch the kids. There's a new restaurant in town. Rafe and I have been looking forward to trying it out."

"Thank you," Lucy said. "I'd like that very much."

"And please invite Mason Fletcher along. It's all over town that the two of you are seeing each other."

Lucy winced. "That was fast. Hang on, he's right here. I'll ask him if he can join us." She held the phone so that the mouthpiece was pressed against her shoulder. "This is Teresa Vega. She's inviting both of us to join her and her husband for dinner. Are you free?"

"Sure," Mason said. "Tell her I said thanks."

Lucy put the phone back to her ear. "We're both delighted to accept. Meet you at the restaurant."

"Perfect. Got a pen?"

"Yes."

Lucy scribbled down the name and address of the restaurant, said good-bye and ended the call. She cleared her throat.

"Something you should know before we go out to dinner with Teresa and Rafe Vega tonight," she said.

"I'm listening."

"Evidently, word has gotten around town that you and I are seeing each other."

"That was fast."

"Exactly what I said. You were right, one thing about Summer River has not changed over the years. It is still a small town in some ways."

Mason's mouth quirked faintly. "Probably why we got invited out to dinner as a couple. Teresa and Rafe want the latest hot gossip on the murder."

"Oh, I'm sure of it. But here's the thing. I don't doubt that Teresa and her husband will try to pump us for inside information, but we will be able to return the favor. Teresa was raised in Summer River. She knows everyone."

"What about her husband?"

"I think Sara said he's relatively new in town. Teaches high school."

"Gosh, this is exciting."

She eyed him warily. "What are you thinking?"

"Just that this will be date number three for us." He held up one hand and extended his forefinger. "On date number one we discovered a dead body." He extended a second finger. "On date number two we were entertained with various and assorted veiled threats from a bunch of rich clowns wearing too much wine-country casual." Mason raised one more finger. "Date number three is going to be all about interrogating local witnesses."

"Your point?"

He gave her a wolfish smile. "My point is that this relationship of ours is getting off to an interesting start."

The word *relationship* sent a frisson of uncertainty through Lucy. Mason was teasing her, she thought. She would follow suit.

"Well, I don't think you can call three dates a relationship," she said lightly. "But I can tell you that

198

both of the dates we've had so far were a lot more interesting than all thirty matchmaking agency dates I've had in the past few months."

"You said none of those arranged matches got past two dates, right?"

"Right. Most didn't get past the first date, actually."

"We are now on date number three. Given your track record, that constitutes a relationship."

CHAPTER
TWENTY-TWO

The restaurant was exactly what one expected in wine country — a bistro-style setting and an innovative West Coast menu. A display of local wines arrayed in floor-to-ceiling racks decorated one wall. Long-stemmed glassware sparkled on the tables. The menu earnestly assured diners that almost everything, from the arugula and the cheese in the arugula-and-fried-goat-cheese salad to the handmade ravioli, was organic and had been produced within a fifty-mile radius of the establishment — in some cases by the farm that was operated by the restaurant's owner and chef.

Lucy wore the twilight dress that she had purchased for the winery reception. At least she would get two nights of wear out of it before it went to the back of her closet when she returned to Vantage Harbor. She had, however, indulged in some new high-heeled sandals. A woman could always use another pair of shoes.

Maybe it was just her imagination, but it seemed to her that when the party of four was escorted to a table they were followed by a lot of discreetly curious glances. Find one lousy body in your aunt's fireplace and the first thing you know everyone is talking.

The evening started off with surprising ease. Rafe and Mason got along well from the start. When Rafe discovered that neither she nor Mason considered themselves wine connoisseurs, Rafe ordered a bottle of dry Riesling for the table after kindly explaining that it was *very approachable*. The waiter discussed the menu in reverential tones using language that belonged to the realm of poetry. Selections were made and orders taken.

And then the politely conducted mutual interrogation began. You had to give a little to get a little, Mason had advised going in. Lucy knew he was right. It was, after all, the first rule of gossip. For the most part, she and Mason answered the questions in a forthright manner until the entrées arrived. The only things they refrained from mentioning were her suspicions about the car accident that had killed Sara and Mary and her conviction that the house had been searched. Mason had stood firm on those two key points. *You are not going to make an even bigger target of yourself than you have already* were the precise words he had used. Put like that, it was hard to argue the point.

"Not surprised you're running into some pressure from the Colfaxes," Rafe said. "It's no secret that they all want those shares back. They say Warner Colfax almost had a stroke when he discovered that someone outside the family had inherited a controlling interest and had the right to sell or give the shares to whoever she wished."

"I'm sure Colfax will pay well for them," Teresa said. "You'll come out of this a wealthy woman, Lucy."

"The trouble is, everyone in the family wants to buy those shares from Lucy," Mason explained. "Money, evidently, is no object."

"Well, for what it's worth, Warner is definitely the richest one in the clan," Rafe observed. "So he can probably afford to give you the best price."

"Yes, I know," Lucy said. She ate a bite of the thinly sliced, delicately sautéed Brussels-sprouts-and-shallots dish that had accompanied her pasta. "Speaking of the past, do either of you remember much about what happened around the time that Tristan Brinker disappeared?"

Teresa and Rafe looked at each other, and then Rafe shrugged.

"You'll have to ask Teresa," he said. "I didn't live here thirteen years ago."

"I certainly remember the reaction when we got the news that Brinker had gone missing," Teresa said. "Every teen in town was talking about it." She glanced at Mason. "You were still here at the time. You must recall the commotion."

"I remember," Mason said. "But I was a little busy at the time."

Teresa smiled. "I know. You were working in the hardware store and fixing up that old house and generally holding things together for yourself and your brother while your uncle was away."

"I heard some of the talk at the store, but I wasn't in high school, so I didn't get the younger teen version of events," Mason said.

"It was all typical over-the-top teen conspiracy-theory stuff, for the most part," Teresa said. "There were two variations, as I recall. The most popular version held that since Tristan obviously had connections in the illicit drug market he had probably been the victim of a drug deal gone bad. That turned out to be the police theory as well. The second scenario, of course, was that you had something to do with his disappearance, Mason."

Mason shook his head. "Nope. Wasn't me."

"Well, we know that now," Teresa said. "But at the time there was a rumor going around that you and Brinker had quarreled the night of the last party out at the old Harper Ranch."

"We had words," Mason said. "But that was the end of it."

Rafe gave him a speculative look. "That was the end of it, thanks to Sara Sheridan."

Mason did not respond.

"I can tell you that no one ever suspected her," Teresa said. "I do remember that when it became clear that Brinker really had disappeared and people started saying he was probably dead, some of the kids seemed relieved. I think Jillian Benson — Jillian Colfax now — was one of them, by the way. Nolan Kelly, too. Or at least that was my take on the situation."

Lucy paused her fork in the air. "I got the impression that both Jillian and Nolan liked Brinker. Or maybe I should say they liked being in the circle that hung around him."

"All I can tell you is that when the authorities announced that Brinker was missing and presumed dead, Jillian didn't exactly go into mourning," Teresa said. "But I'm not positive about her reaction. It was just an impression I got. Same with Nolan and some of the other kids. But I was a couple of years younger, as you know, so I wasn't moving in their circles."

"Brinker was a real piece of work," Lucy said. "If it turns out that he was the Scorecard Rapist, he was a lot more dangerous than anyone could have known at the time. He sure had the teens of Summer River under his spell that summer, didn't he?"

"Yes." Teresa shuddered. "Now that I've got kids of my own, I think about him from time to time. And I worry."

Rafe's expression turned grim. "I wasn't here in those days, but I've seen enough in my teaching career to know just how bad things can get in the world of teenagers when you've got a slightly older, charismatic sociopath in the mix."

Teresa picked up her wineglass. "And to think Brinker's father was so proud of his son."

CHAPTER
TWENTY-THREE

Nolan Kelly searched the desk one last time, aiming the penlight into each drawer. There was nothing except neatly stacked papers, old bills, gardening catalogs and the kind of junk that piles up over the years — boxes of paper clips, pens, rubber bands.

He abandoned the desk and turned to survey the room that Sara Sheridan had used as an office. This was his second attempt to locate the old video. Last night had proven fruitless, but he was determined to give it one more try.

Thirteen years ago he had searched for it obsessively. He had gone through the house that Brinker had rented for the summer from top to bottom, but he had found nothing. There had been nothing online, either. In the end, he had told himself that Brinker had never uploaded the damning evidence — probably because he had known there was a possibility that the trail could lead back to him. Brinker had always looked out for number one, always made sure to cover his tracks, Nolan thought.

He figured that Sara must have discovered Brinker's stash of videos. It was the only way she could have known that Brinker was the Scorecard Rapist. And if she had known that much, Nolan thought, she would have known about the drug connection. If the video he was looking for was somewhere in the house, there was a high probability that Lucy would discover it when she packed up her aunt's things.

He checked his watch. He had some time. There was no need to panic — not yet. He had watched Lucy and Mason enter the restaurant with Teresa and Rafe Vega. The meal would be a leisurely affair.

What he could not predict was whether Lucy and Mason would return to the old house after dinner. He had to assume that it was a strong possibility. There were not a lot of convenient beds available to a couple seeking privacy in Summer River. He was sure that if Lucy and Mason were not already sleeping together, they soon would be. He had recognized the dangerous look in Mason's eyes when he had walked into the kitchen that morning. Mason had not liked finding Lucy alone with another man.

If you only knew the truth, Fletcher.

Nolan swung the penlight around the room, taking one last look. He had no personal interest in Lucy. Hell, back at the start, all he had cared about was getting an exclusive listing so that he could sell the property to his Silicon Valley client. But when Brinker's body turned up in the fireplace, he had been shaken to the core. Disaster loomed. It was just like the bastard to come back to haunt him. Some part of him had been waiting all these years for the other shoe to drop, and now it had.

206

He abandoned the search. It was hopeless. There were just too many places the old video could have been hidden in the house — always assuming that Sara had found it in the first place.

He took a deep breath and tried to think. He was running out of time. Since he could not find the video, he was left with only one option. He had come prepared tonight. The can of accelerant was waiting downstairs.

He hated to burn down the house. It really was a jewel. True, it was too small for the client who intended to build a French château and a walled courtyard complete with swimming pool and tennis courts. Nevertheless, the old Craftsman would have made a picturesque guest cottage on the estate. But the bottom line was that it was the size of the property and the location that were worth a fortune to the client — not the small house.

He went out into the hall, the narrow beam of the penlight spearing through the shadows.

Somewhere in the darkness of the first floor, a door squeaked on its hinges. A draft of night air shifted in the atmosphere upstairs. No one turned the lights on. Whoever had just entered had no more right to be here than he did.

Belatedly, he remembered to switch off the penlight. Footsteps sounded on the stairs. The beam of a flashlight bounced in the shadows. Nolan knew there was nowhere to run, nowhere to hide. He switched his own light back on in self-defense.

He pinned the intruder at the top of the stairs and breathed a sigh of relief. Instinctively, he fell back on his only real talent — a talent for sales.

"I should have known," he said. "I suppose you're here for the same reason I am. Let's talk. Maybe we can figure out how to deal with our mutual problem."

CHAPTER
TWENTY-FOUR

They took their time over coffee and dessert. It was late when the four of them left the restaurant. Main Street was quiet at that hour. The boutiques and shops were dark. Teresa and Rafe expressed a desire to get together again before Lucy left town and then got into their car and drove off.

Mason put an arm around Lucy's waist. She did not pull away. He tugged her a little closer, savoring the thrill he got every time he touched her. The pretty dress she wore somehow managed to look demure and seductive at the same time. In the silence, the high heels of her sandals tapped a blood-heating staccato on the sidewalk.

He considered his options. The last thing he wanted to do was take her back to the inn. But, as he had been forcibly reminded last night, there were not a lot of places a couple could go and be assured of privacy in such a small town. He doubted that Lucy would appreciate being invited to engage in a little foreplay and possibly more in the backseat of his car.

Not that he would care. He would have been delighted to have sex with her anywhere, under any conditions. But a man had his pride. He wanted to impress Lucy. That was hard to do in the back of a car. There was a motel on the edge of town, but he was pretty sure that would sound like a tacky idea, too. There was also the strong possibility that someone would drive past and recognize his vehicle.

If, on the other hand, they drove a little farther — say, to Healdsburg or Santa Rosa or even over to the coast — they might be able to find a suitable motel. Surreptitiously, he checked his watch. It was after ten. It would be close to midnight before they found an anonymous place to spend the night, always assuming Lucy would go for the plan.

And then there was the problem of how to handle returning Lucy to the Harvest Gold Inn tomorrow morning. He did not want her feeling as if she was doing the walk of shame when he brought her back. But half the town was sure to find out that she had spent the night with him. Would she care? Would she even go for the idea in the first place?

Decisions, decisions.

The inn was only one block away now. He had to come up with a plan, and fast. He wondered if Lucy was also contemplating the possibility of sex.

"I thought it was interesting that Teresa mentioned Jillian as one of the people who seemed relieved when Brinker disappeared," Lucy said. "Did you see her after I left town?"

Mason stifled a groan. That answered one question. Lucy had not been contemplating the prospect of having sex with him in an anonymous motel. He pulled his thoughts back from the edge and called up memories.

210

"Jillian? Sure, I saw her around town a few times, but I think she deliberately steered clear of me after that night at the park."

"Not surprising. She would have known that you blamed her, at least in part, for what nearly happened to me."

"Brinker must have used her to lure you there. She was his accomplice."

"That's harsh. She probably didn't know what Brinker intended."

"She knew."

A siren shrieked somewhere in the distance, shattering the silence of the darkened town. He felt Lucy flinch under his hand. He tightened his fingers on her hip. She relaxed.

"In the city you become so accustomed to sirens you tune them out," she said. "But when you hear one in a small town, it gets your attention."

A second siren screamed in the night.

"County fire trucks," Mason said. "Must be something big."

He stopped, forcing Lucy to halt, too. He turned partway around, following the sound of the blaring sirens. The rows of shops that lined Main Street blocked his view, but his intuition kicked in fast.

"Damn," he whispered.

Lucy stilled. "Good grief. You don't think —"

"Those sirens are definitely heading toward the road that leads to your aunt's house. Only one way to find out for sure."

He released her waist and grabbed her hand. Together they sprinted for his car. He wondered briefly how a woman could run in high heels, but there was no time to reflect on the particular skill set required for the task.

He had the engine revving and was pulling away from the curb before Lucy finished fastening her seat belt. She sat tensely beside him.

"It could be something else," she suggested. "A barn, maybe."

"Maybe."

"But it isn't going to be a barn, is it?"

"I don't think so."

The house was engulfed in flames. The fire roared through both floors. Black smoke billowed into the night sky. Fire trucks, police vehicles and an aid car crowded the driveway. Hoses coiled like pythons on the ground. Streams of water ran down the driveway.

Mason found a place to park on the side of the orchard lane. He and Lucy walked toward the scene. The heat was intense, even from a distance.

Mason approached one of the cops.

"This is Lucy Sheridan," Mason said. "She owns the house."

The cop nodded at Lucy. "Heard Sara Sheridan left the house to a niece."

"I was getting it ready to put on the market," Lucy said. "But stuff seems to keep happening."

"Yeah, like finding the body of a rapist in the fireplace," the cop said. "Now this. The chief is not going to be happy."

Someone yelled at the cop. He hurried away.

One of the firefighters came forward. The name on his jacket was Leggett.

"You're the owner, ma'am?" he asked.

"Yes," she said.

"Any chance that there was anyone at home tonight?"

"No, thank heavens." Lucy folded her wrap around herself. "The house was empty. I'm staying in town."

"That's some good news, then," Leggett said. "Sure hope you had insurance."

"Yes, the premium was paid through the end of the year," Lucy said. "Do you have any idea what might have started the fire?"

"Not yet," Leggett said. "The house was old. Could have been any number of things, from wiring to transients. There will be an investigation after things cool down. That will take a couple of days."

He walked away to rejoin his crew.

Lucy looked at Mason. "I'm betting it won't be the wiring."

"That's a sucker bet," Mason said. "I'm not taking it."

"I seriously doubt that the fire was the work of transients, either."

"Might depend on your definition of *transient*," Mason said.

"Why in the world would anyone burn down Sara's house, and why now?"

"Maybe because whoever did it couldn't find what he was looking for last night and figured that the safest way to make sure any incriminating evidence disappeared was to torch the house."

"What evidence could Sara possibly have possessed?" Lucy asked.

"She knew that Brinker was the Scorecard Rapist. Maybe she knew other things as well."

"Maybe. But in that case, I would have thought she would have concealed it with the body."

"Not if she concluded that innocent people might be hurt if the evidence was ever found," Mason said.

"You're right." Lucy thought about it. "But if she believed that was true, trust me, she would have destroyed the evidence thirteen years ago."

"Whoever burned down the house couldn't have been certain of that."

Lucy contemplated the burning house. "I guess this takes care of the problem of packing up Sara's things and bringing in an appraiser."

"I'd say so."

"One thing for sure, this date didn't end the way I thought it would."

"Yeah, I had a different ending in mind, too," Mason said. "I think we should leave town for our next date."

Lacy glanced at him. Her face was unreadable. Her eyes were mysterious pools.

"Got any suggestions?" she asked.

"What do you say we drive over to the coast tomorrow?"

"This isn't going to be a real date, is it?"

"When I hit a wall in a case, I sometimes find that it helps to visit the scene of the crime."

"Wow, an out-of-town date to visit a crime scene," Lucy said. "See, this is what was missing in all those matchmaking-agency dates."

"What?"

"Originality."

CHAPTER
TWENTY-FIVE

Lucy sat in the passenger seat and watched the rural scenery flow past. The drive from Summer River to the coast was only about forty miles, but the road was a two-lane highway that wound through a rolling landscape. A few miles back, the picturesque vineyards had given way to small farms. Goats and dairy cattle wandered across grassy fields. Signs advertising homemade cheese and antiques appeared at the side of the road.

Lucy could not escape a sense of adventure. They were on their way to a crime scene, but in her imagination the drive to the coast loomed as a turning point of sorts in her relationship with Mason.

She was not sure how she felt about that. But for reasons she did not want to examine too closely, she had tucked a few personal items into her tote. She knew that Mason was probably thinking along the same lines, because she was sure she had seen him slip a small leather overnight kit into the trunk of the car. Then again, maybe he was in the habit of always taking a few masculine essentials with him when he set out on a short road trip.

"It's a relief to get away from Summer River for a while," she said. "I'm tired of being the main attraction at the inn. This morning all anyone wanted to talk about was the fire."

"Can't blame everyone for being curious." Mason slowed for a righthand turn. "This is the road Sara and Mary would have taken to visit the old commune, right?"

Lucy caught a glimpse of a weathered sign. The lettering was so faded that it was difficult to make out the words *Rainshadow Farm*.

"Yes, this is it," she said. "Sara and Mary brought me out here a few times. They met each other on the farm. Eventually, they moved to Summer River, but Sara often returned to give yoga and meditation lessons to the small crowd that hung on at the commune for a few years. The last of the Rainshadow Farm residents abandoned the place a year or two after Sara sent me away from Summer River. But Sara and Mary always made it a point to stop there on their way to the coast. It was very special to them."

"Do you happen to know who owns the land?"

"Sara mentioned that when the last members of the alternative community left, they donated Rainshadow Farm to a nature conservancy."

The narrow strip of blacktop had not been patched or repaired in a long while. Mason slowed the car, easing over the gashes and wounds in the road.

The remains of the blacktop gave way to an ancient graveled track, and then the wooden skeletons and

217

rusted trailers that had once housed the residents of Rainshadow Farm came into view. Mason stopped.

Lucy opened her door and got out. Mason came around the front of the car to join her. Together they contemplated the remains of the commune.

"Doesn't look like the new owners have taken much interest in this place," Mason said.

Lucy put on her sunglasses and studied the weathered buildings. "Maybe they've forgotten about it. Or maybe they just don't have the funds to clean up the area. There's a great view from up there in the trees. Come on, I'll show you."

The old path was still partially visible. It climbed the hillside, cutting through low-lying scrub that swiftly transitioned into Douglas fir and a thick undergrowth. The light breeze stirred the leaves and carried the scents of the woods.

It felt good to be out here sharing the warmth of the summer day with Mason, Lucy thought. Her spirits rose. For the first time since she had arrived in Summer River, she began to relax.

"We should have brought a picnic basket," she said.

"Stop," Mason said. It was an order, and it was given in very soft tones.

Her first thought was that he had spotted a snake. She paused and looked at him over her shoulder.

"What?" she asked.

But he wasn't paying any attention to her. He was studying a thick, green patch of bamboo.

"Oh, crap," she whispered. "Definitely not native."

"It's a screen to cover the line," Mason said.

Then she saw it, too; a thin black tube snaked through the bamboo.

"I guess we can forget the scenic view," she said.

"Right." He looked around, quartering the landscape. Light sparked on his sunglasses, but evidently he did not see anything unduly alarming. He took her arm and positioned her in front of him, pointing her back down the hillside. He gave her an urgent little push. "Go."

She did not argue.

"Can you drive a stick shift?" Mason asked.

"Well, yes, at least in theory."

"Good. You're driving."

He gave her the keys. She got behind the wheel and took a deep breath. *I can do this.*

Mason slid into the passenger seat. "Go."

He leaned over, reaching under the console. She heard a click, as if a lock had just opened. Out of the corner of her eye she saw him remove a gun from the concealed compartment.

Crap. He was serious.

"Guess that explains why you don't do rental cars," she said.

Mason did not answer.

She got the engine going without any problem, but there was a distinct lurch when she put it in gear. Gravel spit under the wheels. She winced.

"Sorry," she said.

"Just drive."

She drove, gritting her teeth every time the sleek car bounced over a pothole.

Mason was half turned in his seat, watching the trail behind them.

She checked the rearview mirror and breathed a sigh of relief when she saw that there was no one behind them.

Mason did not turn around in the seat until they reached the end of the gravel road and jolted onto the main road. Only then did she sense him relax.

"We lucked out," Mason reported. "No sinister-looking SUVs with blacked-out windows and no motorcycles with armed riders on board behind us. A good day to go sightseeing at an illegal pot farm."

She took another breath, possibly the first one since she had put the car in gear.

"Okay, that was a little scary," she said. "I wonder if the nature conservancy that bought Rainshadow Farm knows that someone is growing pot up there on the hillside."

Mason stowed the gun in the console box. Lucy heard another click when he locked it.

"Probably not," he said.

"It looked like they were using the line to draw water from the old well on the property."

"That pot farm might explain what happened to Sara and Mary," Mason said. "If that's the case, it blows your Colfax family conspiracy theory all to hell."

"Do you think Sara and Mary may have been the victims of drug thugs protecting their crop?"

"It's a possibility. But that bamboo looked like it had been planted fairly recently to cover the waterline. Sara and Mary might have come along just as the growers were setting up the plantation. The big illegal farms often bring in armed guards along with their own crews of migrant workers to tend the plants. There's a lot of money to be made, and sometimes innocent bystanders get killed."

"So someone might have followed Sara and Mary from the farm and forced them off road?"

"It would be a convenient way to get rid of a couple of women who had seen too much."

"True," Lucy said. "But the growers are drawing water from the old well. Sara and Mary knew Rainshadow like the backs of their hands. I think they would have noticed the waterline and the new bamboo immediately. They would have known what it meant, just like we knew. They wouldn't have hung around, either."

"I think you're right. There's something else here that doesn't quite fit. Forcing a car off the road is a messy and inefficient way to get rid of two people. You can't guarantee the results. People survive car wrecks all the time. Also, a crash scene always attracts cops. If the growers wanted to use lethal force, they would most likely have shot Sara and Mary, buried the bodies somewhere in the woods and dumped the car a long ways from here."

Lucy tightened her hands on the wheel. "And what does this tell us?"

There was a moment of silence before Mason spoke.

"It indicates that whoever murdered Sara and Mary — assuming they were murdered — is not a pro. The car accident feels like the work of a determined amateur, maybe someone who has seen one too many car-chase movies."

"Someone with very little impulse control."

"Lack of impulse control is a defining characteristic of about ninety-eight percent of the criminals I've encountered."

"What about the other two percent?"

"They're strategic thinkers. They are more likely to have realistic exit strategies. But the vast majority of bad guys never do good contingency planning. Probably because they're too obsessed with achieving their goals. Obsession is another defining characteristic of the ninety-eight percent."

"They don't know when to walk away from the table."

"More like they can't bring themselves to walk away."

"Sara had excellent impulse control," Lucy said. "Probably all that yoga and meditation. She was also very smart."

"Which is why the murder of Tristan Brinker remained unsolved until after she was gone. Like I said, the best plans usually revolve around the three basics."

"Shoot, shovel and shut up."

"Right. You can stop here; I'll take the wheel now. Nice driving, by the way."

The praise warmed her for some ridiculous reason.

"A little rough, I'm afraid," she said. "It's been a while since my father taught me how to drive a stick shift. He said it was a skill that gave a driver a more intuitive feel for the handling of a car."

"I think Deke said something like that when he taught me how to drive. Also, the only vehicle we had at the time was the truck."

She pulled over to the side of the road. "But now you drive a stick shift because you *like* to drive a stick shift."

Mason smiled. "I like to work with good tools."

She stopped the engine and looked at him. "Like that gun you keep in the console safe?"

"Believe it or not, I hardly ever use a gun in my job. But on the rare occasions when I do need one, I take comfort knowing it's a good gun."

CHAPTER
TWENTY-SIX

A couple of miles farther down the highway, Mason turned off onto Manzanita Road. Lucy remembered it well. When she was a girl, it made for an exciting thrill ride. The winding strip of crumbling blacktop was cut into the hillside. The pavement was so narrow there was barely enough room for two vehicles to squeeze past each other. Not that there was ever much in the way of traffic, Lucy thought. Manzanita Road had been abandoned years earlier when the highway to the coast had been built. But the old road remained a favorite of adventurous backcountry drivers, bicyclists and motorcycle enthusiasts.

What made the drive an adventure was the dramatic manner in which the hillside dropped steeply away from the ragged edge of the serpentine road.

Lucy shivered. "I see they still haven't bothered to install a guardrail."

"No," Mason said. He glanced at the GPS readout. "We're coming up on the curve where Sara's car went over the edge. There's nowhere to pull off the road, but there's also no traffic. I'll stop on a straight stretch and put on the flashers. We can walk back to the scene."

A short time later, Lucy stood with Mason at the edge of the road. Together they surveyed the steep slope and the rough terrain below.

"It's hard to believe people died here," Lucy said quietly. "There's no sign of the crash."

"It's been three months. Nature heals quickly." Mason studied the tight curve. "It's the ideal place to try to force a vehicle off this road."

"The killer must have known that," Lucy ventured.

"It could have been a murder of opportunity, but I'm with you. It's more likely that it was the work of someone familiar with the road. Whoever did this could not have picked a more dangerous curve."

"I suppose that doesn't exclude the pot farmers."

"No, but given what happened to Sara's house last night, I'm leaning toward your theory."

Mason went silent. She looked at him and saw that his attention was on the scene.

"What are you thinking?" she asked.

"I'm thinking that if I had gone to the trouble of setting up a car crash with the aim of killing two people, I would follow up."

"I don't understand."

"I'd make sure the plan had worked."

"Oh." A whisper of shock went through her. "Yes. I see what you mean. Oh, my God, do you think that the killer went down there with the idea of making sure they were dead?"

"There hasn't been much rain this summer. Dry conditions are good for preserving evidence. I'm going to take a look."

He got a pair of gloves and a small, lightweight backpack out of the trunk of the car. He walked to the edge of the road. After a couple of minutes' contemplation, he started down the hillside at a steep angle, using the manzanita bushes and scrub for handholds.

When he reached the bottom, he walked slowly around the area, pausing now and again to take a closer look at something she could not see from her position on the road.

At one point he picked up what looked like a fist-sized rock and examined it closely. She watched him drop it into the pack. He put his arms through the pack straps and made his way back up the hillside.

"What is it?" she asked. But she had a horrible feeling that she knew what he had found.

He removed the pack and took out the rock. There was a dark, long-dried stain on the stone. She stared at it, dread seeping through her.

"Blood?" she whispered.

"Maybe. I think so, yes."

"Dear heaven. You were right. The killer went down there to make sure."

They got back into the car.

"It's not proof of murder," Mason warned. "There's always a lot of blood at the scene of a bad crash."

"One or both of them was still alive." She clenched her hands together in her lap. "The bastard used that rock to crush their skulls and finish the job. You think that's what happened, don't you?"

He hesitated. "I think it's a very likely possibility."

226

"But why wouldn't the authorities have noticed the injuries?"

"There's always a lot of trauma at a crash site," Mason said gently. "And no one had any reason to believe that it was a case of murder. You don't find evidence unless you go looking for it."

Neither of them spoke for a while.

CHAPTER
TWENTY-SEVEN

A few miles later they crested the last hill and started down toward the coast highway. The sweeping view of the dazzling Pacific Ocean exploded into sight. The mostly empty shoreline stretched for miles, raw and wild.

They stopped in a tiny, weathered community that huddled on a small bay and found a restaurant on the wharf. They ate rich, creamy clam chowder served with generous portions of sourdough bread. They did not talk a lot, but Lucy did not find the silence uncomfortable. It was as if viewing the sight of the crash had cast a somber spell on both of them.

When the check came, she automatically reached for it. Mason deftly swiped it off the little plate and handed it back to the waiter along with his credit card. Lucy waited until they were alone.

"Thank you," she said, somewhat stiffly. "But that wasn't necessary. We're here because of the investigation. I should be picking up expenses."

Amusement gleamed in his eyes. "Do you always do that when you're on a date?"

She hesitated. "We're not on a real date. But to answer your question, yes, I always pay my own way."

He narrowed his eyes a little. "You do that to make certain that the guy knows that the balance of power is equal in the relationship."

She tensed. "Most men appreciate it."

"Probably because they don't understand what's really going on."

She raised her brows "Do you always psychoanalyze your dates?"

"No." He smiled. "Just the interesting ones."

She blushed. "I'll take that as a compliment."

"It was meant as one. Did you handle money that way with your fiancé?"

"Absolutely. We split all expenses."

"Rent? Utilities?"

She frowned. "We didn't live together, so rent and utilities weren't a problem. Paying my own way for everything else made things a lot simpler when we split up. There was no arguing over money."

"Sounds like you were planning to go into the marriage with one foot already out the door. Wait, I take that back. You didn't even have a foot in the door, because you weren't sharing living quarters."

"Let's just say I was ready to adjust to changing circumstances."

Mason nodded once. "Right. You had one foot out the door."

She was starting to get annoyed. "You're not in any position to talk. How long did your marriage last?"

"About five minutes. I told you, I'm a lousy communicator."

"Is that the reason you didn't have kids?"

"No." He smiled briefly, but there wasn't much humor involved. "That particular kind of communication I understand. I just wasn't good at the verbal kind."

Intuition told Lucy to hold her tongue.

There was a beat of silence, and then Mason exhaled slowly.

"Irene said she wanted to wait to have children until we were both making more money. She found someone else who was already on the fast track financially. That was before Fletcher Consulting became successful."

The waiter returned. Mason signed the slip, tucked his credit card back into his wallet and got to his feet. Lucy rose and collected her windbreaker. She hesitated.

"Thank you," she finally said. She was going for simple and gracious, but she knew that it didn't come out that way.

Mason looked amused. "Now who's having trouble communicating?"

Face burning, she headed for the door. "You know, this has actually been a very nice getaway in spite of the stop at Rainshadow Farm. Back in Summer River I feel like I'm always on guard, waiting for another Colfax to spring out of the bushes."

"Things have definitely been lively since you arrived in town," Mason agreed. "We've got time. Let's take a walk on the beach before we drive back."

"Sounds like a plan."

Mason drove a short distance out of the small community and found a lay-by on the bluffs above a rocky beach. He parked the car, and they made their

230

way down to the water, pebbles skittering beneath their shoes. The snapping breeze off the ocean whipped Lucy's hair and sent a rush of pure, unadulterated delight through her. It was good to be here, alone on a beach, with Mason.

She glanced at him, smiling to herself at the sight of his tousled hair. He looked delicious in his black windbreaker, jeans and sunglasses. She was no longer sixteen, but the hormones she thought had matured and perhaps gone a little stale in the past thirteen years were playing havoc with her senses and emotions.

Stop staring, woman. You've got him all to yourself for a while. Do what Aunt Sara would tell you to do — be in the moment.

That bit of enlightenment advice was all well and good, except that she wanted the moment to go on indefinitely. Not a realistic option.

She refocused her attention on the rough beach and stuffed her hands into the pockets of her own windbreaker to restrain herself from doing something rash like, say, grab Mason and kiss him senseless. Assuming she *could* kiss him senseless. Her commitment issues had some disappointing side effects when it came to sex. But given the hot embrace at the river's edge the other night, she had cause for hope.

"What are you thinking?" Mason asked.

Caught off guard, she groped for words and finally came up with the question that had been on her mind since she had walked into Fletcher Hardware and found Mason behind the counter.

"Why did you return to Summer River?" she asked.

She didn't expect a straightforward answer, so she was more than a little stunned when she got one.

"I screwed up," he said. "Someone died."

It took her a moment to process the information. Shaken, she came to a halt and turned to stare at him. He stopped, too, and looked at her. They were both wearing sunglasses, so she could not read his eyes, but she could see the grim line of his jaw.

Shadows, she thought. Sara said that everyone carried a few around.

"What happened?" she asked.

Again, she did not expect an answer. But she got one.

"We were consulting for a small-town police department. Twenty years ago there were three murders, all within a hundred-mile radius of the community. The victims were hitchhikers who had been picked up by the killer. They were homeless men."

"Victims who had no family to push for a thorough investigation."

"The crimes were clearly the work of one person, but the victims appeared to have been chosen at random. The killings stopped within a few months, but the killer was never found. The cases went cold. The locals didn't have the money or manpower to pursue the investigations. But a few months ago they called us in when a new murder occurred."

"A new crime that looked like part of the old pattern?"

"Right. The current chief of police had started out on the force twenty years earlier as a rookie cop. He recognized the pattern and asked for our help. We ran the program, but the results were too vague to be useful. All we got from Alice was the standard unhelpful profile of a serial killer. It described over half the adult males in the community."

"Alice usually gets closer than that?"

"Much closer. Aaron's program is good. But like any computer program, Alice depends on the data that is fed into it. The basic gi-go rule has never changed."

"*Garbage in, garbage out.* I'm very familiar with that particular rule in an investigation," Lucy said. "I come up against it frequently in my work."

"I looked over the files that had been sent to us and decided there was something wrong with the data. So I visited the scenes of the crimes myself, to see if I could get a feel for what was off."

"You said it helped to go into the field sometimes."

"It took me a while, but it finally hit me. The killer had to know how the program worked."

"Good grief, the new murderer was someone who worked for you?"

Mason's mouth twisted. "He was an employee who had left a year earlier to establish his own investigation business. Gilbert Porter, one of our first hires. He knew some of the trapdoors, and he also knew some of the key algorithms Alice uses to analyze data."

"So he was able to manipulate the results by leaving false clues at the scenes of the crimes."

Mason angled his head slightly. "You know, you really are good at this kind of stuff."

"I thought I'd made it clear, I am also in the investigation business."

"I'm starting to get that."

"About time," Lucy said. "Go on with your story."

"As you said, Porter deliberately staged the crimes in ways he knew would throw off the results. When I finally realized what was going on, I was fairly certain I knew who we were looking for, but Aaron ran the program again to double-check. He looked for a killer with an insider's knowledge and a strong desire for revenge against Fletcher Consulting. Gilbert Porter's name was at the top of a very short list."

"Why did he want revenge?"

"Because I fired him," Mason said. "I caught him embezzling from the company using some sophisticated code. I knew he was pissed at the time, but I thought that if he came after anyone, it would be me. Actually, I didn't think he would do anything violent. Figured if he tried to take revenge the assault would come in the form of a cyber attack on Alice. But I was wrong. He killed two men before I caught up with him."

Lucy used one hand to hold her flying hair back from her face. "You did your job. You solved the crime."

"Too late for two homeless hitchhikers. Hell, Fletcher Consulting — the company that's dedicated to hunting human predators — created a killer."

"*Bullshit.*"

Mason looked bemused by her sudden fierceness.

"You didn't make him kill anyone. He was a monster, and he managed to hide in plain sight for a time because he was perfectly camouflaged. But you did identify him, and you caught him. If you had not done that, he would have continued to kill. You saved all of his future victims. In addition, you discovered a blind spot in your program that will help you catch more killers. That's what matters. You did your job. What happened? Is Porter in jail?"

"No, I set him up," Mason said evenly.

She caught her breath. "I don't understand."

"I drew him into a trap. I knew if he felt cornered he would try to shoot his way out, and he did. I killed him."

Understanding flashed through her. "You knew that if he went to trial, he might walk."

Mason looked out at the restless ocean for a long moment before he answered.

"I didn't have enough evidence to get him convicted," he said. "Porter was very good at concealing his handiwork."

"That's what you're having a hard time dealing with, isn't? The fact that you set a trap and he fell right into it."

"Maybe. It was the first and only time that I've killed a man. Hell, most cops go through their entire careers without ever firing a gun except on the practice range. And I wasn't even a cop at the time — I was an investigative consultant who carried a weapon. I don't regret Porter's death, but I knew I had another option that night. I could have taken him alive and hoped that the system would find him guilty. But I didn't."

"Instead, you think you committed the sin of acting as judge, jury and executioner. But that's not how it went down."

"It is how it went down. Exactly how it went down. I knew Porter cold by then. I'd studied him. I knew what he would do if he was cornered."

"You trapped a killer who tried to shoot his way out of the trap. The fact that you were pretty sure he would attempt to murder you doesn't make you responsible for his final decision. Gilbert Porter challenged you to a duel to the death, and he lost."

Mason did not speak.

"What about the old cases?" she asked after a while.

Mason's face tightened as if he had to make an effort to pull his thoughts together. "We closed all three. The reason the killings had stopped was because the first killer was doing time for another murder in another state. He'll do life now."

"You're a decent man, born to protect others," she said. "You know you're supposed to come down on the side of law and order. That night you took a different path, a more ancient path. That's a heavy burden for a good man, an honorable man, to carry. But you will find a way because there are other people to save, other bad guys to catch. That's your mission, and you will fulfill it because if you don't, people will die and the bad guys will win."

Mason just stood there, looking at her, for a very long time.

"I don't want to go back to Summer River today," he said finally. "I want to spend the night with you, here, where no one knows us and we can be alone together."

She caught her breath. But she had known all day that this was coming. It was why she had tucked those few personal items into her tote. Mason had known it, too. It was why he had quietly stashed an overnight kit in the back of the car. Now the moment of decision was upon them, and he was leaving it up to her.

She took a deep breath.

Be in the moment.

"Yes," she said. "I would like very much to spend the night with you."

He took her hand, closing his fingers tightly around hers. They continued walking along the beach in silence.

CHAPTER
TWENTY-EIGHT

He was exhilarated, thrilled, and walking an invisible high wire without a net. Hot anticipation stirred his blood. Lucy had said yes.

It was only three o'clock. The night was still a long way off. Getting through the rest of the afternoon and evening without making a fool of himself was going to take a lot of willpower. But he would not ruin things by hauling Lucy off to the nearest no-tell motel. He wanted the day and the night to be memorable, to be important to her. Definitely something more than a damned matchmaking-agency date.

He did not let go of her hand until they'd finished the long walk on the beach and started up the path to the car. Part of him did not want to release her, even then. He did not just want her, he needed her. She was a bright ray of sunlight cutting through the cold, gray fog that had enshrouded him for the past couple of months.

That was crazy talk, and he knew it. Okay, he had some issues because of what had happened two months ago, but he wasn't *that* messed up. His problems were mere ripples on the surface of a pond compared to the dark waves that Deke had survived in his years as a warrior.

But he knew now that the lightning bolt that had struck him the other day when Lucy walked into the hardware store had not been a fluke. The universe was, indeed, trying to tell him something. One look at her and the fog had begun to clear. He was once again aware of the warmth of the sunlight. He felt reenergized.

That first awakening was nothing compared to what he was experiencing now.

Lucy was going to spend the night with him. Tonight would be a very important night, possibly the most important night of his life. He would not screw it up.

When they got back into the car he did a quick check on his phone, searching for the address of the hotel he had found online that morning. Before leaving town, he had spent an hour going through the short list of establishments in the vicinity of the small coastal community. He had wanted a nice place, a classy, upscale place. Just in case.

At the time he'd had no real reason to hope that Lucy would agree to spend the night with him, but if she did say yes, he wanted to be prepared. He was not going to take her to some cheap, grungy dive.

He had found a lodge that looked like it met his requirements. The price was definitely right — several hundred bucks a night — but he did not mention that little fact to Lucy. The last thing he wanted was another argument about splitting the bill.

He drove the short distance to the Ocean View Lodge and was relieved to see that outwardly, at least, it lived up to its advertising. The handsome, rustic building was perched on the hillside and commanded romantic views of the coastline. He parked the car at the entrance.

"I'll be right back," he told Lucy.

"I'll come with you to register," she said. She started to reach over the seat for her tote.

"No," he said. "I'll take care of this."

She blinked and looked uncertain for a moment. Maybe his tone of voice had been a little too firm. Maybe he'd screwed up already.

Her damned cell phone chose that moment to give a mocking chirp. Lucy took it out and glanced at the screen.

He closed the car door very firmly and went into the lobby.

He booked the best room the desk clerk could offer and went back outside. He moved the car to the small parking lot. There was a potentially awkward moment when he took his overnight kit out of the rear of the car, but Lucy pretended not to see it. At least there were no sarcastic comments about him having come prepared to spend the night.

When she reached into the backseat for her huge purse, he could tell that it weighed a ton. It seemed to him that women always carried an incredible amount of stuff in their bags and purses, but this one appeared unduly heavy. He dared to hope that maybe Lucy, too, had come prepped for a stolen night away from

240

Summer River. The possibility put a definite spring in his step.

To his relief, the room looked good. The large bathroom sparkled with polished tiles and glass. The towels were soft and thick. The bed was artistically made. When he looked at Lucy's face, he thought she looked pleased.

"This is lovely," she said.

Yes. She liked the room. He was already light-years ahead of the damned agency dates.

Satisfied, he dropped his kit on top of the chest of drawers. Lucy set her tote on the table. She took a much smaller bag out of the big bag and slung it over her shoulder. That answered one question, he thought. She didn't actually haul the massive tote with her everywhere.

They went back downstairs and walked the short distance into the village. Lucy took obvious delight in the handful of small shops on the wharf, although, in his opinion, the array of seashell and driftwood souvenirs did not look like her kind of art. He did not pretend to be a connoisseur, but he thought the watercolors in the local gallery looked uninspired as well. Nevertheless, he dutifully accompanied Lucy around the wharf shops. He wanted her to enjoy the day.

When she paused to look in the window of yet another little shop, he sneaked a glance at his watch, wondering how early he could suggest drinks and dinner.

"Are you starting to feel like you're in the middle of one of those television commercials for erectile-dysfunction medication?" Lucy asked. Her eyes glinted with laughter.

Startled, he felt himself turning red. He could not recall the last time he had blushed. "What?"

"You know, those ads that feature happy couples dashing through the rain, dancing in the kitchen, buying flowers at a roadside stand and driving through the countryside in a convertible with the top down. There's always a pounding waterfall or suggestively surging surf thundering in the background."

"Oh, those ads," he said. He smiled slowly. "I don't think I'll be needing any of the meds they're peddling."

It was her turn to blush. She cleared her throat. "Well, just in case, we do happen to have a lot of surging surf in the vicinity." She gestured in the general direction of the ocean.

He laughed. A few strollers on the sidewalk turned to look at him, smiling a little.

He kissed her lightly, getting a taste and letting her feel some of the heat that was firing his blood and his imagination. Then he followed her into the shop.

It was a good day, the best he'd had in a long time, maybe in forever — even if he did have to browse through souvenir shops and look at boring watercolors. Lucy had said yes.

CHAPTER
TWENTY-NINE

"What are we going to do?" Ashley said. "You're the one who told me that the merger will fall apart if we don't get control of those shares."

"Calm down," Cecil said. "I'll take care of everything. That's my job." He smiled. "It's why Colfax is paying me the big bucks and why he gave me the corner office, remember?"

He was not behind his desk in the executive suite of Colfax Inc. at the moment. Instead, he was standing at the window of a dilapidated single-story house deep in the woods. The faded sign in the front yard read *For Sale, Kelly Realty*.

The house had been on the market for more than six months. He had determined that much after a quick online search of the real estate listings in the area around Summer River. He could see why it hadn't sold. It offered none of the amenities that people moving to wine country demanded. The house was a tear-down, which would not have mattered, had the property not broken the cardinal rule of real estate: *Location, location, location*. The location was lousy — a remote section of the county that was accessed by a badly neglected side road. The trees grew close around the place, shrouding it in perpetual gloom. There was no view, and the lot was small. There was not enough property for a vineyard.

All in all, it fit his requirements perfectly, Cecil thought. It made an ideal location for screwing the client's wife. The only item of furniture left in the place was an ancient brass bed.

"The shares were not supposed to end up in Lucy Sheridan's hands." Ashley paced back and forth across the bare living room. "Warner told me that the last he knew, Mary planned to leave the shares to Quinn. At the time he was infuriated that she wasn't going to leave them to him, but he assumed that he could control Quinn's vote if it ever proved necessary to do so."

Warner was wrong this time, Cecil thought. He turned away from the perpetual twilight of the woods.

"Obviously, at some point Mary changed her will," he said patiently.

Ashley came to a halt. "So what are you going to do about it? Warner is sure to offer Lucy more for those shares than we can afford to give her. She'd be a fool not to sell to him."

"Everyone has a price," Cecil said, "but that price isn't always a matter of dollars and cents."

"What do you mean?"

"If Lucy Sheridan was simply after the highest price she could get, she would have made that clear up front. Instead, she's holding out for something else."

Ashley spread her hands. "What else is there?"

"I'm not one hundred percent positive, but I think she may want answers."

"Answers to what?"

"I think she's got some questions about her aunt's death."

"That's ridiculous. Sara Sheridan and Mary Colfax died in a car accident. End of story."

"It might have been easier for Lucy to believe that if she hadn't discovered Brinker's body in her aunt's fireplace."

Ashley turned her back to him, wrapped her arms beneath her breasts and stared out into the trees.

"According to the media, Sara Sheridan murdered Brinker thirteen years ago," she said. "What can his death possibly have to do with those shares?"

"I don't know." Cecil moved to stand behind her. He put his hands on her shoulders and kissed the side of her throat. "Stop worrying. I'll figure out what is going on, and then I'll deal with it."

"You'd better deal with it quickly. The clock is ticking now."

"What do you mean?"

"Warner is getting impatient. I've stalled as long as I can. We've been married for over eight months. According to the terms of that damn prenup, I won't get a dime out of him if I'm not pregnant within a year of the wedding."

"I know."

"I'm not about to have his baby, so my only hope of getting my money is that merger. If Warner finds out that I'm using protection, he'll file for divorce immediately."

"Just give me a little more time."

"Tell me you have a plan to deal with Lucy Sheridan."

"I have a plan."

"Don't lie to me." Ashley spun around. "It would be bad enough if Warner dumped me because he believed that I couldn't get pregnant. If he found out that I have no intention of trying to give him a spare heir — that I'm just hanging on because of the merger — I'm not sure what he might do. He's got a temper."

Cecil frowned. "Do you think he might become violent?"

"If he thinks I've betrayed him, yes," Ashley said. She shivered. "Yes, I think he might become violent."

Cecil tipped up her chin. "Don't worry. I'm in this for the money, just like you and Quinn and Jillian. If the merger doesn't happen, I don't get my payday, either. Trust me, I've got all of our best interests at heart."

"I know." She sighed. "It's just that sometimes I get scared."

"I'll take care of you."

Ashley gave him a misty smile. "I know."

He drew her down the hall and into the bedroom. It was such a rush to screw the client's wife.

CHAPTER
THIRTY

Lucy was braced for Mason to try to hurry her through dinner, but much to her amazement, he did no such thing. It was as if they were lovers who had been together long enough to be comfortable with what lay ahead, she decided. No rush. No pressure. But she had seen the masculine anticipation in his eyes all afternoon and sensed the heat of a low-burning fire inside him. Every time he touched her she was aware that he wanted her.

That afternoon, while he was inside the lodge, she had silenced the notification chirps on her phone. It was her way of making a commitment, she thought. Not a long-term commitment, just a commitment to the night. But it was a commitment of sorts.

She knew that he was impatient, marking time until they went back to the lodge. But now, after a slow meal of crab cakes and roasted sweet-potato fries, he seemed willing to linger indefinitely over coffee and the ice cream they had ordered for dessert.

It was as if now that he knew the end of the sensual game was in sight he was content to let her take her time before he took her to bed.

She wondered if he knew that he was not the only one balanced on the precarious cliff above the dark waters of desire. She was thrilled, but at the same time more nervous than she had expected. The truth was that, deep down, she was a little scared. She was not sure how to deal with the complex mix of emotions that he had stirred up inside her.

Feminine intuition was warning her that whatever happened between them tonight would change everything. He had been right when he'd remarked that she'd had one foot out the door throughout her engagement. She'd had one foot out the door in each of the handful of other serious relationships she'd been involved in as well.

But she had the feeling that tonight she was not taking a tentative step into a strange room to see if she wanted to stay or not. An entirely different metaphor was required. Tonight she would be jumping into an unknown sea without a life preserver.

The thought made her smile. Maybe there was something to all that thundering-water imagery in those erectile-dysfunction commercials. She could swim, but that did not mean she would escape unscathed when things ended. And in her experience, things always ended. Furthermore, they tended to do so sooner rather than later.

But for now she was determined to live in the moment. Sitting across from Mason at the candlelit table, she could see that he had made a similar decision. They were two adults going into the night with their eyes wide open. Tomorrow would take care of itself.

248

When the check arrived, she did not offer to bring out her credit card. Mason was trying to give the night to her as a gift. She had to respect that. Someday, if they stayed together long enough, she would give him something special, too.

He finally put his empty cup down on the saucer and looked at her.

"Ready to go?" he asked.

An unfamiliar sense of certainty settled into her. She wanted this night; she wanted it with all her heart.

"Yes," she said.

They walked back along the wharf to the lodge and through the lobby. Lucy's certainty did not waver, but she could not deny the tension building inside her. She had to be prepared to give the best performance of her usually insipid love life. In her admittedly limited experience, most men had no difficulty believing in a well-acted orgasm, but she had a feeling Mason might be able to detect a fake unless it was a very good replica.

He opened the door and waited for her to move past him into the darkness. She took one step inside the room and stopped. *Crap.* Maybe this was a really huge mistake.

"One foot out the door already?" Mason asked quietly. "Because if that's the case, I'd rather you left now. I can get another room for you tonight."

"No." She spun around. "No, I don't want to leave."

He closed his eyes briefly. When he opened them, she saw the darkly glittering hunger in him.

"Good," he said. His voice was rough and raw. "That's good to know. Because for a moment there you scared the hell out of me. I thought you were going to make a run for it."

"No," she whispered. "I'm not running anywhere."

He moved into the room, reached for her with one hand and used his other hand to close the door. She heard the click of the lock sliding home.

The room was steeped in shadows. The only illumination was the small nightlight that burned in the bathroom and a slender wedge of moonlight that slipped in at the edges of the curtains.

Reflexively, she tried to find the light switch on the wall, but she could not move because both of Mason's arms were around her, trapping her.

His mouth came down on hers with all the urgency, all the pent-up anticipation that she had sensed in him that afternoon.

Be in the moment.

She could do this. In any event, she did not have time to dwell on the future, because Mason was already undressing her. She struggled with the buttons of his shirt, inhaling his scent as she worked. He smelled good, indescribably sexy and thrillingly male. A strange, lightheaded euphoria infused her senses.

He tugged her sweater off over her head and unfastened the clasps of her bra.

His palms closed gently over her breasts. He drew the pads of his thumbs across her nipples. She was so sensitive now that the caress surprised a small, startled squeak out of her. She shuddered.

He stilled as if he had been shot.

"I hurt you," he said.

250

"No, no, really, you didn't."

She went back to work on his shirt.

He touched her breasts again, slowly, carefully. She sighed and leaned into him. He kissed the curve of her throat.

"You smell so good," he said.

His hands moved from her breasts down to her waist. He started to unfasten her jeans.

That was all it took to dampen her panties. She couldn't believe it. They hadn't even made it as far as the bed, but she was already soaking wet. It would have been embarrassing if she hadn't been too hot to worry about it. Later, maybe.

She fought through the last of the buttons on his shirt. He shrugged out of it and then yanked off the black T-shirt. With a soft sigh of delight, she flattened her palms on his bare chest. He sucked in his breath. She felt the hard, contoured muscles beneath his warm skin grow even more taut.

He got the front of her jeans open and shoved them down over her hips. She stepped out of her shoes and then out of her pants, nearly losing her balance in the process. Mason wrapped one arm around her waist to steady her and moved his free hand between her legs. He cupped her, feeling her through the silky fabric of her panties.

"You're ready for me."

Masculine satisfaction and an edgy, reckless desire smoldered in the words. He slipped his hand inside her panties. She was flooding now.

251

She had never responded like this. She wanted to get closer, wanted to sink into him. Maybe the intense desire was the result of having gone for months without a serious relationship. But that didn't explain things, either. She had never been this worked up with any other man.

"What are you doing to me?" she whispered, a little dazed now.

"I want to know what works for you." He found the swollen little nub at the top of her sex. "Because whatever works for you works for me."

She thought about telling him that the only thing that really worked for her was a vibrator and she had not brought one with her. The last thing she had expected when she set out for Summer River was a torrid one-night stand.

Determined to give as good as she got — which was looking to be very good indeed — she moved a hand down to the front of his jeans. He was steel-hard and big. Very big. She rested her forehead on his broad shoulder and touched him through the fabric of the jeans, feeling the size and shape and heaviness of his arousal. He gave a low, harsh groan.

"Oh, my," she said against his skin.

She squeezed gently.

"Probably not a good idea," he said. His voice was hoarse and rough.

"Okay, I've got a better one," she whispered.

She unfastened his belt with shaking fingers and lowered the zipper of his jeans. Reaching inside his briefs, she wrapped her fingers around him slowly, measuring and wondering, more than a little awed.

"Keep that up and I'll come in your hand," he said into her ear. "And while that would be nice, I'd much rather be inside you, *deep* inside you."

She released him and moved her palms up the front of his chest. "That sounds like an interesting scenario."

He gave a husky laugh, wrapped both hands around her waist and lifted her off her feet. He carried her the short distance to the bed and set her back down on her feet.

He hauled aside the quilt and top sheet, picked her up again and settled her lightly in the center of the bed. She realized she was still wearing not only her very damp panties but also her socks. Concluding that the socks did not add much to the sensual atmosphere, she hurriedly stripped them off and tossed them on the floor.

By the time she finished with that small project, Mason was out of his own clothes. He crossed the room to the chest of drawers. She heard him unzip his overnight kit. When he returned to the bed, she caught a glimpse of a small foil packet.

He sheathed himself and came down onto the bed beside her. He gathered her close and kissed her until she forgot about the lack of a vibrator. His erection pressed firmly against her thigh. She knew that he was ready. She reached down, took him in her hand and tried to guide him to the hot, wet place between her legs.

"Not yet," he said.

He caught her wrists in one hand and anchored them above her head. Then he leaned over her, gently forcing her onto her back. He took one of her nipples into his mouth. He tugged just enough to make her catch her breath.

At the same time he moved his hand back down to the scorching hot place between her legs and stroked slowly. Her hips began to move in response. He eased two fingers inside her and used his thumb on her clitoris.

"Show me how powerful you are," he said.

"What?"

"I want to see how strong you are down there. Squeeze my fingers as hard as you can."

Bewildered, she instinctively did as instructed, clenching him with every ounce of strength she could summon from her lower body.

"Tighter."

A rising tide of urgency flashed through her. She gasped, startled by the reaction of her own body. *Okay, that works.*

Evidently, it worked for Mason as well. He made a husky sound that was halfway between a growl and a groan, and slowly withdrew his fingers.

She clenched herself ever tighter in a desperate effort to keep him inside. The tension built deep within her. He eased his fingers back into her and pressed upward. She started to pant. A strange desperation seized her. She drew herself tighter, attempting to imprison him.

"You are going to drive me crazy," he said.

The tension was unbearable. She could not stand it. She strained harder to hold on to him. She knew she was on the brink, and there was no vibrator involved.

The release came out of nowhere, sweeping through her in a series of convulsive little waves. She wanted to laugh or cry or scream, but she could not catch her breath. The pleasure made her giddy and reckless and euphoric.

She was savoring the delight, glorying in the remarkable powers of her own body, when Mason changed position. He released her wrists and moved between her legs.

He thrust into her, hard and deep. She had never felt so full, so tight and so incredibly sensitive. Dazzled, all she could do was grab him and hang on for dear life. Beneath her clutching fingers, his back was damp with sweat.

He drove into her again and again. Another series of waves crashed through her. A moment later he went rigid, back arched, and then his own climax slammed through him, pounding into her. He gave an exultant, half-choked shout.

They hung there together as if suspended over a vast darkness.

And then Mason collapsed, sprawling heavily on top of her.

For a few minutes she waited for him to move, but he showed no signs of doing so, at least not in the immediate future. She prodded him a little.

"Mason?"

"Mmm."

"Mason, wake up. You're very heavy."

"Sorry."

He eased himself out of her and flopped onto his back. He lay still.

She propped herself up on her elbow and looked down at him. In the shadows she could not make out his expression, but she was sure his eyes were closed. She'd experienced sex often enough to know that men were usually relaxed, even sleepy, afterward, but Mason's version of the postcoital glow seemed a little extreme.

"Are you okay?" she asked.

"Define *okay*," he mumbled.

She switched on the bedside lamp. Mason shielded his eyes with his arm.

"Are you always this bouncy after sex?" he asked.

She smiled, thinking about it. "Now that you mention it, I do feel rather energized."

"Energized?"

"Usually I just want to go home and take a shower."

He raised his arm and looked at her with half-closed eyes. "You're a real romantic, aren't you?"

"Sorry. I don't usually —" *Too much information, woman.*

But it was too late. Mason had already figured it out.

"You don't usually spend the night?" he said.

"No. It just feels too —" She broke off, again, sensing that she was digging the hole deeper and deeper.

"Too intimate?" Mason finished for her.

256

"Maybe. Sleeping with someone, sharing a bathroom, having breakfast together. It's just too weird."

"Weird," he repeated neutrally.

She sat up, holding the sheet to her chin to cover herself. "I'm not doing a very good job of explaining this. Probably be best if I just stopped talking."

His mouth curved in a wicked smile. "Ah, but can you stop talking? That is the question."

She picked up the nearest pillow and tossed it at his head. He warded it off with one hand, got to his feet and disappeared into the bathroom.

"If it matters," he said, "I think I know what you mean."

"About what?"

The toilet flushed. Water ran in the sink. Mason reappeared in the doorway.

"About the weirdness factor," he said. "Since my marriage ended, I've developed a thing about spending the night, too. You're right. Feels weird."

Her heart sank. All of the bouncy energy that had animated her a moment earlier evaporated. Was Mason hinting that he wanted to leave now that they had had sex?

"Do you want to drive back to Summer River tonight?" she asked.

"Hell, no. I'm not having a problem with the weird factor tonight." He watched her steadily. "What about you?"

She smiled, relief washing through her.

"I'm not having a problem with the weird factor, either," she said. "That's what I was trying to explain."

He smiled slowly. "That makes it easy, then. We stay until morning."

He went to the dresser and took out a couple more foil packets. When he returned to the bed, she saw that he was already half aroused. He tossed the packets onto the nightstand, where they would be conveniently at hand. Then he turned out the light, climbed back into bed and pulled her down beside him. She resisted.

"What now?" he asked.

"There's something else I want to tell you," she said quickly. "Tonight was different for me."

He touched her cheek. "Me, too."

"I mean, very different."

"Yeah? How so?"

The darkness made her feel bolder and seriously more reckless. She put her hand on his thigh, stroking him with her palm. "You didn't get the opportunity to applaud my acting talents."

He kissed her shoulder. "You mean I didn't give you a chance to impress me with an Academy Award-winning fake orgasm?"

She sat up so quickly she almost clipped him on the chin. "You knew?"

"After all that chatter about your commitment issues, I figured that's probably what you had in mind. I thought it would be good to get the issue out of the way before you screwed things up by going onstage at the wrong time."

For a few seconds, she was speechless.

"Why, you arrogant —"

That was as far as she got, because she was suddenly giggling too hard to continue the harangue. She grabbed the pillow and began to pummel him with it. He was laughing, too.

He ripped the pillow out of her hand and pulled her down across his chest. He wrapped one hand around the back of her head and brought her mouth closer to his.

"Tonight is different," he said.

"Yes," she said.

He kissed her. She went with him once again into the night.

CHAPTER
THIRTY-ONE

Mason savored his second cup of coffee, along with the morning coastal fog, the last bite of a waffle doused in butter and syrup and the sight of Lucy sitting on the other side of the breakfast table. He could get used to mornings like this one.

Every time he looked at Lucy, which was pretty much all the time, hot memories of the night stirred his blood. It felt good to be here with her in the small café, looking forward to another day together. More than anything else at the moment, he wanted to be able to look forward to another night together. But he knew that wasn't going to be possible, at least not immediately. The situation in Summer River had to be cleaned up before he and Lucy could figure out their relationship.

Her phone rang just as he was about to polish off the waffle. At least it wasn't another one of the damned chirps that indicated a message from the matchmaking agency. But Lucy frowned when she glanced at the screen, and he knew the prospect of a really good day had just gone south.

"Yes, this is Lucy Sheridan . . . No, I'm out of town . . . Yes, I plan to return to Summer River today . . . I see . . . Good heavens, are they sure? . . . I understand . . . Yes, of course, but I'm afraid I have absolutely no idea what is going on." She glanced at her watch. "We should be there by noon . . . Yes, Mr. Fletcher is with me . . . Where? We're over on the coast . . . Yes, all night . . . One o'clock today. Fine. We'll both come down to the station."

She ended the call and looked at Mason. "That was Chief Whitaker. The fire investigators went to Sara's house this morning. They found a body in the ashes."

"Damn." Mason felt the old familiar chill. The past had come back to haunt someone in Summer River. That was the way it always was with cold cases. They never really went away. They shadowed the living until they were closed. Methodically, he finished the bite of waffle and put down his fork. "Do they have an ID?"

"No." Lucy hesitated, her eyes darkening with anxiety. "The body was badly burned, but there are some indications that it's Nolan Kelly. Chief Whitaker says no one has seen him since he left his office late yesterday afternoon. They found his car parked in the woods about a quarter of a mile away."

"Huh."

"It's horrible to think about. I was talking to him there in my kitchen yesterday morning, and now he's dead. What a ghastly way to die."

"Assuming he was killed by the fire."

She blinked. "What are you thinking?"

"I don't know yet. Just asking questions. Do the investigators believe that Kelly set the fire and got caught in the blaze?"

"Whitaker didn't say. There's going to be an autopsy."

"It may not tell them much if the body was badly burned."

"What on earth was he doing in my house in the middle of the night?"

"No way to know yet, but I can think of one possible theory."

Mason raised his hand to signal for the check. "Kelly may have been the intruder who searched the house the previous night. He didn't find what he was looking for, so he went back a second time to try to destroy any evidence that might have been hidden inside."

"Evidence that would have proven that he was the photographer who helped Brinker?"

"Maybe. But there are other possibilities."

"Such as?"

The waiter approached with the check. Mason reached for his wallet. "Kelly was in sales his whole life. He started out dealing pot in high school. According to the rumors, Brinker made some kind of hallucinogen available to his inner circle. And if he was the Scorecard Rapist, we know he used drugs to subdue his victims."

"Do you think Nolan was supplying Brinker with the drugs?"

"Brinker was getting those pricey designer phar-maceuticals from someone. He was probably too smart to make the deals himself, but it wouldn't surprise me if he convinced Kelly to get the drugs for him, assuming Kelly had the connections."

A visible shiver went through Lucy. "Kelly was only eighteen at the time, just a couple years older than me."

"Brinker was in the business of attracting and manipulating young people." Mason put some money down on the table. "When you think about it, he was running a kind of cult, preaching a religion that featured sex, drugs and rock music. All the simple pleasures of youth."

CHAPTER
THIRTY-TWO

Leonard Whitaker was in his early sixties. He had left a mid-sized police department in Southern California to take over the Summer River department five years earlier, and he made no secret of the fact that he was looking forward to retirement in another year. He wanted what he called the Sheridan situation cleaned up before he stepped down.

These days, everyone was concerned about the legacy thing, Lucy thought.

Whitaker asked a lot of questions, which she dutifully answered while Mason stood behind her, one shoulder propped against the wall, arms folded. He did not interfere in the questioning, but he made his presence felt. Like a bodyguard, she thought.

She did her best to answer Whitaker's questions, but most of her responses were variations on *I don't know.*

At the end of the interview, Whitaker lounged back in his chair and studied Lucy over the rims of his reading glasses. "One more time, Miss Sheridan. Are you absolutely certain you have no idea why Kelly wanted to torch your house?"

"I told you, all I can give you are speculations," she said quietly. "I suppose it's possible that he thought

264

there was something in the house that connected him to Brinker and the past, but I have no proof."

"We're looking into that angle," Whitaker said. "What about the house itself? You say he was determined to get the listing."

"Yes," she said. "He was very insistent. He said he had a client in Silicon Valley who wanted to open a winery and that the property was ideal."

"But you were stalling. Were you planning to try to do the deal yourself and cut him out? The agent's commission on that property would be substantial."

She drummed her fingers on the arm of the chair. "I am dealing with some other estate issues at the moment."

Whitaker elevated his brows. "The other issues being those shares of Colfax Inc. that you inherited?"

"I see you've heard about them," Lucy said.

Whitaker snorted. "Everyone in town knows about them. They also know that the Colfax family is tearing itself apart over a merger offer. I don't have an MBA and I don't know squat about mergers, but if I were you, I'd sell Warner Colfax the shares and get out of that dogfight before you get bitten."

"I appreciate your views on the matter," Lucy said.

Mason stirred and straightened away from the wall. "There is one other angle here that might be worth considering."

Lucy and Whitaker looked at him.

"What's that?" Whitaker asked.

"The orchard land is valuable, but the house itself may not have been important to the buyer that Kelly had lined up. The place was a nice example of the Craftsman style, but it's small. You know how it is with the folks who come here to start wineries. They tend to build big houses and large compounds. At most, Sara's place would have made a nice little guest house or a residence for a property manager."

"So burning it down wouldn't have done much damage to the overall value of the property," Whitaker said.

"Right," Mason said. "Kelly would still have made a big commission on the sale of the land."

"But that doesn't explain why he torched the house," Whitaker concluded.

"Maybe he thought it would force Lucy's hand," Mason said. "With the house out of the way, she no longer had any reason to stall on the listing."

"Huh." Whitaker did not appear convinced.

"Yeah, I don't like it, either," Mason said. "But the only thing that explains the arson is just what Lucy suggested to you. Kelly must have been afraid there was something in the house that might incriminate him. Lucy was getting ready to start packing up all of her aunt's belongings and papers."

"And Kelly was worried that she might come across something that could hurt him," Whitaker finished.

"Whatever it was, it has to be connected to the past and to the discovery of Brinker's body," Mason said. "There's no indication that Kelly was concerned about the house as anything other than a real estate listing until that point."

Whitaker sat silently for a moment. Then he made a note on the pad of paper in front of him.

"That's it for now," he said. "Thank you for your cooperation, Miss Sheridan."

"Of course." Lucy got to her feet and picked up her tote. She started to turn toward the door, but she paused to look at Whitaker.

"I'm not in law enforcement, but I have had some experience with investigations that involve complicated family relationships," she said.

"Right." Whitaker glanced at his notes. "You work for a genealogy firm. Quite a business. I've got an uncle who paid a hefty amount of money to have one of those family trees drawn up, and guess what? We're all descended from royalty. Who knew? Got a genuine family crest, and my uncle is now sporting a seal ring on his pinkie."

"Chief Whitaker, what I'm trying to say —"

"I have to tell you I got a little suspicious when I checked out the family tree that my uncle commissioned. Couldn't help but notice that the so-called investigative genealogist Uncle Bud hired had overlooked one of my brothers who happens to be still alive and kicking, by the way. The so-called expert genealogist also managed to get the middle name of my father and at least two other relatives wrong. I didn't bother to go back any farther on the family tree."

"As I was saying," Lucy continued, "I am a forensic genealogist. In my experience, the answers to the kinds of questions we are all asking at the moment usually lie somewhere in the family dynamics."

"If you're talking about Brinker," Whitaker said, "he didn't have much in the way of family. No one has even come forward to claim the body. That case is closed as far as I'm concerned. For reasons we will never know for certain, but most likely because he attacked her, your aunt crushed his skull with a poker. If I was a betting man, I'd say the original theory of the crime was correct. It probably was a drug deal gone bad."

"Now, just one damn minute." Lucy stormed back toward the desk. "Are you saying my aunt was involved in drugs? That's an outrageous lie."

"Whether or not it's true doesn't matter to me. I just told you, that case is closed. Kelly's death is what interests me now, and I don't think you're going to find any answers in his family dynamics, either. His father died a few years ago. His mother remarried and moved to Florida. As far as I can tell, there is no one else."

Mason looked at him. "What's your theory of the case?"

Whitaker exhaled slowly. "When I come up with one, I'll be sure to let you know."

CHAPTER
THIRTY-THREE

"What's this about, Jillian?"

Jillian took a deep breath. "I want to know how much Warner offered you for those shares. Whatever it is, Quinn and I will match it. If we don't have the cash up front, we'll get it when the merger goes through."

"I've got other things on my mind right now," Lucy said. "In case you haven't heard, Nolan Kelly died in the fire that burned down my aunt's house."

They were at Harper Ranch Park, standing at the edge of the river. Lucy wasn't sure yet why she had suggested the park as a meeting place. But for some reason, it was the first location that had come to mind when Jillian had called her, pleading for another meeting. Jillian had sounded as if she had been crying.

The park where Brinker had held court on those summer nights thirteen years ago was a different place these days. The infusion of money into the local economy combined with a city council that was big on community space had wrought wonders. No longer neglected and overgrown, the land had been transformed. The grass was lush and green. There were paths for walking, running and bicycling. Families ate picnics at the wooden tables set out under the trees. There were two off-leash areas — one for large dogs and one for small dogs. Everyone knew that the owners of each size were, themselves, very different breeds and needed to be separated.

"I know about Nolan," Jillian said. She slanted Lucy a quick, searching look. "I was horrified to hear about his death. We were in high school together, you know. People are saying that he went to your aunt's house with the intention of setting it on fire and that he got caught in the blaze."

"That's the current theory."

"I also heard that the police chief questioned you and Mason Fletcher today," Jillian said.

"Yes, he did. Do the people who are spreading the rumors have any idea why Nolan would have wanted to burn down my aunt's house?"

Jillian hesitated. "No. Well, some are saying that you were stalling on giving him the listing. You made a point of letting people know that you wanted to do some upgrades. Everyone knows it's the property that's valuable, not the house."

"I don't think he burned it down in an attempt to push me into giving him the listing." Lucy watched the river. "I think his reasons must have had something to do with the discovery of Brinker's body. It's hard to keep the past buried."

Jillian was silent for a moment. When she finally spoke, she sounded exhausted and resigned.

"No matter how hard you try, it comes back to haunt you," she said.

"Did you ever wonder what happened to Brinker when he disappeared?"

270

"Every minute, every hour, every day of my life for weeks, months and years I wondered what had happened to him," Jillian said.

Lucy looked at her, startled. "Did you?"

"Yes. Because I could never really bring myself to believe that he was dead."

"You . . . missed him?" Lucy asked, treading cautiously now.

Jillian clenched one hand into a fist around the strap of her shoulder bag. "No one was happier than me when they officially pronounced him dead, but I was afraid to believe it. Deep down, I was sure that someday he would come back to torment me. That was his favorite sport, you know, tormenting people."

Lucy went still. "I thought you liked him."

"Sure, at first. Until I became one of his victims. By the time I realized that he was a complete sociopath, it was too late."

"Will you tell me what happened, Jillian?"

Jillian's mouth tightened. "Why?"

"Because it might help me understand why Nolan Kelly died setting fire to my aunt's house."

Jillian thought about that for a long time. Then she started walking along the shady riverfront path.

"I suppose it doesn't matter now," she said. "My whole life is falling apart. There's not much left to protect."

Lucy fell into step beside her.

"Was Kelly dealing drugs thirteen years ago when Brinker was doing his Pied Piper thing here in Summer River?" Lucy asked.

271

"Pied Piper." Jillian shook her head. "Yes, that does describe the bastard, doesn't it? He had us all under his spell. Well, everyone except for Mason Fletcher, of course."

"Tell me about Kelly."

"All I can tell you is that at the time everyone knew that he was the one supplying Brinker with those designer drugs that always seemed to be available in his vicinity. Nolan had the connections. He always had connections, remember?"

"No. I was only here during the summers and sometimes on weekends. I didn't go to school here in Summer River, so I wasn't aware of much of the local teen gossip. Besides, Kelly was two years older than me."

"Funny how time changes some things, isn't it?" Jillian said, bitterness dripping from every word. "Thirteen years ago Mason Fletcher considered you a kid. Now the two of you seem to be very close."

"Word gets around."

"Everyone knows you went out of town together yesterday and didn't come back until this morning." Jillian glanced at her. "I heard you went to the coast."

"It wasn't a secret," Lucy said. "Can you tell me anything else about Nolan Kelly?"

"I don't know what else to tell you. Thirteen years ago he was the dealer who scored those drugs for Brinker's parties. I assume Brinker paid him very well, because Nolan always had the hottest clothes and the coolest tech gadgets."

"Kelly's parents didn't wonder how their son could afford all the latest stuff?"

"His parents were divorced. Neither one of them paid a lot of attention to Nolan."

Lucy came to a halt on the path. "What did Brinker do to you to make you fear him, Jillian?"

Jillian stopped. She slipped her sunglasses out of her shoulder bag and put them on. "It doesn't matter now."

"You said you were one of his victims. Did he drug you and rape you and record it all on video?"

Jillian went slack-jawed for a few seconds. Rage and panic flashed across her face.

"How did you know that?" she got out in a voice that sounded as if she was being strangled.

"It's what he planned to do to me the night of the party here in the park, isn't it? How many other local girls did he hurt and humiliate that way?"

"I don't know." Jillian had a death grip on the strap of her shoulder bag. "I can't be sure, because Brinker was good at keeping his own secrets. But I can tell you one thing, I don't have any trouble believing that he was the Scorecard Rapist."

"Did he ever post a video of your rape?"

"No." Jillian's mouth twisted. "Don't you get it? He used the video to blackmail me."

"He was rich. What did he want from you?"

"Not money," Jillian said. "He wanted me to pimp for him."

Lucy went cold. "Yes, of course. That explains why you invited me to the party here at the park that night."

"You were my first assignment, so to speak. I know this is going to sound freaky, but I think he had his eye on you because he hated your aunt."

"He wanted to punish Sara? Why? What did she ever do to him?"

"I'm not sure of any of this. It wasn't like Brinker confided in me. But looking back now, I think that he was . . . afraid of her."

"Why? She couldn't possibly have hurt him. He was Brinker, the son of Jeffrey Brinker. How could she have been a threat?"

Jillian sighed. "Maybe because she saw him for what he was — a monster. He told me once that Sara Sheridan was a witch. He said it sarcastically — tried to make a joke out of it — but I remember thinking at the time that it didn't ring true. If he wasn't actually afraid of her, I think he was worried about her for some reason. He wanted some hold over her. That's why he told me to bring you to the party that night."

"He believed that a video of me being raped would give him leverage over Sara?"

"It would allow him to hurt her," Jillian said. "Brinker was into that kind of torture. Speaking personally, I will be forever grateful to your aunt for getting rid of the bastard. I just wish I had known for certain that he was actually dead all these years. I would have slept better."

"If Brinker was the Scorecard Rapist, do you think Nolan Kelly might have been the one who filmed the rapes for him?"

274

"What?" Jillian looked floored. "Nolan? Wait a minute, are you saying there was someone else involved with the rapes?"

"It's a possibility. One of the investigators at the time theorized that there may have been two people who committed the crimes, Brinker and the photographer."

"I never heard that. I'm sure Nolan wasn't in the room the night Brinker raped me. I was half awake. Brinker wanted me to know what was happening. But even if he had an accomplice for the other rapes, I can't see it being Nolan. For one thing, he wouldn't have been able to keep his mouth shut."

"Good point."

"Any way you look at it, Sara Sheridan did the world a favor," Jillian said. "There's no telling how many women she saved."

"I'm sorry she wasn't able to save you, Jillian."

"In a way, she did," Jillian said. "She made Brinker stop before he could force me to find him another victim. You were my first and last target."

Understanding whispered through Lucy. "And you chose to try to save me by going to Mason, didn't you? You knew he wouldn't stand by and allow a kid like me to get raped."

Jillian looked at the opposite shore of the river. "I didn't know if telling Mason what Brinker planned would work or not, but I couldn't think of anything else to do. I was frantic that day, knowing what was going to happen. I was terrified of Brinker, but I didn't want to be responsible for you getting hurt."

"So you told the one person you knew who could be trusted to come up with a rescue plan. Mason Fletcher."

"Brinker wanted to control Mason the same way he controlled the other teens who circled around him. But Mason was the one guy Brinker couldn't manipulate. You should have seen his face that night when Mason walked through that crowd here at the ranch to get you and take you home. Brinker was laughing like the devil himself at first. He thought another victim had just stumbled into his little circle of hell."

"Brinker made the mistake of going up against a guardian angel."

"Trust me, Brinker wasn't laughing after Mason took you away. I saw the look in his eyes. Scared me to death, to tell you the truth."

CHAPTER
THIRTY-FOUR

"Give me a break," Mason said. "You actually believe Jillian's version of events?"

"Yes," Lucy said. "I do. She was barely eighteen, and she was dealing with the equivalent of a sociopathic cult leader, a guy who had drugged her and raped her and was threatening blackmail. She felt helpless to defend herself against Brinker. She was afraid to go to her parents or the cops. She was scared to death. The bastard was holding the threat of a video over her head to force her to do what he wanted, which was to lure me to him. So she turned to the only person she thought might be able to save me. That would be you."

"A plan which also had the advantage of keeping Brinker from finding out that she had double-crossed him," Mason said.

He reached into the shipping box that he was unpacking and took out a handful of screwdriver kits. Each kit contained an assortment of precision screwdrivers in various sizes. The grips of the screwdrivers were neon pink. The vinyl storage cases were done in a matching shade. Deke had discovered that women were wild about attractively packaged screwdrivers. He had ordered fifty kits, all in shocking pink.

"Well, it was certainly better than no plan at all," Lucy snapped.

They were in the back room of the hardware store. Mason had retreated to the crowded space to think. There was something about organizing plumbing supplies, hinges and screwdrivers that was conducive to the thinking process. Lucy had come through the door a short time earlier. He had heard Deke and Joe greet her, and then Deke had sent her into the stockroom.

Mason had taken one look at her serious expression and had known that there had been a new development. As soon as she had told him about the meeting with Jillian, he had said the first words that came to mind: *What the hell did you think you were doing meeting with her alone?*

That had not gone over well. He had seen the irritation and stubbornness in Lucy's eyes and had to acknowledge that he had screwed up. He had growled a weak apology, which only made things worse because she had proceeded to inform him that the meeting had taken place at Harper Ranch Park and that there had been a number of people around at all times. He had to admit she had been careful, but he couldn't shake the bad vibe that had hit him when he found out what she had done.

"Damn it, you should have called me before you agreed to see her," he said.

"Give me one good reason why I needed your permission," Lucy said.

278

He thought about it. "I haven't got a good reason."

"That's right, you don't. Going to you thirteen years ago to tell you about Brinker's plan was the only way Jillian could protect both me and herself."

Mason put the pink screwdriver kits on a workbench. "You really bought that story, didn't you?"

Lucy cleared her throat. "For your information, she didn't try to convince me that was what had happened. It just sort of came out after we started talking."

"Wait, don't tell me, let me guess. You're the one who told her that contacting me was probably what saved you that night, right? You *gave* her the story that made her look like a heroine, not an accomplice."

Lucy winced. "Okay, maybe I did put the words into her mouth. But that doesn't mean it didn't happen just as I said, even if she wasn't entirely aware of her own reasoning at the time. But she agreed with me."

"Yeah, I'll bet she did. All right, what's done is done. Just remember that the only reason Jillian wants to be your new best friend is because she's desperate to get those shares."

Lucy crossed her arms, leaned one nicely curved hip against the side of the workbench and looked stubborn. "Maybe. Maybe not. By the way, it has been brought home to me yet again that this is one very small town."

"How's that?"

"Turns out that Chief Whitaker is not the only concerned citizen who knows that we spent the night over on the coast. Evidently, it's all over town."

"You know as well as I do that there was bound to be talk."

"Well, yes, but geez, you'd think people would have something better to gossip about."

Mason smiled. "Now, see, as far as I'm concerned there isn't anything better than what happened between us over on the coast."

Lucy turned the same shade of pink as the screwdriver cases. "That's not the point —"

"Hold that thought."

"Why?"

"Because I'm leaving."

She unfolded her arms and looked suspicious. "Why?"

"I came in here to do some thinking." He started toward the door. "I have now had a genuine thought. Your meeting with Jillian has inspired me."

"Where are you going?" she called after him.

"To talk to Quinn Colfax. I've got a few questions for him."

Deke looked up from some paperwork at the counter. "You two finished arguing?"

"For now," Mason said.

"Too bad," Deke said. "It was just getting interesting."

"Keep an eye on her. I'm going out to the Colfax Winery."

Lucy emerged from the stockroom. She had one of the bright pink screwdriver cases in her hand. "Maybe I should come with you, Mason."

"Nope," Mason said. He kept moving. "The conversation I plan to have with Quinn is going to be one of those man-to-man conversations. You don't want to be there."

"I thought you didn't communicate well," Lucy called after him.

"I know how to do this kind of talking."

He had his hand on the doorknob when Lucy spoke again. But she wasn't talking to him.

"Deke, how much are these screwdriver sets?" she said. "I'd like three of them. One for myself and two more for my friends back at Brookhouse Research."

CHAPTER
THIRTY-FIVE

Deke waited until he heard the outer door close behind Mason before he turned to Lucy.

"Don't know what it is about those pink screwdriver sets," he said. "Women love 'em. Gave one to Becky for her birthday. You'd have thought it was a diamond necklace."

"Are you kidding? It's the perfect gift. Practical and stylish at the same time." Lucy smiled. "But I hope you gave her some jewelry as well."

"Oh, yeah. Nice set of earrings. You can never go wrong with screwdrivers or jewelry, I always say. You're welcome to three screwdriver sets. Take them as a thank-you gift."

Lucy looked bewildered. "What are you thanking me for?"

"Mason's been brooding around the store and the cabin ever since he landed on my doorstep a couple of weeks ago. Figured he'd come around in time, but it was taking a while. Everything changed the minute you showed up, though."

She blinked a couple times, assimilating that information, and then she smiled. "I think he just needed a job, something that required his kind of talent and energy."

She understood, Deke thought. Not every woman did.

"Right," he said. "He needed a mission."

She shrugged. "A job, a mission, whatever. And as it happened, I needed an expert like him."

Deke searched her face, looking for the truth.

"A win-win situation for both of you, is that it?" he asked, keeping his tone neutral.

"I certainly hope so," Lucy said. "Because if it doesn't work out that way, I have a horrible feeling that someone is going to get away with murder."

"You're talking about Sara and Mary?"

"The deeper Mason and I go into this thing, the more I'm convinced that they were deliberately forced off that bad curve on Manzanita Road."

"I'm not arguing the point. Mason told me about the bloodstained rock. I agree with you, the timing of their deaths is damn suspicious. But there's no one better at figuring out what's going on in a situation like this than Mason."

"I believe you."

"He'll find your answers for you," Deke said. "You know, I was away when that business with Brinker went down all those years ago, but Mason emailed me that night to tell me that there had been some trouble at the park and that he'd had a confrontation with Brinker. I emailed him back, telling him to be careful. Brinker sounded like the kind of guy who would come looking for revenge. Mason contacted me again to tell me that

Brinker had disappeared and that the police had come to the hardware store asking questions. I knew that Brinker's dad had the local chief of police in his pocket. I started making arrangements to get back here. But before I could leave, the cops concluded that Brinker had been the victim of a drug deal gone bad. Whatever the case, there were no charges against Mason."

"I didn't know until recently that Mason had been a suspect."

"*Person of interest* is how the cops put it."

Lucy studied him intently, her eyes very green. "Did you ever wonder if Mason had something to do with Brinker's death?"

"Sure. It wasn't beyond the realm of possibility that Mason had been forced to defend himself, killed Brinker in the process and then decided that it would be best to make the body disappear."

Lucy's mouth fell open. "You thought he could manage that kind of thing at nineteen?"

"I'd taught him pretty much everything I knew by then."

She swallowed hard. "I see."

"But Mason told me that he hadn't had anything to do with Brinker's disappearance."

"And you believed him?"

"Mason wouldn't lie to me. He might not tell me something if he figured I'd be better off not knowing, but he wouldn't outright lie to me. Besides, there would have been no reason for him to tell me anything but the truth."

284

"He knew that you would have kept his secret," Lucy said.

"Sure. We're family. Besides, in my opinion, sooner or later someone would have had to do something of a permanent nature to Brinker. But Mason was off the hook as far as the law was concerned. That was all that mattered to me. The search-and-rescue operations were eventually called off. Brinker's father spent a fortune on private investigators, but they all came up empty. Then Jeffrey Brinker died of a heart attack, and that was the end of the investigation."

"And all the while Brinker's body was hidden inside Sara's fireplace. We — her family — never had a clue, you know. She kept the secret to the end."

"I expect there was at least one other person who knew that body was in the fireplace."

"Mary?" Lucy nodded. "I've wondered about that. She and Sara were very close. But if that's true, Mary kept the secret as well."

"They were more than close friends. They were family, too."

"Yes."

"One more thing you should know about what happened thirteen years ago," Deke said.

"What?"

"Everything settled down here in Summer River. Aaron went off to college that fall. Mason sold the fixer-upper he had been working on. Did all right with it, too. The market was just starting to heat up around here. He socked away some of the cash to pay for Aaron's tuition and bought himself a new car. But then he went over to the community college and enrolled in some classes. Started working on his degree in criminal justice."

Lucy smiled. "I knew he'd end up in law enforcement. If ever someone was born to catch bad guys, it was Mason."

"Here's the thing," Deke said. "I always figured he was cut out for business. That first fixer-upper wasn't his last. He's made good money in real estate over the years. But it's not his first love. When I asked him why he wanted to become a cop, he said it was all your idea."

"Good grief." Lucy started to laugh, and then she shook her head. "It was a passing comment that I made to him the night he yanked me out of Brinker's party. At the time, I didn't think he was even paying attention. He was too busy lecturing me about not getting involved with Brinker and his crowd. I seem to remember telling him that I didn't need a professional guardian angel and that if he was going to insist on saving people he ought to go into law enforcement."

"Seems to me everyone could use a guardian angel at some point in their lives. Or maybe someone who just happens along at the right time and aims you in the right direction."

"I won't argue with that," Lucy said. "Mason certainly came along when I needed someone to rescue me that night thirteen years ago. I never realized the danger I was in until I returned to Summer River. What about you, Deke? You survived in several war zones. You must have had some people looking out for you."

"Over there I had my buddies to watch my back. But I had a couple of guardian angels back here, too — Mason and Aaron."

"How did they save you?"

"Let's just say they pointed me in the right direction. They gave me a reason to come home."

CHAPTER
THIRTY-SIX

There was a single long black limousine with the words *Summer River Winery Tours* parked in the otherwise empty lot at the Colfax Winery. It was still early in the day for wine tasting.

Mason left his car at the foot of the terraced steps and started toward the tasting room's entrance.

Beth Crosby emerged from the large building that housed the fermentation tanks and bottling room. When she saw him, she waved. She was dressed in jeans and a denim shirt. Sunlight glinted on the lenses of her serious black-framed glasses. She changed direction and walked toward him. He stopped.

"Don't tell me you decided to drop by for a tasting," she said. "I thought you said you were a beer man."

Mason smiled. "I'm here to talk to Quinn. Is he around?"

"Oh, sure. I saw him a few minutes ago." She gestured toward the building where the tasting room, souvenir shop and the offices of Colfax Winery were located. "He was headed for his office, I think. It's a couple of doors down from the tasting room. Keep to the right after you go through the entrance. You can't miss it."

"Thanks."

"Is it true they found Nolan Kelly's body in Sara's old house?" Beth squinted against the sun. "They're saying he torched the place and got caught in the fire."

"That's how it looks," Mason said. "But there are still some questions about his motives."

"Know what I think?" Beth lowered her voice to a conspiratorial tone. "I'll bet he wanted to force Lucy's hand. She was telling everyone that she intended to do some upgrades before she put the house on the market. Kelly probably got impatient. Everyone knows that the land is a lot more valuable than the house. Prime vineyard property."

"I've been hearing that theory a lot today. You went to high school with Kelly. Do you think he would commit arson just to get a listing?"

"Maybe. If he was desperate. I mean, he was the main pot dealer back in high school. Why would he hesitate to commit arson if there was money in it?"

"Any reason to think he might have been that desperate for money recently?"

"Who knows?" Beth sighed. "It's true, I knew Nolan for years. We were the same age, but we were never close. He ran with a different crowd back in high school. I was with the nerds, remember? But Nolan was always trying to get into the A-list circle. I think that's why he set himself up in the drug business. He was the dealer of choice that year here in Summer River. The A-list kids let him into their gang because they wanted what he could supply."

"So he had the connections to do some high-end drug deals?"

"I guess so. All I know is that he seemed to be able to supply whatever the A-list crowd wanted."

"And what Tristan Brinker wanted."

Beth grimaced. "Yeah, everyone said that Nolan was the one who brought in the drugs for Brinker's parties that summer."

"Where did Kelly get them?"

"Who knows? The city, I suppose. They say you can get anything you want in San Francisco. Listen, it's none of my business, but you might want to be careful when you talk to Quinn."

"Why?"

Beth hesitated and then let out a long sigh. "In case you haven't heard, things are more than a little tense in the Colfax family at the moment. I'm just the winemaker, so I don't know much about business. But in my position working here at the winery, I hear things. I can tell you that there's a lot of friction."

"What's your take on the feud?"

Beth shrugged. "It's simple enough. Everyone in the family except Warner wants to take the merger offer. But Warner didn't realize that until recently. He's been paying more attention to the winery than he has to Colfax Inc. Now that he knows the family is ganging up against him, he's furious. He blames Quinn, I think."

"Because Quinn has been leading the charge to take the merger?"

"That's what I'm hearing."

290

Mason studied the ornate façade of the winery and the elaborate landscaping. "Looks like Colfax spared no expense building this place."

"It's his pride and joy," Beth said. "He loves seeing his name on the labels. He's really excited about the Reserve."

"What about the rest of the family? Do they get a charge out of those fancy labels?"

Beth grew thoughtful. "Well, the winery is their ticket into wine-country society. I think they all like that, especially Jillian and the new brood mare — I mean, the new Mrs. Colfax. But they also know that the winery is not the source of the Colfax fortune. It hasn't even turned a profit yet. A lot of boutique wineries never do."

"With the exception of Warner, the Colfaxes seem determined to sell the goose that lays the golden eggs. Any idea why?"

"It's simple enough. My understanding is that the merger would make everyone involved a multi-millionaire. It's none of my business, but personally, I think Warner Colfax should have the deciding vote on whether or not to go through with the merger. Colfax Inc. is his company. He's the one who built it from scratch."

"He and Jeffrey Brinker."

"Well, yes, but Brinker has been gone for years now. Warner is the one who built the company into what it is today."

"But he turned the day-to-day management over to Cecil Dillon."

Beth gave him a quizzical look. "Everyone says that hiring an outside CEO is common practice in closely held businesses. Warner wanted to retire and devote himself to his wines."

"I see."

Beth glanced at her watch and then pushed her glasses up higher on her nose. "I'd better get back to work. Nice to see you again, Mason. You know, a lot of people around here figured you'd end up working some dead-end job your whole life. They always said your brother was the smart one in the family."

"Aaron *is* the smart one in the family."

"Maybe, but you've certainly done all right." Beth smiled. "I'm glad things worked out for you."

"You did all right, too." He angled his head toward the large tank room. "Warner Colfax isn't the only one building a reputation here. His label wouldn't mean much without a great winemaker behind it."

"Thanks. I had a lot of advantages from the start. Warner was willing to go state-of-the-art in everything, from the pressing and fermentation processes to the aging techniques and the bottling." Beth chuckled. "You wouldn't believe how many different kinds of corks I tried before I settled on the one that allowed just the right amount of air to reach the wine."

"Obviously, you are very, very good."

"I like to think so. My goal is to be the best." She walked away, lifting a hand in farewell. "See you later."

Mason continued on up the steps and pushed through the glass doors of the tasting room.

The wine tourists from the limo were lounging against the bar, listening intently as the attractive woman on the other side poured small, measured amounts of a white wine into their glasses.

"A very fresh, dry Riesling with notes of apricot and pear," she said. She broke off in mid-lecture when she saw Mason walk toward the hallway labeled *Offices*.

"Can I help you?" she asked quickly.

"I stopped by to see Quinn Colfax," Mason said. He did not pause. "We're old acquaintances."

"I'll let him know that you're here," the woman said, her tone sharpening.

"It's okay," Mason said. "Quinn and I go way back."

He turned the corner and went down a paneled hallway decorated with framed photographs of sunny vineyard landscapes. He stopped outside the room labeled *Marketing & Sales*. The door was open. Quinn was seated behind the desk, studying a computer screen full of colorful images of wine country. He had a phone to one ear.

"All right, I understand," he said into the phone. "I'll deal with it." Sensing the presence in the doorway, he swiveled around in his chair. He frowned when he saw Mason. "I've got to go now." He ended the connection and eyed Mason warily. "What do you want, Fletcher?"

"I have some questions for you," Mason said. He closed the office door.

"Is this about Lucy's shares?" Quinn asked.

"No, those shares are her business. I'm here to talk about Brinker and Kelly and the past."

"Shit. I was afraid of that. I remembered enough about you from the old days to know that you were not going to give up and go away quietly. Have a seat. I wouldn't be much of a marketing exec if I didn't offer you a glass of wine."

"No, thanks."

Quinn looked pained. "Fine. Have it your way. Coffee?"

For some reason, people tended to talk more freely when they were sharing a drink or food with another person. Probably something primal, Mason thought. Regardless of the psychology involved, he had learned long ago that it worked.

"Thanks," he said.

Quinn hit a button on his phone. "Letty, would you please bring my guest some coffee? Tea for me, as usual."

"Certainly, sir."

"Appreciate it," Quinn said. He sat back and looked at Mason. "Sit down and tell me what this is all about."

Mason moved deeper into the room. There was no telltale scent of alcohol in the atmosphere. Either Quinn confined his drinking to after business hours or he used some very good breath mints.

"You heard about Kelly?" Mason said.

"Everyone in town has heard about Kelly by now. The idiot tried to burn down Sara Sheridan's house and got caught in his own fire. It's all very sad, but what has it got to do with you being here in my office?"

Mason examined the photographs on the wall. "Nice pictures. Did you take them?"

"Yes, as a matter of fact, I did."

"And the ones in the hallway?"

"Yes. What the hell do my photographs have to do with this?"

Mason turned back to him. "Let me tell you where I'm coming from. Unlike most people, I don't think Kelly torched Sara's house because he wanted to push Lucy into giving him the listing for the property."

"Why don't you buy that angle?" Quinn's brow creased. "Makes sense to me. Kelly wanted the listing pretty badly, and Lucy was stalling."

"You don't think maybe torching the house is a little over-the-top, even for a desperate real estate agent?"

"Look, Kelly was a good salesman, but he wasn't exactly known for his high ethical standards. I don't know if you were aware of it at the time, but thirteen years ago Kelly sold pot to half the kids in town. Everyone knows he was Brinker's dealer as well."

"I've heard that. Any reason to think he was still in that line?"

"No." Quinn rose and went to stand at the window. "Furthermore, I'm strongly inclined to doubt it. I think there would have been some talk if that were the case. What I'm trying to tell you is that there is no reason to think his standards have improved. He wasn't above doing something illegal if he thought he could get away with it."

There was a light tap on the door. Quinn crossed the room to open it. The young woman who had been pouring wine for the tourists out front stood in the hall.

She held a tray with two mugs. One mug had a tea bag string hanging over the edge.

"Thanks, Letty." Quinn took the tray from her and set it down on a side table. "That's all for now. Please tell Meredith to hold my calls until we're finished here."

"Yes, Mr. Colfax."

Letty left, closing the door behind her.

Mason went to the window and looked out at the rolling, vineyard-covered hills.

"Sugar or cream?" Quinn asked.

Ever the gracious host, Mason thought. He did not turn around.

"Black," he said.

Behind him, he heard Quinn open a sugar packet.

"Nice view," Mason said.

"If you like vineyards."

Mason turned away from the view. Quinn handed him the mug of coffee and picked up his tea.

"You might as well sit down," Quinn said. He went behind his desk and lowered himself into his own chair.

Mason took one of the two chairs that faced Quinn. He tried a sip of the coffee. It was good. Probably freshly ground, using beans ethically sourced from an organic farm that used sustainable growing and harvesting techniques, this being Summer River and all.

Quinn drank some tea.

"Have you ever wondered what happened to Brinker's accomplice?" Mason asked.

"*Accomplice?*" Quinn stiffened. A little tea splashed over the rim of his mug. "What the hell are you talking about?"

"I pulled the old police files relating to the Scorecard Rapist. There was some indication that there was a second person involved in the rapes."

"I never heard that." Quinn scowled. "What are you getting at?"

"When you think about it, there are at least two people who might have had reason to worry after Brinker's body fell out of the fireplace the other night. The accomplice and the person who was supplying the drugs to Brinker."

"I told you, Brinker got his drugs from Nolan Kelly." Quinn swept that issue aside. "But what's this about an accomplice?"

Mason took another sip of the coffee. "It was just a theory at the time. Makes you wonder, though."

"You're going way out on a limb here, Fletcher. But say you're right. Maybe there was an accomplice. Seems to me the most likely suspect would have been Kelly. He would have done anything to get close to the guy with all the power."

"The power broker being Brinker?"

Quinn's mouth tightened. "Yeah."

Mason drank some more of the coffee and looked at the photos on the wall. "If there was a second person involved in the rapes, there's reason to think that individual was handy with a camera."

"You son of a bitch," Quinn said. He put his mug down very carefully. His eyes went hard. "Are you accusing me of being the second rapist just because I've got some photos hanging on my wall?"

"I'm not making any accusations — not yet. Just asking questions."

"You want a suspect who was good with a camera?" Quinn said, his voice tight with rage. "Kelly fits the profile."

"What makes you say that?"

"Who do you think took all the photos and videos of his listings? Kelly did his own marketing work. He was very good at it, too. Check out his website." Quinn groaned and slumped deep into his chair. "Look, I'm sorry I lost my temper, but you have to admit that when you barge into a man's office and accuse him of aiding and abetting rape, you've got to expect some pushback."

"Sure."

"I swear I had nothing to do with the videos."

"You were as close to Brinker as anyone that summer. Are you saying you didn't know he was the Scorecard Rapist?"

"That's exactly what I'm saying." Quinn rubbed the back of his neck. "But you're right. I probably knew Brinker better than most. And you know what that amounted to? Virtually nothing. In spite of all the teens who flocked around him, Brinker was the ultimate loner. He kept his secrets."

"What did Brinker say and do that night after I left the two of you alone together at the ranch?"

"Brinker was in a rage, of course. I'd never seen him like that. Behind that smile he was ice-cold. But after you left, he really went off. Made a lot of threats. Said he'd make you pay and pay and pay. At the time I didn't know how much to believe. But he scared the shit out of me, I can tell you that much."

"Did he threaten to kill me?"

Quinn's jaw tightened. "No, at least not immediately. He wanted to torture you first. He wanted you to suffer. He wanted to humiliate you and hurt you."

"How did he intend to do that?"

Quinn rose and went to stand at the window, his back to Mason.

"He said that the best way to crush you was to go after Sara and Lucy Sheridan. When he was finished with them, he planned to do something to your brother. He didn't get specific."

"But he mentioned Sara Sheridan by name?"

"Yeah. I could tell he hated her, maybe even feared her for some reason."

"Why?"

Quinn turned around. "I have absolutely no idea. It made no sense at the time. But that night when he was wild-eyed with rage, for some reason he blamed her."

"For what?"

Quinn shook his head. "I don't know. I swear to you I don't have any idea what he was talking about. He was crazy mad. After you left, I got into my car and I went home. I was freaked, let me tell you. The next day Brinker left town. I never saw him again. I figured the threats he had made were all bluster. But within twenty-four hours he was reported as missing. Everyone started to talk about a drug-deal-gone-bad scenario. I wanted to believe that, but —"

"What?"

"Brinker was very careful when it came to the drugs. I couldn't see him making a connection directly. He used Kelly as the broker. And I could tell that Kelly had no idea what had happened to Brinker. In fact, I got the impression that Nolan Kelly was as relieved as everyone else when word went around that Brinker was probably dead."

"How did you and Brinker end up as buddies that summer? The two of you didn't have a lot in common as far as I could tell, aside from the fact that your fathers were partners, that is."

Quinn's mouth twisted into a humorless smile. "Here's a nice slice of irony for you. My old man figured Brinker was a good role model for me."

The sunlight slanting through the window behind Quinn had become uncomfortably bright. Mason decided it was time to leave. He set the mug down on the desk.

"Thanks for the coffee," he said. He got to his feet and went to the door. The knob was very cold to the touch. He paused and looked back at Quinn.

"After Brinker was reported missing, what did you think had happened?" he asked.

"I assumed he was playing some game at first," Quinn said. "But when the authorities concluded that he was dead, I decided that you had probably killed him."

The sunlight was painful now. Mason took out his sunglasses and put them on. "Is that what you told the cops?"

"No," Quinn said. "I just said that there had been an argument between you and Brinker, but that's all. As far as I was concerned, if you had killed him, you'd done me and a lot of other people a favor."

Mason opened the door. The knob had been cold a few seconds ago, but now it felt like it was made of ice.

"One thing you might want to know," Quinn said quietly.

Mason looked at him. "What?"

"I did warn one person about Brinker's threats."

A knowing sensation crackled through Mason. "You told Sara Sheridan that he had threatened to hurt her and Lucy and my brother, and that he would probably go after me eventually."

"I couldn't sleep that night. I got out of bed about four in the morning, dressed and drove out to the orchard. I parked in the trees and walked the rest of the way to her house. I never even got a chance to knock on the door. It was as if Sara had been waiting for me — or maybe keeping watch at the window. She came out onto the back porch in her robe. I told her about the threats that Brinker had made. We spoke in whispers. I knew she didn't want to wake Lucy."

"What did Sara do after you told her your story?"

"She smiled at me in that way she had, as if she could see straight through you and knew all your secrets. She thanked me and told me that she would take care of everything. And then she told me to go home and forget that I had ever talked to her. She said Brinker must never find out, because there was no telling what he would do. She was right."

301

"Talk about a coincidence. I had a similar conversation with her later that same morning."

There was a short silence. The office was starting to look like a brilliantly lit stage.

"It never occurred to you that she was the one who killed Brinker?" Mason said.

"No." Quinn gave a weak laugh. "I mean, Sara Sheridan? A murderer? She was first in line at the antiwar protests. She led classes in meditation and yoga. She was vegan before vegan was cool."

"You've got to watch out for those vegans," Mason said.

CHAPTER
THIRTY-SEVEN

He let himself out into the hall and closed the door. He stood still for a moment, wondering why it was so dark. Belatedly, he remembered that he was wearing his sunglasses. He took them off, stuffed them into his shirt pocket and walked into the tasting room. The wine tourists were gone. So was Letty.

He went outside. The glare of the sun was so dazzling it hurt his eyes. He fumbled with his sunglasses, got them on again and made his way down the broad steps to the parking lot.

He climbed behind the wheel and sat quietly for a moment, enchanted by the way the sun filtered through the leaves of the trees and splashed on the ground. Liquid gold. He would like to make love to Lucy in the beautiful light. But Lucy was not here. He needed to find her.

He got the car going after a couple of tries and drove out of the parking lot. The road that followed the river seemed to have more curves than he remembered. It twisted into infinity. He was struck with a sudden flash of insight. The answers he was looking for were at the end of River Road. All he had to do was keep driving. Lucy would be waiting for him.

The world had a crystalline purity, as if his vision had been enhanced. Everything from the boughs of the trees to the white lines on the pavement was as sharp and clear as if it had been made of glass. The colors were amazing. He had never been so aware of the many shades of nature.

Even the scene in his rearview mirror was vivid. The large black SUV coming up fast behind him had a cinematic quality. He laughed, wondering if he had accidentally taken a wrong turn and driven into a movie.

The SUV was closer now. The windows were heavily tinted. He could not make out the driver's face. Probably a stuntman. It was starting to look like one of those films in which the bad guy tried to force the good guy off the road.

Just as someone had forced Sara and Mary off the road.

But the accident had happened out on Manzanita Road. This was River Road.

He wondered if he should tell the stunt driver that he was on the wrong road.

The lookout point above the river was coming up soon. One more curve.

The SUV pulled out to pass. Now, that was just stupid. It was also illegal as hell. But this was a movie. The bad guys did stupid, illegal things in films and got away with it, at least until the very end.

Okay, fine. If the bad guy wanted to risk his neck passing on a curve, that was his problem.

But he didn't want to be in a movie, Mason thought. He wanted to find Lucy and make love to her in the liquid-gold sunlight streaming through the trees. Oh, yeah, and find the answers at the end of the ride.

The big SUV was alongside now. Close. Way too close. Suddenly the script became crystal clear, just like everything else. This was it, the big scene where the bad guy tried to send the good guy over a cliff.

But the good guy was not in a mood to act. He just wanted to find Lucy. Damned stuntman was in the way.

Mason hit the brakes hard, slamming to a halt. There was a screech of metal as the rear fender of the SUV clipped the front of the car.

The stunt driver must not have expected that change in the script, because the SUV overcorrected wildly, barely managing to stay on the pavement. In the next instant it was gone, vanishing around the next curve.

Mason sat quietly for a time, contemplating the view through the windshield. Adrenaline flooded through him, temporarily clearing his thoughts. He eased the car onto the lay-by and shut down the engine.

The dazzling sunlight and the crystalline world blazed around him. He was once again lost in the wonder of it all. Where had he been going? Lucy. He was on his way to find Lucy. But for some reason he did not think it would be a good idea to drive any farther.

He took out his phone and looked at it for a while, admiring the illuminated screen. Who did he want to call?

Lucy.

With exquisite care he tapped the screen with her name on it. She answered on the first ring.

"Hi," he said. "I want to make love to you, but I don't know if there's going to be time because I might die. So I called to say good-bye."

"*Mason.* What's wrong?"

"I was in this movie and the stuntman tried to force me off the road."

"Good grief. You sound drunk."

"Nope. Just had a cup of coffee is all."

"Where are you?"

"River Road, I think. Let me check." He surveyed his surroundings. "Everything is very sparkly, but I'm pretty sure it's River Road."

"Where on River Road?" She sounded tense but very patient, as if speaking to a child.

"Lookout Point," he said. "You know, that place where the tourists pull over to take pictures of the river."

"Lookout Point? You're sure?"

"Pretty sure." He heard a heavy engine revving in the distance. "Oops, gotta go. I think the stuntman is coming back."

"What stuntman? Listen, don't move. Do you understand? Stay right where you are. Deke and I are on our way."

"Good-bye, Lucy."

The big vehicle was coming closer now. The engine was slowing.

"I think I should get out of the car," Mason said.

He cut the connection and fumbled with the seat belt. Another wave of adrenaline sluiced through him. He managed to get the gun out of the glove compartment and then proceeded to engage in close-quarter combat with the door until he got it open. He stumbled toward the trees, not sure why he needed to get out of sight but not questioning the instinct.

His head was spinning, but he made it into the woods. He hunkered down behind some rocks and waited, the gun clutched in both hands. There was a small pool of the liquid-gold sunshine nearby. He watched it, fascinated.

He heard the vehicle cruise slowly past the lay-by, but it did not stop. Mason remembered that he had left the driver's-side door of the car open. He wondered what the person behind the wheel of the SUV made of that.

Probably thinks I jumped into the river. Joke's on him.

He heard the big engine rev once more, an angry predator deprived of its prey. And then the SUV was gone.

Mason put the gun down very carefully on a rock and sat there, losing himself in the wonders of the crystalline landscape and thinking about Lucy until he heard another vehicle arrive. Tires squealed. Car doors slammed.

"Mason?"

Lucy's voice pulled him to his feet. He collected the gun and worked his way back through the trees. He saw her standing at the guardrail, staring down at the river, anguish on her face. She was not alone. Deke was with her.

"Hi," Mason said.

Lucy whirled around at the sound of his voice. So did Deke.

"*Mason*," Lucy said. "Dear heaven. For a moment there we thought . . . Never mind."

She rushed toward him.

"What the hell is going on?" Deke demanded, striding across the graveled lay-by. "Here, give me that gun. You're in no condition to handle it."

"I know," Mason said. "Couldn't think of anything else, though. Seemed like a good idea at the time."

Another wave of dizziness swept over him. He gave the gun to Deke.

And then Lucy was in his arms and that was all that mattered. He stopped fighting the darkness and fell into the deep.

CHAPTER
THIRTY-EIGHT

The movie continues . . .

CUT TO:
EMERGENCY ROOM

There is a team of medical personnel dressed in scrubs. Lucy is standing at the foot of the bed, anxious. Deke is behind her, one hand on her shoulder. He is grim-faced.

DOCTOR
No signs of trauma. Vitals normal.

Doctor checks patient's arms and then moves to foot of bed, forcing Lucy to step back. Doctor examines patient between the toes.

DOCTOR
No needle tracks.

LUCY
Outraged.
Of course there are no needle tracks. Mason doesn't do drugs.

DOCTOR

With AMS, we have to assume drugs are a
possibility. We'll know more when the labs
come back.

PATIENT

I'm okay.

No one pays any attention. They haven't heard him.

LUCY

What's AMS?

DOCTOR

Altered mental status. You're sure there's no
history of drug use?

DEKE

She's right. A couple of beers or some wine in
the evening. That's it.

DOCTOR
*Speaking to other members of
the medical staff.*
Take him to X-ray. I want a CT scan of his
head.

PATIENT
Louder this time.
I'm okay, damn it.

Everyone looks at patient. Lucy smiles, relieved.

                    LUCY
He's okay.

                   PATIENT
Right. I'm okay. I want to go home.

                   DOCTOR
          Gives patient a stern look.
Do you remember what you ate or drank
before your wife and uncle brought you in
here?

                   PATIENT
     Looks at Lucy, winks and smiles.
Hi, wife.

*Lucy frowns in warning. Patient gets the message. She
and Deke lied about Lucy's relationship to the patient
in order to get Lucy into the exam room.*

                   DOCTOR
          Speaking firmly to patient.
Mr. Fletcher, do you remember what you
ingested before you got here?

                   PATIENT
          Concentrates hard.
Coffee. I think.

DOCTOR
Do you remember the hallucinations?

PATIENT
I think I was in a movie.

DOCTOR
Are you still in a movie?

PATIENT
Realizes there probably is a right answer and a wrong answer. Takes a chance.
Nope. Movie's over.

DOCTOR
Looking like he doesn't believe patient.
Glad to hear it. But just to make sure the film has a happy ending, you're going to spend the night with us, Mr. Fletcher. If your vitals remain stable and your neurological signs look good, you can go home in the morning.

PATIENT
Shit.

CHAPTER
THIRTY-NINE

Stop looking at me like that," Mason said.

"Like what?" Lucy asked.

"Like you're wondering if I'm going to keel over at any minute." Mason drank some of the lemonade in his glass. "I feel fine. The overnight in the hospital was the worst part."

They were on the front porch of Deke's cabin. Lucy and Mason were on the swing. She had one leg tucked under her thigh and one foot on the wooden floor. Mason lounged next to her. Deke was braced against the porch railing. Joe was sprawled at the top of the steps, dozing.

It had been a very long night for Deke and herself, Lucy thought. They had spent it at Mason's bedside, watching closely as he slipped in and out of a restless sleep. But by morning, the effects of the hallucinogen had fully dissipated. A social worker had stopped in long enough to suggest counseling for any *self-medication* problems he might be having. Mason, Lucy and Deke had glared at her. The social worker had gotten an odd look on her face and had hurried out of the room. The ER doctor, no longer worrying about being sued for malpractice due to having discharged a patient too soon, cleared Mason to go home. He had been released with two pages of instructions that he had wadded up and tossed into a trash can on the way out the door.

"Last night was bad," Lucy said. "But the worst part was not the hospital. The worst part is that Quinn Colfax tried to kill you."

"Yeah, that wasn't so good," Mason admitted. He swirled the lemonade in his glass and looked thoughtful. "Assuming it was Quinn."

"He drugged the coffee," Deke said. "That's the only reasonable explanation. Good thing you didn't finish it."

Lucy shuddered. "I find it hard to believe that Quinn Colfax cold-bloodedly tried to poison you right there in his own office."

"Well, it wasn't like there was a more convenient place," Mason said. "Got to hand it to him. He worked it like a pro. I never saw it coming. Hell, we almost bonded over our mutual gratitude to Sara."

Deke snorted. "Well, one thing for sure, the poisoning wasn't premeditated. It had to be a spur-of-the-moment action. Quinn didn't know you were going to confront him at the winery. That means he had to have the drug somewhere real handy."

"What a horrible thought," Lucy said. "I'll never drink any more wine from the Colfax Vineyards."

"You might want to skip the coffee they pour there, too," Mason said.

"Probably organic," Deke said. "Got to watch that stuff."

314

"What the hell is going on here?" Mason said.

"Quinn Colfax tried to kill you, damn it." Deke gripped the porch railing, his eyes going very dark and cold. "He drugged you and then tried to force you into the river at the most dangerous place on River Road. You might have survived the crash, but you would have been sliding into unconsciousness because of the drug, so you would have drowned. That's cold-blooded attempted murder. The only reason I didn't call the police was that we don't have a shred of proof. So what are we going to do about this situation?"

Mason took another swig of lemonade and set the glass aside. "We are going to figure out what the hell is going on and then find some proof."

He got up from the swing. Lucy watched uneasily, but Mason was steady on his feet as he went down the steps and examined the front fender of his car. She rose and followed him. Deke pushed himself away from the railing and joined them. Joe padded after them.

They all contemplated the damage to the front fender.

Lucy folded her arms. "All I can tell you is that I didn't do it when I drove the car back here."

"I have some memory of the impact," Mason said. "I braked hard to let the driver of the SUV get past me."

"That's probably what saved you," Deke said. He took a closer look at the deep scratches in the fender. "Black paint. Remember anything about the vehicle that sideswiped you?"

"Not much," Mason said. "I was hallucinating wildly at the time — the movie thing. I remember wondering if I was in the middle of a car-chase scene. A big vehicle was coming up fast behind me, an SUV, I think. Black. Tinted windows. There was a lot of glare off the windshield. Couldn't see the driver."

"*Big black SUV with tinted windows* describes about half the vehicles on the road in this part of the state," Deke said. "One of them just happens to belong to Quinn Colfax. Be interesting to find out if there's any damage to his fender. I could drive up to the winery and see if I can spot his car."

Mason considered that briefly and then nodded once. "If it was his vehicle in that car-chase scene, I doubt he'll leave it parked out in the open, not if it was damaged. But you never know."

"I'll take a look," Deke said.

"Use Lucy's compact," Mason said. "Everyone in town knows your truck and my car."

"Good plan." Deke glanced at Lucy. "Is that all right with you?"

"Sure," Lucy said.

She walked across the graveled drive to the compact and retrieved her tote from the front seat. She tossed the keys to Deke, who snagged them neatly out of midair with the same effortless coordination that characterized Mason's catches.

Deke started to get behind the wheel. Joe leaped to his feet and looked hopeful.

"Okay if I take Joe with me?" Deke said.

"No problem," Lucy said.

Deke opened the rear door of the car. "Joe. Car."

Joe raced down the steps and vaulted into the compact.

Lucy and Mason watched the car pull out of the driveway.

"If I didn't know better, I'd say your uncle was enjoying himself," Lucy said.

"Yeah, I got the same impression."

"What if he gets caught checking out the winery vehicles?"

"He won't get caught. Uncle Deke knows what he's doing. What do you say we take a walk along the river? I need to clear my head and think."

Alarmed, she peered at his eyes. "What do you mean? Are you feeling woozy again? Are you seeing things?"

"No, I'm fine. Stop checking out my pupil size. I just want to walk and think for a while."

He caught her hand, threaded her fingers through his, and started down the sloping hillside into the trees that bordered the river.

Lucy felt the strength in his hand and told herself to relax. Mason was back to normal.

"What almost happened to you today is probably what happened to Aunt Sara and Mary, isn't it?" she said after a while.

Mason gave that some thought.

"Maybe," he said. "But if they were drugged, it means someone not only had to know that they were going to the coast that day but also had access to the contents of their picnic basket. Can you figure out how that could have happened?"

Lucy thought about it. "They always picked up the baskets at Becky's Garden. But I can't imagine that Becky would have any reason to hurt either Sara or Mary."

"No, and I'm sure she has no financial interest in Colfax Inc. But it's possible that someone else got to the picnic basket that day."

"The killer would have had to follow them the whole way, waiting for the opportunity," Lucy said.

"Maybe there was no drug. Maybe the killer simply forced Sara and Mary off the road. It happens. Usually in the movies, but it happens in real life, too." Mason paused. "But in real life it requires a very good driver behind the wheel of the assault car. And like I said, results are not guaranteed. It's a sloppy way to get rid of a target. I still think we're dealing with a desperate amateur."

"Doesn't make him or her any less dangerous."

"Makes him or her more dangerous in some ways. Less predictable. We've identified two fault lines in this thing — money and drugs. We've been focusing on the drugs. I think we need to pay closer attention to the money."

Mason stopped and released her hand. She sensed the energy in the atmosphere around him. He took his phone out of his pocket and hit a coded number.

"Aaron — yes, I'm fine. Deke called you? Yeah, well, he overacted. Yes, there were drugs involved, but we're not dealing with a drug gang or a cartel here. There's money in this thing, though. I want you to use Alice to

318

follow it. I need to know everything you can find out about the status of a company named Colfax Inc."

Lucy went closer to the water.

Behind her, Mason continued to talk to his brother. He rattled off the location of the Colfax company.

". . . Yes, I know it's a privately held corporation. But that doesn't mean there won't be plenty of rumors about the merger. Go ask Alice. Plug in all the data you can find and see what she says. I'm looking for signs of financial problems that may have been covered up at Colfax. Right. Call me as soon as you get anything solid. Thanks."

Mason ended the connection and dropped the phone back into his pocket. He came to stand directly behind Lucy. His hands closed over her shoulders. She smiled and reached up to cover one of his hands with one of her own. She sensed his chained anticipation. The part of him that had been born to hunt the bad guys was aroused and ready.

"Go ask Alice?" she asked.

"Aaron loves that line," Mason said.

"You're onto something, aren't you?" she asked.

"Maybe. I can envision a scenario in which Cecil Dillon, the second Mrs. Colfax, Quinn and Jillian aren't just anxious to make the merger happen because they want to take the profits and run. Maybe they're desperate to make it happen because they know something about Colfax Inc. that Warner doesn't know, something that could bring down the company. They want to get out while the getting is good. If they don't, they might lose everything."

"That would explain their united front. But why wouldn't they tell Warner?"

"Because it's his company, his empire."

"His legacy," Lucy said.

"If he finds out that there's something rotten at the core, he'll want to try to save Colfax Inc. and rebuild — not sell it to an unsuspecting buyer."

"But the others wouldn't want that, because it would put the whole company at risk. There's a good chance they would end up with nothing."

"Plenty of motive to go around in that family."

"But it was Quinn who poisoned you," Lucy said. "That makes him the most likely suspect in the murder of Sara and Mary. Same setup in both cases — drugs and a car accident."

"It's looking like Quinn, but something doesn't feel right," Mason said. He tightened his fingers on her shoulders and turned her around to face him. "Yesterday, when I was in the middle of that damn movie —"

"You mean when you were hallucinating."

"When I was hallucinating, I pulled over into the lay-by and took out my phone. I was aware enough of what was happening to know that I should call nine-one-one, but I also knew that whoever had tried to force me off the road might come back to finish the job. Just in case, I wanted to say good-bye to you."

She cupped his face in her hands. "You scared the daylights out of me."

His mouth crooked at the corner. "Yeah, sorry about that. I was too messed up to realize how you would react." He wrapped his hand around the back of her neck. "Lucy, the night together over on the coast was the most important night of my life. The best thing that ever happened to me."

She knew that the declaration was fueled, at least in part, by the charged emotions generated by his near-death experience. But in that moment she did not care. She, too, was dealing with some strong emotions, mostly the aftershocks caused by the forces of fear and anxiety followed by overwhelming relief at the knowledge that Mason had not died.

"That night on the coast was the most important night of my life, too," she said. "I will never forget it."

He did not look satisfied with her answer, but he did not push for more.

"Lucy," he said. He drew her closer. "Little Lucy. Now that you have come back into my life, I don't want to let you go."

He kissed her before she could demand a clarification of that enigmatic sentence. She reminded herself that he had been through a lot in the past twenty-four hours. He might be saying things — feeling things — that he might not say and feel when reality had once again fully asserted itself. Maybe the same went for her.

But in the meantime she could not think of any sane reason not to abandon herself to the hot rush of desire and the intense intimacy that she experienced when she was in Mason's arms.

She returned the kiss with all of the passion that he ignited in her. His mouth was hot, fierce and exciting.

He held her close and tight against him, making her aware of his own arousal.

He finally raised his head and did a quick scan of their surroundings. She knew they were alone. No one was likely to come hiking along that stretch of the river, but Mason shook his head.

"Not here," he said. "Not safe."

The realization that he had just nixed making love out in the open not because he was afraid someone might happen along but rather because he did not think it was safe made her catch her breath.

"Do you really think someone might be watching us?" she asked, glancing around.

"I can't imagine Quinn sneaking up on us with a loaded gun, but I'd rather not take any chances. When I make love to you, I prefer to concentrate on the sex, not listening for footsteps."

"When you put it like that —"

"And there's always the potential problem of poison oak," he added. She laughed. "I never thought of that. You're right. We definitely don't want to do this kind of thing in the woods."

He laughed, too, his masculine anticipation and triumph ringing in the clear, sun-warmed air. He caught her hand and ran with her through the trees to the cabin.

CHAPTER
FORTY

The exhilaration he felt knowing that in a few minutes he was going to be making love to Lucy set fire to his blood. They dashed up the stairs to his old room together. Lucy was a little breathless. Her eyes were brilliant with feminine mystery and desire.

He tumbled her onto her back on the bed and came down on top of her, bracing himself on his hands. He looked down at her, savoring the knowledge that, for now, at least, she was his. She wanted him, and that was the most intoxicating drug of all.

He used one hand to open the front of her shirt. Her bra was a sexy little scrap of black lace. He unsnapped the front clasp and freed her dainty breasts.

"You are so lovely," he marveled.

She smiled. "I don't know about lovely, but when you look at me like that, I definitely feel hot."

"That, too." He kissed one pink nipple. "Very, very hot."

"It's your fault," she said. She started to unfasten the buttons of his denim shirt. "Do you think that we might accidentally set fire to the sheets?"

"Who cares?" He opened the front of her trousers. "There are more where those came from."

He got her out of her clothes and impatiently shed his own. He lowered himself back down onto her, inserting his leg between hers, separating her thighs. The scent of her arousal hardened every muscle in his body. He moved his hand down her hip and then to her hot, warm core.

He groaned, pulling on all of his willpower to keep himself from coming then and there.

He put his mouth on the soft skin of her shoulder and bit gently. "I love how you get so wet so fast for me."

He stroked her, finding the trigger spots that he had learned in the course of their first night together. She clenched herself around the two fingers he had inside her. He probed gently, deliberately. She sucked in her breath. Her nails bit into his shoulders.

"There," she got out. "Yes, there."

He gave a hoarse laugh. "You learn fast."

He used his mouth on her, starting with her breasts and moving lower and lower until she gasped and clutched at his head, snagging her fingers in his hair.

"What are you doing?" she yelped. "No, wait, I'm not sure —"

But it was too late, she was already climaxing. He could feel the delicate waves shivering through her lower body, taste the essence of her. She shrieked.

"*Mason.*"

When it was over she collapsed, laughing, breathless, blushing.

"That was amazing," she said, sounding and looking stunned. "Absolutely amazing. I've never wanted

324

anyone to do that before. I wasn't sure I wanted you to do it."

"You are delicious," he said. He kissed her shoulder. "Everywhere. I like it when you scream my name the way you did just then. I like it a lot."

She used her palms to push him slightly away from her.

"Show me what you like," she said.

Curiosity and determination illuminated her eyes.

He smiled slowly. "Trust me, I like everything you do to me."

"I'm serious. I want to know what works for you — what really works."

She slipped her palm down the front of his chest and captured him in her hand. She pumped him slowly, tightening her fingers until he thought he would go a little mad.

"That works," he managed, his voice suddenly tight. "That definitely works."

She giggled, rolled him onto his back and kissed his throat, his chest, and then she went lower. When he felt her tongue on him, he knew he had reached the breaking point.

"Now," he said. "I need to be inside you right now."

He caught hold of her arms and pulled her back up his body so that she sat astride him. He used one hand to guide himself into her, holding his breath while he strained violently against his own self-imposed control.

Then he was surging deep into her snug, wet heat. She tried to glide up and down on him, but he caught her hips, forcing her to let him set the rhythm. She tightened herself around him. So tight. Impossibly tight. He could not take any more.

His climax hit him in a shattering rush. He abandoned himself to the tide and let it sweep him out to sea.

CHAPTER
FORTY-ONE

It was all falling apart.

The carefully conceived plan was going to crash and burn, Quinn thought. Hell, his whole life had been going in the wrong direction since what he had come to think of as the Summer of Brinker.

It was as if he had been driving down a dark road for years and was now thoroughly lost. He had taken any number of wrong turns along the way, trying to find the right route, but each miscalculation had made things worse. He should have walked away from Colfax Inc. that summer when Brinker had swept into his life like a sorcerer — fascinating, dangerous and seemingly invincible, until the night Mason Fletcher had confronted him.

Brinker's rage that night had been terrifying. Infuriated by his inability to lure Mason Fletcher into his web, he had vowed a long and horrible revenge. Quinn was certain that someone would die. And in the end, someone *had* died — Brinker.

But Brinker's disappearance had not changed the course of his own life, Quinn thought. He had kept going in the wrong direction. Except for Jillian. She was the only right move he had ever made, and now he was going to lose her.

He swallowed some of the vodka and orange juice he had mixed for himself and went to stand at the window. He stared, unseeing, at the elegantly laid-out vineyards. He hated the winery, just as he loathed Colfax Inc. There had been a time in his life when he had believed that he would one day inherit the empire his father had built and go on to make it even larger and more powerful. He had clung to those dreams for years, desperately trying to please a father who could never be appeased, let alone pleased.

It was his parents' divorce that had finally opened his eyes. When Warner immediately remarried the bitch it had all become clear. Warner never intended for his firstborn son to inherit the Colfax empire. He planned to beget himself a new heir.

Quinn knew that he'd had another chance to walk away at that point. Instead, he had allowed Jillian to talk him into staying. And then had come the news of the merger offer, and with it the opportunity of a lifetime to exact revenge. If the merger went through, Colfax Inc. would be swallowed up and effectively cease to exist. He and Jillian could walk away with a great deal of money.

Once again he had chosen to stay. He needed the money if he was going to have a chance in hell of hanging on to Jillian.

He heard the heavy footsteps in the hall and dropped down into his chair. He took another swallow of the vodka and orange juice to fortify himself and waited.

The door of the office slammed open. Warner Colfax stormed into the room.

"What the hell is going on?" Warner demanded. "I heard that Mason Fletcher came here to see you yesterday afternoon. This morning it's all over town that he was in a car accident and wound up in the hospital. What was he doing here?"

Quinn lounged back in his chair and stacked his heels on the corner of the desk. He took another pull on his drink.

"You mean the great, all-knowing Warner Colfax hasn't figured out what's happening? There was a time when you knew everything that was going on in your kingdom. Careful, Dad. You're slipping."

Warner's face flushed a dull red. "It's three-thirty in the afternoon. How much have you had to drink?"

Quinn contemplated his glass. "First one all day. I decided it was time to celebrate."

"Celebrate what?"

"My departure from Colfax Wines. I'm quitting as of today. What else would I be celebrating?"

Warner planted both hands on the desk and leaned forward, eyes glittering. "What are you talking about?"

Quinn rolled the glass between his palms. "Where to begin? Shall I start with the fact that I strongly suspect that Lucy Sheridan is refusing to sell her shares to you or anyone else because she thinks Sara and Mary were murdered?"

"That's ridiculous. They died in a car accident. Everyone knows that."

"Not sure Lucy is buying that."

Warner's brows snapped together. "That's why she's being so damn stubborn about the shares?"

"I think so, yes. Got a hunch she isn't the only one who believes there was something suspicious about the accident. Hence the visit from Fletcher yesterday."

"Damn it. What did he want from you?" Warner asked.

"Answers. He seemed mostly interested in the past. So I told him what he had already guessed — that thirteen years ago, Brinker was furious because Fletcher refused to join the merry little band of acolytes who worshipped the awesome Brinker. I also told him that Brinker was enraged because Fletcher rescued Lucy Sheridan the night of the final party at the ranch."

"Rescued her from what?"

"I think Sara Sheridan was right," Quinn said. "I think Brinker was the Scorecard Rapist. There is no doubt in my mind that he intended to make Lucy one of his victims. Fletcher heard rumors the afternoon of the party. That's why he showed up that night."

"You knew Brinker was the rapist? Or are you just guessing?"

"I didn't know it at the time. But I'm dead certain of it now. He used me like he used everyone else, but we weren't friends. He never confided in me. However, he was so pissed off that night after Fletcher warned him never to go near Lucy Sheridan again that he sort of lost it. He started making threats. When I left him there by the river he was practically frothing at the mouth. I decided I'd do my one good deed of a lifetime and warn Sara Sheridan that Lucy was in danger. But

330

Brinker was gone by morning. I figured that in spite of all his bluster he really was scared of Fletcher."

Warner looked dumbfounded. "You never told me any of this."

"Why would I?" Quinn laughed. "You thought Brinker was a terrific role model for me, remember? You kept telling me how strong he was, how he would one day be a real force to be reckoned with in the business world. And maybe he would have been, if he had lived." Quinn winked. "Between you and me, I always assumed that Fletcher was the one who punched Brinker's ticket. Who knew Sara Sheridan had it in her?"

"I don't believe any of this. You're drunk, and you're making up the whole story."

"In that case, you probably don't want to hear that your handpicked, high-priced CEO is screwing your new brood-mare wife, either."

Warner stared at him. "Shut your damn drunken mouth."

"Give me a break — everyone knows. Any heirs you get from her will have Cecil Dillon's DNA. But it's moot, anyway, because I doubt that Ashley has any intention of getting pregnant by either of you. She's in this for the money, pure and simple. Big mistake on her part. But she's smart enough to know when to cut her losses. As soon as she realizes that the merger is going to fail, she'll grab the jewelry and the Porsche and disappear."

"It's not true." Warner's face was splotchy with rage. "None of it's true. I swear, if you don't stop talking like this —"

"You'll do what?" Quinn slammed the glass down on his desk and surged to his feet. "Cut me out of your will? Go for it, Dad. Damned if I care."

"You won't walk away from Colfax Inc.," Warner said again. But his voice was shaky now. "You're mad because I didn't let you take control of my company. But you didn't deserve to take the helm of Colfax Inc. You were too weak to run the business."

Quinn smiled. "You know what? You're right. I don't have the stomach for Colfax Inc. Good thing for me that I socked away a fair amount of cash six months ago when I started to get suspicious of those glowing company financials."

"Glowing financials? What are you talking about?"

"Come off it, Dad. You know what they say in the investment world. If it looks too good to be true, it probably *is* too good to be true."

"Are you saying you know something I don't know about my business?"

"I'm telling you that I'm damn suspicious of Cecil Dillon and those incredibly good numbers he's been producing for you these past few months. I'm also telling you that I'm damn sick of this job here at the winery. Which is why I'll be handing in my resignation this afternoon."

Warner blinked. His mouth was open, but for a few seconds no words came out. Evidently, it had never dawned on him that his son might one day simply walk away.

"What about Jillian?" he finally rasped. "She'll have something to say about you leaving the wine country."

"Jillian will do what she wants, but I think it's safe to say she won't be coming with me. In spite of appearances, I'm not stupid. I realize that she has stuck around as long as she has for the same reasons the brood mare has stayed. She liked the money and the social status here in the valley."

The possibility that Jillian would leave him now was shredding his insides. She was the reason he had stayed as long as he had. He knew how important it was to her to be connected to the Colfax family. Deep down, he was pretty sure it was the reason she had married him in the first place. It was his own damn fault that he loved her.

"I don't believe any of this." Warner's voice was thin and whispery now, his rage so great he could hardly talk. "It's all a pack of lies."

Quinn shook his head. "Believe whatever you like. It's not my problem anymore. Never was, come to think of it. Just took me all these years to realize it."

Warner spun around and stalked out of the office.

Quinn waited until the door closed. Then the fury and the pain overwhelmed him.

He picked up the half-empty glass and flung it against the wall. Shards rained down on the floor. The vodka and orange juice splashed across a picture of the Colfax family vineyards.

The small act of violence was strangely clarifying. For the first time since the Summer of Brinker, Quinn knew what he needed to do. It was time to grow up and become a man.

Jillian appeared in the doorway. She stared at the broken glass and the juice running down the wall. When she looked at him he saw the dread and fear in her eyes. His heart ached.

"What just happened in here?" she said. "Warner was leaving as I was coming in. He's in a rage."

"What happened is that I just quit my job. I won't be working for Colfax Winery in the future. In fact, I won't work for my father in any capacity whatsoever in the future."

Jillian studied him for what seemed like forever. "What are you going to do?"

"I have no idea." He took a deep breath and put it all on the line. "I'm walking away from everything, Jillian — the company, the winery, the money. I will understand if you don't want to come with me."

She moved into the room and closed the door. "Do you think I married you for the Colfax name and the Colfax money?"

He shrugged. "I don't know."

"I will tell you the truth," Jillian said. "But first I need to tell you about the past."

CHAPTER
FORTY-TWO

Mason was buckling the black leather belt of his jeans when his phone rang.

"Perfect timing," he said to Lucy. He crossed the small space to the end table.

Lucy was in the process of buttoning her blouse over the lacy black bra. She smiled at him in the dresser mirror.

"You look good like that," he said. He could feel his body heating again.

She tucked her blouse into the waistband of her trousers. Her eyes gleamed with sexy mischief.

"I look good dressed?" she asked.

"That way, too, but you look really, really good after hot sex. You're all sort of pink and soft and cuddly." He gave up trying to find the right words. "I don't know. Good."

The phone rang again. He glanced at the screen and his incipient arousal instantly metamorphosed into another kind of heat.

"What have you got for me, Aaron?"

"Maybe something," Aaron said. "Maybe nothing."

Lucy sat down on the bed to put on her shoes. The aged springs creaked loudly.

"Is there someone else with you?" Aaron asked. "Uncle Deke?"

"Lucy's here," Mason said. He was suddenly conscious of the fact that he was taking the call in his bedroom. "Never mind. Tell me what you've got."

"Well, as we both predicted, what few financials I could find all appear to be clean. A little too clean. I had Alice look them over. Alice says they look fine, too. Actually, she said they look more than fine. They look surprisingly good, given the fluctuations in the market over the past few years. But here's the kicker — two months ago one of the accountants at Colfax Inc. was let go with no notice. He just stopped showing up for work. Evidently, there were some social-media rumors going around at the time to the effect that he had been fired because he was caught embezzling."

Mason watched Lucy bustle around the bedroom, tidying the tumbled bedding. She looked adorable. The old headboard scraped against the wall when she tucked in one corner of the sheet.

"What's that?" Aaron asked.

"Nothing. Have you got anything else for me?"

"Alice highlighted the fired accountant as a red flag, even though it's routine for companies to keep quiet about embezzlement problems. So I got curious and looked a little deeper. Turns out there were some other rumors buzzing around in a couple of Internet chat rooms where disgruntled employees from various financial firms hang out."

"What kind of rumors?"

Lucy was tucking in the corners of the quilt now. The headboard groaned.

"Is Lucy moving furniture or something?" Aaron asked.

"Tell me about the rumors, Aaron."

"Where are you guys?"

"At the cabin. The rumors. Now."

"Oh, yeah, right, the rumors. There were some veiled references to Colfax Inc. from one member of the chat room. Alice and I both think there's a high probability that the comments were posted by the fired accountant. He indicated that he had been forced out because he had uncovered some discrepancies in the company's financials."

"Go on."

"According to him, when he took his concerns to management he was told someone would look into the matter. The following day the accountant was terminated without notice and given the impression that he was suspected of embezzlement. He was assured that no charges would be brought if he went quietly. He was escorted to his car by a security guard."

"Any chance you can find the accountant?"

"I've got his address."

Lucy walked past Mason and paused in the doorway. "I think I hear a car in the drive," she whispered. "Probably Deke."

She disappeared out into the hall. Her footsteps echoed on the stairs.

"What did she say?" Aaron asked.

"Nothing." Mason went quickly out of the bedroom and started down the stairs. "Deke took off about an hour ago to have a look around the Colfax Winery. Whoever drugged me yesterday tried to run me off the road. We think the vehicle may have belonged to the winery."

"What the hell? Uncle Deke didn't tell me about that part. Are you okay?"

"I'm fine. But the situation is getting complicated. That's why I need you to talk to the accountant. I want to know what he found in the Colfax financials that caused him to take his concerns to upper management."

"What if he doesn't want to talk?"

"That's your problem." Mason started down the stairs. "I'm sure you'll think of something. If all else fails, try a bribe."

"Hey, you're on the stairs now, aren't you?" Aaron said. He sounded pleased with himself, as if he had just solved a puzzle. "I can hear your footsteps. You and Lucy were upstairs in your old bedroom when I called. It was the bed I heard creaking a couple minutes ago."

"Go find the accountant."

Mason ended the connection and went swiftly down the stairs. By the time he reached the hall, Lucy had the door open. Deke and Joe came up the front steps. Joe immediately headed for the kitchen to check his food and water dishes.

Deke gave Lucy an appraising look. Mason gave her a quick glance, too, and realized that her hair was

338

different. It had been in a casual twist before the lovemaking. Now it was down around her shoulders.

Deke raised his brows. A knowing smile edged his mouth. But he had the good sense not to comment on the change of hairstyle. Instead, he closed the door and looked at Mason.

"The bad news is that it wasn't Quinn's black SUV that clipped you yesterday," he said. "His car was sitting in the private parking lot behind the winery. Not a scratch on it."

"Is there any good news?" Mason asked.

"Depends how you look at it. There is a small fleet of black SUVs at the winery — company vehicles. Quinn could have grabbed one of them rather than use his own car. No way to know if one of the winery vehicles is missing."

"I think it's time to have a talk with the CEO," Mason said.

Lucy grabbed her tote off the table. "I'll come with you."

Mason followed his first instinct.

"No," he said.

She glared at him. "Has it occurred to you that you're inclined to say no to everything on general principle?"

"In my experience, no is usually the safest answer in any given situation."

"Don't be ridiculous. Think about this. Cecil Dillon wants something from me — namely, those Colfax shares. If he's getting desperate, as we suspect, he's more likely to blab if I'm in the room. People start talking fast when they want something."

"The way you're talking right now?" Mason asked.

Lucy raised her eyes to the ceiling in silent supplication.

Deke looked amused. "She's got a point. Besides, you'll both be safe as long as you stick together."

"Exactly," Lucy said, triumphant.

"Given that I don't think Dillon is the one who ran me off the road yesterday, I guess it won't matter if you come with me."

"I love it when you surrender graciously," Lucy said.

She swept out the door ahead of him.

Joe appeared in the hall, once again hopeful.

"What the hell, you might as well come, too," Mason said.

Joe made for the door.

Mason looked at Deke. "Aaron called a few minutes ago. He's got a lead on an accountant who was fired from Colfax Inc. There may have been an attempt to cover up some financial trouble at about the same time that the merger offer was made."

"That would explain why several members of the family want to sell and get out while the getting is good."

"Somehow, I don't think anyone has informed Warner Colfax that his company might be in danger of imploding."

"Why would they?" Deke said. "I doubt that he would be willing to bail under any circumstances. My take on him is that he'd fight like hell to try to save the company. He's planning to hand it over to his second son."

"What second son?"

Deke's mouth twisted. "I do believe that's where the second Mrs. Colfax comes in. Warner is severely disappointed in his current heir. Wouldn't be surprised if he's planning on a replacement for Quinn."

"Lucy came up with the same thought. I wonder if Quinn has figured it out."

"He may be drinking too much these days, but no one ever said that Quinn was stupid."

CHAPTER
FORTY-THREE

Mason studied the small Mediterranean villa that served as guest quarters for Colfax's visitors. The curtains were pulled across the windows. A black SUV was parked in front. His intuition and his pulse both kicked up. *Should have started looking at Cecil Dillon back at the start*, he thought.

There were three more mini-villas scattered around the outskirts of the estate, but the driveways in front of the other guesthouses were empty.

"Don't you think that it's a little weird that the draperies are closed?" Lucy said. "Maybe he's asleep."

"At four in the afternoon?" Mason unbuckled his seat belt. "It's possible Dillon is taking a nap, but I think it's more likely that he wants privacy for whatever he's doing at the moment."

"This could get really awkward if he's in bed with the second Mrs. Colfax."

"We aren't here to discuss his sleeping arrangements. All we care about is what's going on inside Colfax Inc.," Mason said. He paused, thinking. "But that doesn't mean that the second Mrs. Colfax won't be one of the subjects of conversation. Got a hunch she's been in on the financial cover-up from the start."

342

Lucy unfastened her seat belt and climbed out of the passenger seat. Joe whined.

Mason opened the rear door. "You can come, too, but behave yourself. No peeing on the front steps, at least not until we're finished with Dillon."

Joe bounded out of the car, ears pricked. He stood patiently while Mason snapped a lead on his harness.

"I doubt if Dillon will want Joe inside the house," Lucy said.

"Joe can wait outside."

They went up the front steps. Mason punched the doorbell. There was no immediate response. He knocked a few times.

Joe growled softly and fixed his gaze on the door.

"What's wrong with him?" Lucy whispered.

Mason glanced down at Joe. "Damned if I know."

Rapid footsteps sounded inside the house. *A man,* Mason thought, heading toward the back of the house.

"Looks like we did indeed interrupt the CEO in the middle of a briefing," he said.

He loped back down the steps, taking Joe with him. Lucy followed, running to keep up.

They rounded the corner of the villa. Mason paused briefly to open a gate. The rear door of the house slammed open just as the three of them rushed into a small, elegantly landscaped garden.

Cecil Dillon stumbled out onto the back porch. When he saw Lucy, Mason and Joe, he stopped short. He stared at them, stricken.

"You don't understand," he said. "I didn't do it. It's a setup."

343

"Joe." Mason unfastened the leash and gestured toward Cecil. "Guard."

Joe paced forward and took up a position in front of Cecil. Cecil stared at him, horrified and furious.

"Call off the damn dog," he said.

"You're safe as long as you stand still," Mason said. "Are you carrying?"

"No gun, I swear it. The one inside isn't mine."

"Hands behind your back."

Cecil obeyed. Mason took out the plastic cuffs that he carried in his back pocket. He snapped them around Cecil's wrists and then performed a quick pat-down.

"Sit on the ground," he ordered.

Cecil got down on the ground. Joe's attention never wavered. Mason looked at Lucy.

"Call nine-one-one and come with me," he said to Lucy. "Stay within eyesight. I don't want you out here with him. If Dillon moves, Joe will handle him."

"Understood," Lucy said. She took her phone out of her tote.

Mason realized that she appeared strangely fascinated by the transformation that had come over Joe.

"Retired war dog," Mason said.

"I see." Lucy keyed in 911.

"You've got to listen to me," Cecil said. "It wasn't me. The bastard set me up."

"Who is inside the house?" Mason asked.

"Ashley Colfax," Cecil said. "He must have followed her here and shot her. I just got home a few minutes ago and found her in the living room. The gun is still in there. I didn't touch it. He set me up, I tell you."

"Who set you up?" Mason asked.

"Warner Colfax. He obviously discovered that Ashley and I were sleeping together. The stupid bitch probably let it slip."

Mason went into the villa. Lucy followed.

It didn't take long to find Ashley. She was sprawled, facedown, on the floor of the front room. Blood was still seeping steadily from the wound in her back.

Mason turned her over gently. The exit wound was a lot messier. He yanked off his shirt and pressed it tightly over the injury.

"She's still alive," he said. "Tell the operator that we need an ambulance."

CHAPTER
FORTY-FOUR

"The police are talking to Warner Colfax," Mason said. "He admits the gun is his, but he swears he did not shoot Ashley."

"What about Ashley?" Lucy asked.

"She made it through surgery okay. Lost a lot of blood, but the doctor says she will probably survive. According to Whitaker, she doesn't know who shot her. The bullet caught her from behind. She never saw the shooter. She believes that it was Warner Colfax. But Whitaker says they are also looking hard at Cecil Dillon."

"Everyone knows that when a woman gets killed the police always put the husband or the significant other at the top of the suspect list," Lucy said.

Mason and Deke looked at her.

"I watch a lot of police procedural shows," she explained.

"Well, in this case Whitaker has both a husband and a significant other on the suspect list," Deke said.

They were gathered once again on the front porch of Deke's cabin. Lucy and Mason were on the swing. Deke leaned against the railing. Joe was sprawled at the top of the steps, off duty once again.

"For what it's worth," Lucy said, "I'm inclined to believe Cecil."

Mason and Deke looked at her again, this time as if she had said something remarkably dumb.

"Because he said he didn't do it?" Mason asked. "Here's a little inside tip: Suspects in a murder always claim to be innocent."

"I know that," she said. "But think about it. He has an excellent reason to keep Ashley alive, at least until the merger is finalized. Also, I think he's way too smart to kill her inside his own house."

"A lovers' quarrel?" Deke suggested.

"I don't think Cecil Dillon is the kind of man who would let his emotions get in the way of closing a billion-dollar merger deal," Lucy said.

"I'm inclined to agree with you," Mason said. "I don't see him as the careless type, either. Shooting your mistress in the house you happen to be living in at the time is beyond careless. It's flat-out dumb. Unless . . ."

"Unless what?" Lucy asked.

"Unless you wanted to make it look like a setup that will ultimately point the finger at Warner Colfax," Mason said.

His phone rang. He unclipped it, glanced at the screen and took the call.

"Fletcher."

There was a short silence while Mason listened to the speaker on the other end of the connection.

"Thanks, Chief," he said. "I appreciate being kept in the loop. Yes, it does change a lot of assumptions."

347

Mason ended the call and looked at Lucy and Deke. "That was Chief Whitaker. He got the results of the autopsy on Nolan Kelly."

"Good heavens," Lucy said. "With so much going on, I forgot about Nolan. Was there anything that we didn't already know?"

"Yes, as a matter of fact," Mason said. "Turns out Kelly was shot before the fire was ignited."

"My goodness," Lucy said. She tried to process the news. "That changes everything, doesn't it?"

"Certainly puts a new light on the situation," Mason said.

"What in the world is going on here?" Lucy asked.

"I don't know, but I keep coming back to the drug connection. It makes me think that at least part of the puzzle has its roots in the past."

"Maybe it would help if we went back to basics and built a family tree," Lucy said.

Deke snorted. "Which family are we talking about? The Colfaxes? Your family? Our family?"

"None of the above," Lucy said. "The clan that interests me is the one that Brinker gathered around him that summer thirteen years ago."

"How the hell do we do that?" Mason asked.

"Leave it to me," Lucy said. "Building family trees is what I do for a living, remember?"

CHAPTER
FORTY-FIVE

"Thank you for agreeing to help me, Teresa." Lucy put a blank sheet of paper on the table and picked up a pen. "There are software programs that can be used to build family trees, but this tree is a little different."

"I'm happy to help," Teresa said. "It sounds like an interesting project."

They were sitting together at a table in the tree-shaded town square. Two plastic glasses of iced tea from a nearby coffee shop were on the table.

"Why do you want to make a diagram showing all the people who were involved in Brinker's little cult that summer?" Teresa asked.

"Because I think it will help the police figure out who killed Aunt Sara and Mary. It might also point to the person who shot Nolan Kelly and torched Sara's house."

Teresa took a deep breath and let it out slowly. "This thing just keeps getting more and more weird. I could wrap my brain around the possibility that Nolan might have wanted to burn down the house in order to destroy any evidence linking him to Brinker and drug dealing in the past. But I can't fathom why anyone would shoot him."

"Mason says that when drugs are involved, there is always someone around who is happy to shoot someone else. It's just part of the business."

"But that implies that Kelly was still dealing." Teresa grimaced. "That's what I can't quite visualize. I mean, he seemed so normal. He was a member of the Chamber of Commerce, for heaven's sake."

"Let's start with Brinker and Kelly," Lucy said. "Everyone seems to agree that Kelly was supplying the drugs that Brinker used to spike those so-called energy drinks that Brinker made available to the kids who hung around him. That means Kelly was close to Brinker."

She drew a box in the center of the page and put Brinker's name inside it. Then she drew a short line to another box. She wrote *Kelly* in the second box.

Teresa watched intently. "I think your chart is going to look a little like Dante's nine circles of hell by the time we're done. It sounds like Brinker hurt everyone he touched."

"And savored every scrap of the pain he caused."

"Total psycho."

"Oh, yeah."

They worked steadily for an hour. Between the two of them, they managed to remember the names of most of the people who had belonged to Brinker's inner circle thirteen years ago. A couple of times Teresa took out her phone and checked the local listings to refresh her memory. Several of the people who had moved in Brinker's orbit had left town. One had died.

When they finished with the names of those who had constituted the inner circle, they worked steadily outward. At one point Lucy put her own name into a box and then linked it to Jillian and Sara and Mary.

"This gets complicated, doesn't it?" Teresa said after a while. "It's starting to look like everyone in town was linked to someone who was close to Brinker."

"You know the old saying about everyone on the planet being only six degrees of separation away from everyone else?" Lucy said. "But I think we've gone far enough out on the tree. Let's start chopping off a few of the limbs and see what we've got left."

"How are we going to decide who gets the ax?"

"Let's focus on the drugs. Kelly was getting those designer pharmaceuticals from someone. It's not like he was brewing them in his own basement."

"No, Kelly wasn't much good at chemistry," Teresa said. "He was a broker. He scored those drugs from someone else. Probably a dealer in San Francisco."

"If that's true, then he may have maintained his business relationship with the connection he used thirteen years ago."

Teresa looked up, frowning. "Why do you say that?"

Lucy hesitated. Mason had been adamant when he said he did not want her to reveal that he had been drugged.

"Because I'm convinced that someone used a hallucinogenic drug to murder Aunt Sara and Mary," she said.

Teresa looked first startled and then sympathetic. "Lucy, accidents do happen."

"I know, but bodies don't show up in the victims' fireplaces very often. Trust me. Hallucinogens are a connection here, I'm sure of it."

"Okay, I'm not going to argue with you about it. Keep going. Let's see where the drug connection takes us."

"Nowhere," Teresa announced later. "The drug connection starts and ends with Kelly, and he's dead. Now what will you do?"

Lucy studied her diagram. Her forensic genealogist's intuition was aroused. The answer was somewhere in the family tree she had constructed around Brinker. It had to be there.

"I have no clue what to do next," she admitted. She got to her feet and gathered up the papers she had spread out on the table. "Maybe this wasn't such a good idea after all. I'm a genealogist, not a detective. I hope Mason can look at this tree and see some link that I'm missing."

"That's a good idea." Teresa rose and collected the empty cups. "He was three years older than us at the time. He had a different circle of acquaintances."

"Good point. Thanks for the help on this."

"No problem. It was an interesting experience. That's the sort of thing you do for a living?"

"Yes. Usually, I'm looking for lost heirs. This was a different kind of search, which is probably why I didn't get very far."

Teresa glanced at her watch. "I'd better get back to the shop. Summer afternoons are always busy. My assistant will be wondering where I am."

Lucy smiled. "All those tourists looking for wine-country casual outfits."

"It may be a niche market, but it's my market. Let me know if you come up with another approach to identifying Nolan Kelly's drug connection."

"I will."

Teresa walked back through the square and disappeared onto Main Street.

Lucy sat quietly for a time. She was overlooking something important. She was sure of it.

She gave up, hoisted the tote and walked back to the inn. She went upstairs to her room and took a few minutes to refresh herself in the bathroom. When she looked at her image in the mirror she thought about the night of the party. It had been thirteen years, but doing the Brinker tree had brought back memories.

Maybe she had been asking the wrong questions. She and Teresa had been looking at those who had been in Brinker's inner circle. Maybe she should be looking at the wannabes.

She was not the only outsider who had been at the ranch on the night of Brinker's last party. There had been a lot of other kids hanging around the fringes, moths drawn to the flame.

Mason said it sometimes helped to revisit the scene of the crime.

She grabbed her tote and went back downstairs. Outside, in the parking lot, she got into her car and drove the short distance to Harper Ranch Park.

As usual, there were a number of people walking dogs, jogging and sunbathing in the main section of the park. She found a parking place close to the secluded area near the river where Brinker had staged his parties.

She took the charts out of her tote and studied them, one by one, trying to remember who had been where the night of the party.

Teresa's words came back to her. ". . . Kelly wasn't much good at chemistry."

The name in one of the boxes that was very distant from Brinker's box suddenly stood out as if it had been written in neon. She put the paper down on a nearby picnic table and circled the name twice.

It was you, she thought. You were there all the time.

She hurried back to the parking lot, used her key fob to unlock her car and slipped into the front seat. She left the car door ajar to allow in the slight breeze while she took out her phone. She found Mason's name on her contacts list.

The passenger-side door opened abruptly. Beth Crosby slid into the seat. She had a gun in her hand.

"Give me the phone," Beth said.

Lucy handed her the phone. Beth tossed it out the window.

"Now we're going to take a scenic drive along River Road," Beth said. "Close the door."

Lucy realized she was still holding the sheet of paper that contained the Brinker cult family tree. When she turned to pull the car door closed she let the paper slip from her hand. It landed on the ground and fluttered a little. It would no doubt blow away, she thought. But at that moment she could not think of anything else to do.

"Drive," Beth ordered.

354

CHAPTER
FORTY-SIX

"You figured it out, didn't you?" Beth said.

"That you were the one who brewed up the hallucinogens for Brinker all those years ago?" Lucy asked. "Yes. You're the one person on the Brinker family tree who had the skill. You were a star in science class back in high school. That year you were studying for your degree in wine-making at the local community college. Probably taking a lot of chemistry classes."

"I was the science geek back in high school. I loved chemistry. Started playing around with hallucinogens in my senior year." Beth frowned. "What did you mean by a Brinker family tree? Brinker didn't have any family except his father."

"I did a chart showing the names of all of the people who hung around Brinker thirteen years ago. It came out looking a lot like a family tree."

"So that was what you were doing with Teresa this afternoon. It made me nervous watching you two together. But when Teresa went back to her shop a few minutes ago, she saw me on the street and said hi as if nothing was wrong, so I thought maybe everything was okay. When I saw you come out of the inn, get into your car and drive toward this section of the park, though, I got a bad feeling."

"I didn't put it together until I came here and started asking the right questions. Tell me, how in the world did you end up as Brinker's drug supplier? You didn't move in his circles."

"Nolan Kelly was the one who approached me," Beth said. "We went to school together. He knew I could make some very special stuff, and he wanted to impress Brinker."

"How much did Brinker pay you?"

"Nothing."

"You just *gave* him the drugs? Why would you do that? Wait, don't tell me. You thought you were in love with him, didn't you? You wanted to make Brinker pay attention to you."

"Shut up," Beth hissed. "You don't know what you're talking about. Brinker needed me. It was my drugs that made him a rock star here in Summer River that year. And it was my drugs that made it possible for him to make those videos of those whores."

"Please don't tell me that you were the one who filmed the rapes. That would be just too awful."

"They deserved it, all of them," Beth said. "They were the kind of A-list girls who made fun of girls like me."

"You were sure Brinker would fall in love with you once he understood how much he needed you."

"He would have realized he loved me if your aunt hadn't murdered him," Beth said, very fierce now. "I knew when he disappeared that something terrible had

356

happened. He came to see me after that last party, you know."

"What did he want?"

"Drugs. But he said he wanted me to make something extra-special. He wanted something stronger, something that would be lethal. He went on and on about how he was going to kill everyone connected to Mason Fletcher. I got scared."

"Because you knew that if a number of people in a small town like Summer River started to die from an overdose of illicit drugs, there would be an investigation and sooner or later the trail would lead straight back to you."

"I didn't know what to do," Beth said. Her tone slipped from fierce to anxious in the blink of an eye as if she was reliving the emotions she had experienced at the time. "I was afraid that if I didn't give him the drugs he wouldn't want me anymore."

"He never did want you. He just used you."

"Stop saying that. You don't know how it was between us."

"Yeah, right. So what did you tell him the last time you saw him?"

"I told him it would take me a while to come up with the kind of heavy drug that he wanted. The truth is, I thought that once he calmed down he would realize that killing off everyone around Mason was maybe not the smartest move in the playbook."

"Did he calm down?"

"No," Beth admitted. "He just got angrier. Called me all sorts of names and . . . and he hit me. He said he couldn't be bothered to screw an ugly bitch like me, and then he left. I never saw him again. The next day it was all over town that he had left Summer River. Three days later, the rumors that he had been killed in a drug deal gone bad started to circulate."

"Did you ever wonder who started those rumors?" Lucy asked softly.

"Who cares?"

"For the record, I think my aunt might have fired up that gossip."

"It's almost impossible to believe Sara Sheridan murdered Brinker," Beth whispered, sounding a little awed.

"I had a hard time believing it, too, at first, but I've come to the conclusion that Sara really did kill Brinker. I think he returned to Summer River in secret to carry out his revenge. Sara was his first target. But she was waiting for him. She had set a trap of some sort. He didn't take into account all that yoga and wood chopping. The physical activity made her a very strong woman."

"All these years I thought he was dead in a drug deal, and all the time he was in your aunt's fireplace."

"Did you kill Nolan Kelly?" Lucy asked.

"He came to me the day after Brinker's body was discovered." Beth was composed once more. "The fact that Sara had made a point of putting the newspaper with the Scorecard Rapist headlines into the fireplace along with the body had him terrified. He was afraid that she had found some of the videos. He searched the place, but when he couldn't find anything, he came up with the scheme to burn down the whole house."

"Why was he concerned about the videos?"

Beth snorted. "Because he starred in one of them. Brinker secretly filmed Nolan bragging about how he could get some high-end designer drugs for the parties as well as pot and cocaine. Afterward, Brinker showed Nolan the video and warned him that if he ever decided to spill his guts to the cops, Brinker would give the video to the police."

"The video was blackmail material in case Brinker ever wanted to use it against Kelly."

"Yes," Beth said.

"I still don't understand why you killed Kelly."

"Don't you get it? He got scared after you found Brinker's body. I was scared, too. We were both afraid that the cops would reopen the investigation. I knew that if that happened, Nolan would be questioned because half the town was aware of his history as the local pot dealer. Nolan was weak. I knew that if the police came down hard on him, he would break in a second."

"And give you up as the supplier," Lucy said. "If they got that far, the cops might also figure out that you were the one who filmed the rapes."

"At the very least, the scandal would have ruined my career as a winemaker. I couldn't let Kelly destroy everything I've worked for all these years."

"Did Brinker make a video of you, too?"

"Yes, it showed me laughing about the rapes," Beth said, back in anxiety mode. "But I knew he would never use it against me. It was just for fun."

"Right. Still, the fact that it existed and might turn up when I packed Sara's things made an excellent reason to go ahead and burn down the house. Nolan told you of his plan to torch Sara's place. You went there that night, shot him and then set the fire yourself."

"You got it."

Lucy drove around a curve. The Colfax Winery came into view.

"Drive around the back to the employee parking lot," Beth ordered. "No one will see your car there."

Lucy looked at the empty visitors' lot. "Where are the tourists?"

"The winery is closed today because of a family emergency. Haven't you heard? The lovely Mrs. Colfax is in intensive care. The staff was sent home."

"You shot her, didn't you? It wasn't Warner. It was you."

"I wanted to make sure she was dead, but I heard Cecil's car in the drive and I didn't dare fire another shot. I knew he would hear it. I had to get away."

Lucy drove slowly around to the back of the Mediterranean villa. Mentally, she ran through her limited options. She considered ramming the car head-on into one of the buildings in a low-speed crash, but the impact might cause Beth to pull the trigger, whether she intended to or not. The nose of the gun was less than two feet away. Beth could not miss at that distance.

CHAPTER
FORTY-SEVEN

"Someone's got her," Mason said.

He was standing in the nearly deserted parking lot at Harper Ranch Park. He had his phone crushed to his ear. He was holding Lucy's busted phone and a sheet of paper with a weird-looking family tree in his other hand.

"Son of a bitch," Deke said softly.

"Lucy was here at the park but she never got back to the inn. Car's gone. I found her phone. Deke, she figured it out. She's got Beth Crosby's name circled on the damn tree."

"I'm not arguing with you," Deke said. "But we need to think about this before we go charging over some damn cliff. Why would anyone grab Lucy? The merger offer will soon be off the table. Dillon has to know that. It's all going to fall apart."

"She wasn't kidnapped because of the shares." Mason looked down at the heavily circled square that contained Beth's name. "This is personal. It has been from the start."

"But if we're right about Cecil Dillon —"

"I don't think he's the one who grabbed her." Mason climbed into his car and fired up the engine. "He's a rare bird in the crime world, a long-range strategist. I can't see him grabbing Lucy at a public park. No, Beth is the one who took Lucy, I'm sure of it."

"But why?"

"A mix of revenge and panic and a lack of impulse control."

"Bad combination. Where are they headed?"

"Colfax Winery. Beth's out for revenge. She's obsessed, and she's panicking. She'll head there. It's her world — her creation. She'll want to destroy it before she makes a run for it. Probably plans to use Lucy as a hostage. Call Whitaker and tell him what's going on."

He ended the call and concentrated on his driving. If he got to the winery in time — he *would* get there in time — he would be dealing with a classic hostage situation. He needed help from someone who knew the winery. He made another call.

Quinn answered on the second ring. "Fletcher? What the hell do you want now?"

Mason told him.

CHAPTER
FORTY-EIGHT

"You moved on after Brinker, didn't you?" Lucy said. She couldn't think of anything else to do except keep talking. "You found another abusive male to love and admire, Warner Colfax. What happened? Did he turn on you, too?"

"You've got it all wrong," Beth said. "I never loved Warner Colfax. But we had a deal. I'm making the Colfax name a legend in the wine world, and how does he repay me? He plans to betray me."

"Why do you say that? He gave you everything you wanted when you graduated with your degree in wine-making — the latest technology, state-of-the-art equipment — everything."

"I found out the bastard intends to let me go. He's going to bring in another, better-known winemaker."

"I gather that's not going to happen now?"

"No." Beth smiled. "It's not just Warner's company that's going to fail. His precious winery is going down, too. He needed me, but he never appreciated me. I finally realized that."

"Who helped you to see the truth? Wait, let me guess — Cecil Dillon, right?"

"Cecil found out that Colfax plans to replace me."

"Cecil probably lied."

"Why would he do that?"

"Because he needed your help, you twit. For a smart woman, you are about as dumb as a brick when it comes to men."

Beth stared at her. "What are you talking about?"

"Think about it for half a second. It was Cecil's idea to get rid of Sara and Mary, wasn't it?"

"Mary," Beth said quickly. "He just wanted to get rid of her. He needed those shares to go to Quinn, you see. He was afraid that Mary would side with Warner when it came time to vote on the merger. But Sara and Mary went everywhere together. We didn't have any choice when we arranged the accident."

"I believe the polite name for it is collateral damage. You really are dumb. Trust me, Cecil Dillon lied to you from the start. He used you, just like Brinker did."

"What is it with men?" Beth said, clearly bewildered. "You give them everything and they walk all over you. Stop the car."

Lucy brought the car to a halt and slowly unfastened her seat belt.

"Now what?" she asked.

"Give me the keys."

Lucy obeyed.

Beth opened the passenger-side door and backed out of the seat, never taking the gun off Lucy.

"Now you get out," she ordered. "Slowly."

Lucy obeyed. There was an eerie silence around the winery today. The place truly was deserted.

"Shouldn't there be someone here?" she asked. "A security guard or one of the workers?"

Beth snickered. "Not when the boss orders everyone to leave."

"Colfax did that?"

"While I held a gun to his head." Beth angled her chin toward the large building that housed the fermentation tanks, the bottling room and the rest of the equipment required for wine-making. "Inside."

Lucy walked toward the entrance. She stopped in front of the computerized lock.

"I'll give you the code," Beth said. "Key it in."

She rattled off a string of numbers. Lucy dutifully touched the keypad in sequence. She heard the muffled sound of the bolt. Maybe if she could get inside first and haul the door closed behind her . . .

"Stand back," Beth said. "I'll get the door."

So much for plan B.

Beth grabbed the door handle and hauled it open with one hand. "Go inside. Walk slowly and stay where I can see you. Understand?"

"Got it," Lucy said.

When she moved inside, she discovered that only a portion of the cavernous structure was fully illuminated by the overhead fluorescent fixtures. The far end of the room lay in shadow. If all else failed, she would have to make a run for it and pray that Beth was not a good enough shot to hit a moving target.

The lights gleamed on the large, stainless-steel fermentation tanks and the piping connected to them.

The cold glow of the overheads revealed something else as well. Warner Colfax lay, unmoving, on the floor.

"You killed him, too?" Lucy said quietly.

"He's not dead — not yet." Beth smiled. "He drank some of my own private-reserve supply of bottled water. He should be coming around soon. I want him awake to witness the destruction of his precious winery. He's going up in flames along with it."

"What happens now?"

"As long as you're here, you might as well make yourself useful." Beth gestured with her free hand. "Take those bottles out of that rack and put them into the boxes that are sitting on the trolley. When you finish loading the boxes, you will wheel them outside and put them into the back of the van."

"You want me to pick up whole cases of wine and load them into a van?"

"Why not? I do it all the time. You look strong to me."

Lucy went to where the bottles of Reserve were stacked in small clusters in the wine racks. She removed one bottle and placed it gingerly into the wine carton.

"Faster," Beth said.

Warner Colfax chose that moment to groan. Beth glanced at him, frowning.

There wasn't going to be a better chance, Lucy thought. She grabbed two bottles out of the rack and flung one of them directly at Beth. Beth turned back quickly, yelped in panic and managed to dodge the missile. The bottle shattered when it struck the floor, splashing dark red wine on Beth's pants and shirt.

"Damn you," Beth shrieked. "What have you done?"

For a heartbeat or two, her horrified attention was fixed on the valuable wine spilling like fresh blood across the floor.

Lucy was already in motion. Clutching the remaining bottle, she fled for her life, racing to put a row of gleaming steel fermentation tanks between herself and Beth.

The gun roared. Lucy heard shots crack in quick succession. Some sounded as if they had struck the steel tanks.

For the first time in her life she wished she knew something about firearms. As it was, she had absolutely no idea how many shots Beth could fire with the particular gun she was using. Then again, who could count under such stressful circumstances?

She ducked behind a long row of casks stacked as high as her shoulders and tried to breath light, shallow breaths. Mercifully, the HVAC system hummed throughout the building. The low rumbling of the machinery provided some ambient noise.

"How could you do that?" Beth screamed. "You have no concept of what you just destroyed, do you? It took me three years to get that blend the way I wanted it. Three years of my life."

Her footsteps echoed on the floor. Beth moved forward cautiously, stopping every few steps for a short time. Lucy could not see her, but it was all too easy to imagine what was happening. Beth was stalking her through the tank room.

The occasional pause in Beth's footfalls no doubt came when she stopped to peer underneath the fermentation tanks. They were elevated off the floor.

It would not be long before she turned the corner and started down the row of casks where Lucy crouched. Just a matter of time.

Time was exactly what she needed. She had to buy some for herself. Sooner or later Mason would realize that she had disappeared. He would find her.

In the shadows she could make out a door set with translucent glass that looked like it opened onto an office or a storage room. She might be able to make it into the space and lock the door behind her, but she doubted it would do her much good. It would be only a matter of seconds before Beth blasted her way through the lock.

Still, there were possibilities, Lucy thought.

She took off her shoes and experimented with a couple of barefoot steps, hoping the background noise of the ventilation equipment would cover the faint sounds she might make.

Luckily, Beth started talking again.

"Everything has gone so wrong," she wailed. "It wasn't supposed to happen like this. I was going to be a star in the world of wine."

Under cover of the chatter, Lucy managed a few more steps. She was almost at the office door.

Beth was very close now, moving steadily along the tank aisle. In a moment she would turn the corner and see the glass-fronted office door.

Lucy got down on her hands and knees and crawled to the door. She reached up and tried the handle, half expecting to find the room locked. But the knob turned easily.

She opened the door. The interior lay in darkness, but light from the main room glanced off what appeared to be a lot of chemistry apparatus.

"My lab," Beth screamed. "No, don't go in there."

She broke into a run. Lucy slammed the door closed and then retreated behind the casks. She gripped the neck of the wine bottle tightly in both hands.

Beth rushed to the door and yanked it open. She fired wildly into the shadows. Glass shattered, popped and exploded.

The shots stopped abruptly just as Lucy swung the bottle of Reserve at Beth's head.

Beth started to turn, automatically putting up an arm. She managed to deflect some of the force of the blow. But the impact, the breaking glass and the shock of the attack sent her reeling backward into the lab. She lost her balance, bounced off a metal bench laden with what was no doubt state-of-the-art wine-science apparatus and finally went down hard. She did not move. Blood mingled with the wine on the floor.

Lucy struggled to catch her breath. Her heart was pounding. She braced one hand against the doorjamb, transfixed by the pools of blood and wine.

Somewhere a small voice in her head was yelling at her to call Mason — no, 911. She had to get her priorities straight, but it was hard to think. One step at a time. Get out of the damn winery and then call for help.

Okay, I can do this.

Footsteps echoed in the shadows behind her.

Help was already here. Relief washed through her.

She started to push herself away from the doorframe.

"I have to tell you, I didn't see this coming," Cecil Dillon said. "But a good CEO is nothing if not adaptable. I can work with this scenario."

CHAPTER
FORTY-NINE

"Nice work," Cecil said. He glanced at Beth. "I was going to get rid of her anyway."

"I don't think she's dead," Lucy said. "Not yet. She's still bleeding."

"She'll be dead soon enough, another victim of the fire that destroyed the Colfax Winery."

"This would be a really good time to cut your losses and get out of town, Cecil. No one is dead yet."

"Actually, two people are dead. Sara Sheridan and Mary Colfax."

"You killed them. When you realized the car was not going to explode in flames, you went down that hillside and used a rock to murder my aunt and her friend."

"Beth told me about Manzanita Road. We drove there together to check it out. She's the one who made sure the right bottles of water went into the picnic basket that day, but I'm the one who followed Sara and Mary and sent their car off that particular point on Manzanita Road. I couldn't trust Beth not to screw up, you see."

"You're a monster."

"Mary was dead by the time I got down to the bottom of the hillside. I'm pretty sure that Sara was dying, but she was still conscious. She couldn't move, but she watched me with those weird eyes. She watched me pick up the rock. She knew what I was going to do and she just looked at me like she knew everything about me. She smiled."

"How could you kill her like that?" Lucy whispered.

"She spoke, you know. There at the end. She said, *Karma*. And then she said, *You're next*. It was like the bitch had put a curse on me. After that, everything started to go wrong."

"You also tried to kill Mason on River Road."

"No, that was Beth." Cecil shook his head. "And the stupid woman did, indeed, screw up. I knew going in she was a risk, but I needed her help."

"Beth was willing to help you because you made her believe that Colfax was plotting to bring in a new winemaker."

"And also because I told her that I was a long-lost relative of Brinker's, his half-brother, in fact. Unfortunately, Beth turned out to be something of a loose cannon."

"You used her, but in the end you couldn't control her, so now you're going to kill her."

"And you as well, I'm afraid. You can blame Beth for that. I never intended to get rid of you. I do realize it will draw Mason Fletcher's attention."

"You've got a real talent for understatement," Lucy said. "There was a saying here in Summer River in the old days. *Don't mess with Mason Fletcher*."

"I'd rather not deal with Fletcher, but now that you're involved, I don't have any choice. I'm not concerned about him, to tell you the truth. Nothing in this situation connects with me. It will begin and end with Beth. She had motive, opportunity and access to drugs and a firearm. That will be enough."

"You're here to clean up all the loose ends, is that it?" Lucy said.

"Five minutes after meeting you I realized that you were going to be a problem. I could see it in those damned eyes of yours. They're just like Sara Sheridan's eyes. You're the one who dragged Fletcher into this. I understand now why my dear, departed half-brother hated him so much."

A shadow shifted in the gloom that enveloped a row of fermentation tanks behind Cecil. Or maybe it was just her fevered imagination, Lucy thought.

Keep him talking. The bastard has the same character flaws that Brinker had. He thinks he's the smartest man in the room.

"I knew this would all come down to family," Lucy said. "How did you find out that you were related to Brinker?" she asked.

"Pure chance." Cecil smiled. "I grew up with nothing. My mother used to gripe about how her lover gave her a few thousand bucks and dumped her when she got pregnant. He told her to get an abortion and assumed she did just that. But she spent the money on dope. By the time I got old enough to ask questions, she was so deep into the drugs I couldn't believe anything she said. After the old lady died, I found some photos in her closet. I got curious about my family history and went online."

"You discovered that you were Jeffrey Brinker's son and that he had ignored you in his will. So you started digging deeper."

"Imagine my surprise when I realized how badly my old man had been shafted by Warner Colfax."

"And how you, in turn, had been stiffed. You set out to get revenge."

"That's it in a nutshell."

That shadow shifted again. This time Brinker noticed. He started to turn around.

Mason spoke from behind a gleaming tank.

"*Down, Lucy.*"

Lucy reacted instinctively to Mason's command, throwing herself behind a row of casks.

Shots boomed in the room. Lucy heard a gun clatter on the floor.

"You damned son of a bitch," Cecil grated.

Heavy footsteps echoed in the cavernous space.

Lucy peeked around the corner of the row of casks. She saw Cecil running toward the front door, clutching his shoulder.

Mason appeared from behind a tank.

"Get his gun," he ordered.

He went after Cecil.

"He's headed your way, Quinn," he shouted.

Lucy managed to stagger to her feet. She emerged from behind the casks and started toward the gun. She got two steps before she felt the sharp pain in her bare foot. She halted, looked down and saw the blood.

"Damn, damn, damn."

She raised her foot and yanked out the shard of broken glass. Blood rushed from the wound. It should have hurt, she thought, but she felt nothing, just a curiously numb sensation.

She limped forward a few more steps and scooped up Cecil's weapon. She had never held a gun in her life. It was surprisingly heavy.

There was a commotion and some shouting from the other end of the winery. She made her way forward, trailing blood.

"Mason," she yelled.

"Stay back," he ordered.

She stopped, but she could see him now. He had his back to her, his gun in his hand. She took in the situation in an instant.

Warner Colfax was on his feet, dazed but very much aware of what was going on. Cecil had his injured arm around Colfax's neck. There was a large, antique iron corkscrew in his good hand. The sharp tip of the corkscrew was aimed at Colfax's throat. Colfax's face was frozen with panic.

"Give it up, Dillon," Mason said. "It's over."

"It's Colfax's fault," Cecil said, his voice harsh with rage. "Everything. He cheated my father, and my father cheated me."

"Killing him won't fix any of it," Mason said.

Colfax's jaw worked. "I didn't cheat Brinker, I swear it."

"You lie," Cecil said. "You knew he wasn't thinking straight. He'd just found out he had a bad heart and his son had been declared dead. You took advantage of that to make him a lowball offer for his share of the company. I went back and read all the papers, you son of a bitch. This isn't over until you go down."

He pulled the iron corkscrew back a few inches, preparing to sink it deep into Colfax's throat.

"No," Colfax screamed. "No, please. I'll pay you whatever you want."

"I don't want your money," Cecil said. "I was going to destroy everything you had and walk away with millions. But that's not going to happen now, so I want you dead. It's the least I can do to avenge dear old Mom and Dad."

Quinn loomed in the shadows. He had a bottle of wine in his hands. He brought it down on Cecil's skull in a sweeping motion that sent Cecil pitching to the side.

Cecil grunted and collapsed, groaning.

Warner Colfax scrambled frantically away from the fallen man. He stared at Cecil, and then he looked at Quinn, uncomprehending.

Quinn gave him a thin smile. "So much for following your gut when it comes to hiring a CEO."

The sirens were louder now. Lucy heard the first vehicles pull into the parking lot and screech to a halt.

Mason glanced at Lucy again. He started to speak. Then he noticed the blood leaking from her foot.

"You're bleeding."

"It's okay," she said quickly. "I stepped on some glass. Don't worry. Some of the blood on the floor came from Cecil."

376

Mason took the gun from her hand and gave it to Quinn.

"Keep an eye on them."

"They're not going anywhere," Quinn said.

"Watch out for Beth. She's unconscious back there near the lab, but she might wake up."

"Understood," Quinn said.

Mason tucked his own gun into the waistband of his trousers and scooped Lucy up into his arms.

"I'm okay, really," she said.

He carried her out the door into the sunlight.

"We need a medic here," he said in his cop's voice.

Cops, firemen and medics were swarming across the parking lot. Deke and Joe emerged out of the controlled chaos. They headed toward Mason and Lucy.

"Is she all right?" Deke asked.

"I'm fine," Lucy said. "It's just blood."

Someone in a uniform raced toward them, medical kit in hand.

"What have we go here?" he said.

He looked at Mason, not Lucy.

"It's not that bad, really," Lucy said.

Mason ignored her.

"Broken glass," he said to the medic.

"Get her to the aid car," the medic said. "I'll take a look."

Chief Whitaker materialized out of the crowd.

"What's the situation inside?" he asked.

"Under control," Mason said. "Quinn's in charge in there. He'll explain everything. Oh, yeah, you'll need some medics too. Three people down, including Beth Crosby and Cecil Dillon. Those two are the bad guys."

He moved around Whitaker and carried Lucy to the aid car, where the medic waited.

"It's not that bad," Lucy said. "Seriously."

Mason ignored her.

CHAPTER
FIFTY

Two days later they gathered on the front porch of Deke's cabin for what Deke called a debriefing. Lucy was once again on the swing with Mason. His arm was draped around her shoulders, clamping her close to his side. It felt good. Okay, so he was inclined to be overprotective. It was not the worst character flaw in a man, not by a long shot.

Her injured foot was propped on one corner of the seat. A few stitches and a bandage were all she had to show for her close call.

Deke was in his usual position, leaning against the railing. He and Mason had hauled out a couple of kitchen chairs for Quinn and Jillian. Everyone had a glass of the lemonade that Lucy had made.

"I apologize for wasting so much of the Reserve," she said. "I assure you, I would have gone with one of the less expensive Colfax labels if there had been an opportunity to browse the shelves."

Quinn gave a little snort of laughter. "Worth every drop that was spilled. You can't buy publicity this good. The news is spreading all over the Northern California wine country. If there's one thing that people who love wine love even more, it's a good story behind the wine.

The old man's Reserve is suddenly famous, and so is his wine-maker, although maybe not in quite the way either of them had anticipated."

Jillian smiled. "The market price of the Reserve just quadrupled in value. What's more, the glow will spread to the other labels. When Warner gets past the shock of having to acknowledge his own bad judgment in wives and CEOs, he'll be thrilled."

"Hard to believe that everything that's happened here in Summer River in the last few days had its origins in the past," Quinn said.

Lucy used her toe to give the swing a little push. "In my work, we learn that lesson early on."

"Got to say it's usually true in my line, too," Mason said.

Deke nodded somberly. "Goes for my former profession, that's for damn sure."

Quinn raised his brows. "War fighting?"

Deke sucked up some lemonade through the straw and nodded. "If you want to know what makes people fight wars, look at the history involved."

Jillian turned to Mason. "What made you realize that you could trust Quinn this afternoon? Why call him on your way to the winery? Didn't you think that he was the one who had drugged you and tried to force you into the river?"

Mason looked at Quinn. "You were on my list of suspects for a while. But something kept bothering me. You had no way of knowing I was going to show up in your office that day. It was possible, of course, that you kept a supply of the hallucinogen handy in your office to use on folks like me who came around asking too many questions. But I had seen Beth shortly before I spoke with you. She knew I was on my way to talk to you."

"She realized that you were going to question me, and that made her very nervous," Quinn said. "She told police that she called Dillon immediately and told him what was happening. She said there might be an opportunity to drug you because I always offer my guests something to drink. Evidently, Dillon tried to talk her out of it because he didn't trust her to do the job right. But she ignored him. She got a supply of the drug from her lab and followed you into the tasting room."

"No impulse control," Mason said.

"When Quinn called Letty and requested the coffee and the tea, Beth saw her chance," Jillian said. "She offered to pour the coffee and the tea because Letty was busy with the tourists out front. But she made sure that Letty was the one who carried the tray to the office."

"Did you ever suspect Letty?" Quinn asked.

Mason shook his head. "Not for long. She had no close ties to the Colfaxes, Dillon or Summer River, for that matter. For her, working in the wine-tasting room was just a part-time job. But you took the tray from her when she came into the room and I heard you dealing with the sugar packet while my back was turned."

"So I was the obvious suspect," Quinn said. He looked at Lucy. "How did Beth manage to drug Sara and Mary?"

"Like most of the other longtime residents of Summer River she knew Sara and Mary's routine," Lucy said. "She was aware that when they made their weekend trips to the coast they always ordered a picnic basket from Becky's Garden café. If the weather was good, they stopped to eat at the site of the old commune. On that particular day, Beth made sure to be at Becky's when Sara arrived to pick up the basket."

Deke spoke up. "Becky remembers that Beth was wearing a small backpack and that she offered to carry the basket out to the car. She went outside with the basket and stowed it in the back of Sara's car while Sara and Mary paid the bill and chatted with Becky."

"There were two plastic bottles of water in the picnic basket," Mason added. "Beth replaced them with two bottles that she had brought with her in the backpack."

"Which she had drugged and bottled and labeled herself," Lucy said. "Just like she used to do in the old days when she supplied Brinker with his special energy drinks. There was some risk that Sara and Mary might not stop at the old commune site on that day, but the forecast was fine and Beth knew the odds were good that the two would follow their usual routine."

"But it was Cecil Dillon who followed them and killed them," Mason said.

"Bastard," Lucy whispered.

Mason tightened his arm around her.

"How did Beth and Cecil Dillon meet?" Jillian asked.

"Dillon knew who she was right from the start," Mason explained. "In fact, he knew who most of the players were before he formulated his plans, because he did his research."

"But how did he learn Brinker's secrets?" Jillian asked.

"When he discovered that he had a half-brother who had disappeared under mysterious circumstances and a wealthy father who had abandoned him, Dillon became obsessed with getting what he considered his rightful inheritance," Lucy said. "He hit pay dirt when he tracked down Brinker's elderly aunt."

"Brinker was too smart to keep the rape videos and his notes in the house he rented here in Summer River that year," Mason said. "Instead, he made periodic trips to San Francisco to visit his aunt. He stored the videos and the notes in a suitcase in her basement. And that's where they sat until Cecil Dillon tracked her down. When he started asking questions about the half-brother he had never known, she felt sorry for him and gave him the only thing she had of Brinker's."

"The suitcase in the basement," Quinn said. "The videos had probably deteriorated over time, but the notebooks would have been in good shape."

"The videos were of no use to Dillon," Mason said. "He wasn't interested in small-time blackmail. But when he read the notebooks he knew that he had everything he needed to start plotting his revenge."

A sharp, agonized look flashed across Jillian's face. "What happened to the contents of the suitcase?"

"Dillon told the cops that he destroyed everything in the suitcase," Mason said. "For what it's worth, I'm inclined to believe him. So does Whitaker. Nothing showed up when the cops searched Dillon's apartment and his office."

Jillian bit her lip. Tears glittered in her eyes. "But there's no way to be absolutely certain."

Quinn reached out and caught her hand in his. "I told you, honey, it doesn't matter. If those old videos ever reappear, we'll deal with the situation."

Jillian gave him a misty smile and tightened her grip on his hand.

Quinn looked at Mason. "I know Dillon. If he did keep the cache of blackmail materials, they would have been on his computer. He never let it out of his sight."

"Which is where my brother, Aaron, comes in," Mason said. "Whitaker asked Fletcher Consulting for a forensic analysis of Dillon's computer. There was plenty of incriminating material, but it all related to concealing the financial disaster that Dillon had personally orchestrated inside Colfax Inc."

"I knew he was up to something," Quinn said. "I could feel it. But when I tried to talk to Dad about my concerns, he told me that he had a gut instinct when it came to identifying talent. He was convinced that Dillon was brilliant."

"Dillon was every bit as good as his half-brother when it came to dazzling his victims with his charisma and charm," Jillian said.

"A family talent, maybe," Lucy said.

Mason looked at Jillian. "Aaron also did some poking around online. He couldn't find any traces of the old videos."

"But there's no way to be certain, is there?" Jillian asked.

"No," Quinn said. "But it doesn't matter. You can't give in to blackmail. If you do, there's never any end to it. Just like you can't give in to a dictator." He grimaced. "Just ask me. When I think of all the years I tried to prove to my father that I was the man he wanted me to be —"

"Those days are over," Jillian said.

He smiled at her. "Yes, they are."

Lucy looked at Quinn and Jillian. "What happens now?"

"My father came to see me while I was cleaning out my office this morning," Quinn said. "He's still in shock, I think."

Jillian sniffed. "Mostly at the realization that Quinn was the one who saved his life the other day."

"Damned right you saved his ass, Quinn," Mason said. "I would have tried a shot, but the odds of taking Dillon down before he stuck that old corkscrew into Warner's throat were not great. Hell, I might have hit your father instead, for that matter. Or you, because you were right behind both of them. Dillon was bent on a final act of revenge, and that kind of obsession is hard to shut down when the avenger loses his self-control."

Quinn shrugged that off. "Dad made it clear that he's going to file for divorce from the brood — I mean, Ashley — and devote himself to rebuilding Colfax Inc. I wished him well. He offered to put me in charge of the winery."

Jillian looked disgusted. "Warner assumed it was an offer that Quinn couldn't, or wouldn't, refuse."

385

"I declined," Quinn said. "Which infuriated the old man, because it puts him in a bind. He knows he can't successfully revive the company and pay full attention to the winery. He'll have to choose, and he knows it. I'm betting he'll sell the winery."

"Quinn and I have some plans of our own," Jillian said. "We're going to sell some of the properties we've acquired here in the valley during the past few years, thanks to Nolan Kelly's advice and the inheritance from Aunt Mary. We'll use the cash to buy and renovate the old Harvest Gold Inn on the square. We're going to turn it into a real wine-country destination, complete with a spa."

"If there's one thing I've learned working at Colfax wines, it's how to market the wine-country image and lifestyle," Quinn said. "I can put the inn on the map."

Lucy looked at Quinn. "At a rough estimate, what do you think my aunt's old apple orchard is worth?"

Quinn gave her the number.

"Oh, my," Lucy said. She smiled. "I guess Kelly wasn't trying to con me after all."

"No," Quinn said. "Nolan was a damned good real estate agent."

"What about the shares in Colfax Inc.?" Deke asked.

"They aren't worth much at the moment," Quinn said, "but my dad is very, very good at investing. If anyone can salvage the company, he can. I'd suggest that you hang on to them."

"No," Lucy said. "I'm going to give them to you. Those shares are your problem now."

CHAPTER
FIFTY-ONE

Three days later, Mason suggested a weekend at the coast. This time neither of them smuggled a few personal items into the car. Instead, there were two small overnight bags in the trunk.

Mason drove. They took the main highway this time. Neither of them suggested a detour past the site of the old commune and the treacherous stretch of road where Sara and Mary had been killed.

The purpose of the trip was not to revisit the scene of the murder, Lucy thought.

This is all about us.

She knew that she and Mason were both searching for the way forward. Nevertheless, for the duration of the drive, they managed to talk about everything except their relationship.

The morning fog had burned off by the time they crested the last of the hills and saw the long stretch of rugged coastline. Mason parked the car on the bluffs above a beach. They climbed out, put on wind-breakers and sunglasses and made their way down to the water's edge. Lucy was still moving gingerly because of the cut on her foot, but she made it down to the beach with a little help from Mason.

Sunlight sparked and flashed on the water. A crisp breeze tangled Lucy's hair. When Mason reached for her hand, she gave it to him without hesitation. His fingers closed around hers, warm and strong. They walked for a time, not speaking. The relentless roar of the waves crashing on the rocky shore made conversation unnecessary.

Sooner or later they would have to talk, Lucy thought. But a part of her was afraid to start a conversation that might not conclude the way she hoped it would.

I'm afraid.

An image of Dr. Preston sitting behind her desk in the therapy room loomed in Lucy's imagination. She could see Preston's neatly styled gray hair and her impassive, unreadable face.

What are you afraid of, Lucy?

"Well, damn," Lucy said aloud.

"That's not a promising way to start a conversation," Mason said. He sounded wary. "What's wrong?"

"Nothing's wrong." She laughed. "I just realized I don't have commitment issues after all."

Mason relaxed and started walking again, hauling her along with him.

"Congratulations," he said. "But I could have told you that."

"Is that so?"

"Can't see anyone with commitment issues risking her neck and potentially millions of dollars in stock shares to find justice for two women everyone believed had died in an accident. That kind of thing requires a major commitment."

"That's different," Lucy said.

He smiled. "Sure, go ahead, blow it off."

"Pay attention. This is a very big deal. I never had commitment issues. My problem is that I've been risk-averse most of my life."

"Says the woman who cracked a bottle over the head of a crazy killer armed with a gun."

"That's not a good example of risk aversion. I had no choice in that situation."

"Some people freeze in those situations."

She frowned. "What good would that do?"

"None," Mason said. "But a risk-averse person might choose that option. Thinking on your feet is not a natural skill for most people."

"We're getting off-topic here."

"What is the topic?" Mason asked.

"Me and my history of commitment issues."

"So this is all about you."

"Absolutely." She stopped, forcing Mason to halt, too. "Listen up, Fletcher. I have had an epiphany."

He smiled. "And like everyone else who has ever had an epiphany, you can't wait to share it with the rest of the world."

"I don't give a damn about the rest of the world, but I admit I feel compelled to share it with you."

"Why me?" he asked.

"Because you are the person who inspired my epiphany. My therapist was convinced that I had commitment issues, but the truth is I have just been extremely cautious when it came to trusting other people."

"Being cautious is not dysfunctional, it's a smart survival tactic," Mason said.

"Exactly my point. To be fair to Dr. Preston, I've got a feeling that it's easy to confuse a bone-deep caution with an inability to commit. And to her credit, I think she was starting to close in on the real problem toward the end of therapy, but I fired her just before we got to the important revelation."

"Are you sure you're not overanalyzing yourself here?"

"I'm trying to describe my epiphany."

"Right."

"The thing is, there is a difference between being super-cautious and having commitment issues."

"Okay," Mason said. "So what?"

"What I'm trying to say is that after everything that has happened, I have come to the realization that life is too short to be lived cautiously."

"Are you trying to tell me you're going to take up skydiving or bungee jumping?" Mason asked.

"No, I'm trying to tell you that thirteen years ago I got a brief glimpse of the kind of man I would one day want to marry. He was strong and solid, and somehow, even at the age of sixteen, I knew he was a man who, if he made a commitment, would honor it to hell and back. I wasn't consciously aware of it over the years, but in hindsight I can see that I judged every man I've known against the standard he set. It wasn't fair, not to the men I met or to myself. It's not right to make those kinds of comparisons. Everyone is different. Everyone has strengths and weaknesses. But I made the comparison to you anyway."

"Hang on here," Mason said. "Are you telling me I'm the man you used to set your so-called standard?"

"You were the prototype I had in mind when I filled out the online matchmaking questionnaires. Well, except for the poor-communicator thing, of course. I always stipulated that good communication skills were very important."

"Don't try to tell me that you've been carrying the torch for me for the past thirteen years. I'm not buying that."

"I wasn't carrying a torch — not exactly. I had a lot of other things to do during that time. I've been busy."

He looked amused. "Doing what?"

"Growing up, going to college, traveling, meeting new people, finding a career that I love. In short, I've been living my life and it's been good, and when it hasn't been all good it's been . . . interesting."

"Interesting." He smiled. "Is that the optimist's way of saying there were times when the shit hit the fan?"

"My point —"

"You mean you've got one?"

"My point is that one of the things I've had to do along the way was figure out what I really wanted in life."

"Did you figure that out?" Mason asked.

"Oh, yes. And it's the one thing I've been afraid to risk going for."

"You want a family."

She tried to read his face, but it was hard because of the sunglasses.

"How did you know?" she asked.

"Give me a break." he smiled. "I'm a detective."

"Oh, yeah, right." She cleared her throat. "After my big screwup with my engagement, I tried to approach the problem of getting married and having a family as carefully and as scientifically as possible."

"The online-matchmaking thing."

"I met some very nice men. Well-educated, successful men. Interesting men. Men who passed all the criminal background checks."

Mason nodded. "Always a bonus, I say."

"Men who said they wanted what I wanted: a family."

"Could you hurry this up? I think I'm going to suffer a fit of the vapors at any minute here."

She ignored that. "But even though, according to the computer algorithms, some of those men met many or even most of my requirements, none of them was right for me."

"Where are you going with this? Because I'm getting hungry."

Frustration threatened to overwhelm her. "Where the hell do you think I'm going with it? I'm trying to say that the reason I haven't had any luck with the online dating services is because you weren't registered."

"You were looking for me?" he asked.

"Not you." She groped for the words. "Not consciously. I was looking for someone *like* you. Sort of."

"Are you trying to say that I'm not the man of your dreams? If so, I gotta tell you that kind of thing can be awfully rough on a man's ego."

Now she was getting mad. She clutched the front edges of his unzipped windbreaker in two fists. "What I'm saying is that I haven't been looking for a dream man. I've been looking for the real thing. Only I didn't realize it until I walked into Fletcher Hardware and saw you again."

He cupped her face in his hands and smiled his slow, heart-stopping smile. "Well, why didn't you say so back at the start of this conversation? You know I'm not good when it comes to verbal communication."

"Stuff it, Fletcher. You do just fine when it comes to verbal communication. Except when you don't want to do just fine with it."

"I don't see the problem here. You found me."

"Yes. And it's perfect, at least for now."

"You're thinking short-term?" he asked, his voice going hard and flat.

"Yes." Lucy smiled, a glorious sense of daring rushed through her. "Nothing lasts forever. I want you to know that I'm not asking for a lifelong commitment. I'm going to practice what Aunt Sara taught me — I'm going to live mindfully and in the moment. No more trying to control the future. I'm going to break the risk-averse pattern if it's the last thing I do."

"Let me get this straight. You're suggesting that we carry on with what we've started, which is, when you get right down to it, an affair."

"Yes. Right. Exactly. An affair."

"Well, damn," Mason said. "You just ruined my whole day."

Shock reverberated through her. "I did?"

"See, I suggested this trip to the coast so that I could ask you to marry me, or at least think about it."

Her mouth opened, but no words came out. She stared at him, stunned. She could not seem to catch her breath.

"I know it's too soon," Mason said. "I know you're trying to get over your so-called risk-averse issues. I know you want to try to do the Zen thing and live in the moment. And I'm okay with that. For now. I'll give you time. But you should know that I've got my own agenda. I love you, and that's not going to change. That means I'll take you any way I can get you, but what I really want is to marry you. I want to have a life together. I want to have kids with you."

She used her grip on his windbreaker to try to shake him. It was like trying to move a very large boulder.

"Damn it, why didn't you say so?" she yelped.

"Let's see. Maybe because you were doing all the talking?"

She smiled and wrapped her arms around his neck. "I'm through talking. For now."

He touched his fingertip to her lips. "You can't stop, not just yet."

"Why not?"

"Because we poor communicators have to have things spelled out."

"Okay," she said. "I will spell it out. I love you and I am making a commitment to you. To us. Not just for now but for a lifetime."

"That spells marriage to me."

"Yes," she said. "It spells marriage to me, too."

"You said you spent the past thirteen years getting your act together so that you could take the risk of finding the right man. I've spent the time searching for something as well. I just didn't know what I was looking for until you walked into Fletcher Hardware."

"What were you looking for, Mason Fletcher?"

He traced her cheekbones. "My own personal guardian angel. I met her thirteen years ago. I've been looking for her ever since. Now I've found her again, and I'm not going to let her go. I love you, Lucy. That being-in-the-moment thing is all well and good as far as it goes, but when it comes to us I want now and forever."

"Now and forever," Lucy said.

Mason kissed her there in the forever light that flashed and sparked on the surface of the ocean. Lucy realized that they had both just spoken their vows. Later they would make it formal and legal and there would be a celebration. But promises had been made and she knew they would be kept.

Now and forever.

Other titles published by Ulverscroft:

TEMPTING FATE

Jane Green

In 20 years of marriage Gabby has never doubted her love for Elliott — even when he refused to give her the one thing she still wants most of all. But now their two daughters are growing up, Gabby feels restless. And then she meets Matt . . . Intoxicated by this young, handsome and successful man, Gabby is momentarily blind to what she stands to lose. And in one reckless moment she destroys all that she holds dear. Consumed by regret, Gabby does everything she can to repair her mistake. But are some betrayals too great to forgive?

TAKE A LOOK AT ME NOW

Miranda Dickinson

Nell Sullivan has always been known as "Miss Five-Year Plan". But when she finds herself jobless and newly single on the same day, she decides it is time to start taking chances. Blowing her redundancy cheque on a trip of a lifetime to San Francisco, she meets a host of colourful characters, including the intriguing and gorgeous Max Rossi. Very soon the city begins to feel like her second home. But when it's time to return to London, will she leave the "new Nell" behind? And can the magic of San Francisco continue to sparkle thousands of miles away?

THE HOLIDAY HOME

Fern Britton

Two sisters. One House. The holiday of a lifetime . . .

Each year, the Carew sisters holiday at Atlantic House, the family's Cornish retreat, but they are complete opposites. Prudence, hard-nosed businesswoman married to the meek and mild Francis, and Constance, loving wife to philandering husband Greg, who has always been outwitted by her manipulative sibling. Suspecting that Pru wants to get her hands on Atlantic House, Connie won't take things lying down. When an old face reappears, years of simmering resentment reach boiling point. Little do they know that a long-buried secret is about to be exposed. Is this one holiday that will push them all over the edge?

A CROWN OF DESPAIR

Jenny Mandeville

Having sent his last wife to the block, the tyrannical Henry VIII sets his lustful sights upon an innocent and unworldly gentlewoman, the recently widowed, Katherine Parr. In mourning for her late husband, and yet desperately in love with another, Katherine is forced to choose between the man she loves and a crown of despair. In the years that follow, as Henry's terrified sixth wife and queen, she battles to contain her fear and revulsion of her bloated and monstrous new husband. The real threat of execution and the humiliation that she endures only strengthens Katherine's resolve that somehow she will escape the gruesome fate of her predecessors and ultimately be with the man she loves.

EVERY TIME WE SAY GOODBYE

Colette Caddle

It hasn't always been easy, but Marianne has worked hard to give her children a secure and loving home. But then comes the news that changes everything: her husband has been found dead and her future is uncertain. As Marianne struggles to move on, the past keeps drawing her back. For Dominic Thompson was not the man everyone thought he was. In spite of everything, though, she's not quite ready to believe the worst of him, and she is determined to discover the truth. Now, even in her darkest moments, there is one thing Marianne can hold on to: a love that has always seen her through . . .

WHO NEEDS MR DARCY?

Jean Burnett

Mr Wickham turned out to be a disappointing husband in many ways, the most notable being his early demise on the battlefield of Waterloo. And so Lydia Wickham, née Bennet, must make her fortune independently. A lesser woman, without Lydia's natural ability to flirt uproariously on the dance floor and cheat seamlessly at the card table, would swoon in the wake of a dashing highwayman, a corrupt banker and even an amorous royal or two. But on the hunt for a marriage that will make her rich, there's nothing that Lydia won't turn her hand to.